Eric Wilder

Oyster Bay Tango

Gondwana Press

Edmond, Oklahoma

Other books by Eric Wilder

Gondwana Press
1802 Canyon Park Cir. Ste C
Edmond, OK 73013

Front Cover by Gondwana Graphics

ISBN: 978-1-946576-15-6

Acknowledgments

I wish to thank Linda Hartle Bergeron and Don Yaw for beta reading, editing, and providing valuable input involving timeline and character development.

For Marilyn

Oyster Bay Tango

A novel by
Eric Wilder

Chapter 1

A clap of thunder signaled yet another late winter storm moving up from the Gulf of Mexico. It shook Odette Mouton's little pop-tent on the beach, her home since arriving on Oyster Island. Except for the frequent storms, often threatening to blow her tent away, Odette loved it.

Odette was small, shorter than five feet, and usually wore her long blond hair in a braid reaching almost to the crack of her ass. She might have looked Nordic except for her dark Cajun eyes. Though college-educated at L.S.U., she spoke with a discernible Cajun accent.

When lighthouse keeper Jack Wiesinski and Atakapa Indian Grogan 'Chief' la Tortue had visited a Bourbon Street strip club to see the naked girls, they'd met Odette, a tittie dancer at the club. The two older men had shared a flask of Dominican rum and given her a solid gold piece of eight to take care of their tab.

Jack and Chief had found the piece of eight, along with a crate of rare Dominican Rum, in the shallow water beneath the bridge connecting the island to mainland Louisiana. They'd celebrated their discovery with a visit to Rockie's, the Bourbon Street strip club where Odette had worked. The bottles of almost one-hundred-year-old rum proved more valuable than the gold.

After tasting the excellent rum and receiving the piece of eight as payment for Jack and Chief's tab, she'd realized her fortune lay someplace other than stripping on Bourbon Street. Quitting her job, she'd hitchhiked to the island to seek her fortune. Upon arriving on Oyster Island, she learned Jack and Chief had another endeavor.

John Pierre Saucier, a St. Bernard Parish police officer, had convinced Jack and Chief the island was perfect for the location of a service dog training facility. J.P., like Odette, was Cajun. With his dark hair and eyes, he looked like a young Elvis. The service dog training facility was an ongoing project as the group worked on their funding problems.

Mudbug, the mixed-breed dog Odette had rescued from a garbage bag someone had thrown out of a car into a bar ditch, was now her constant companion. Though cozy, the little pop-tent was less comfortable until Odette's friend Paula brought her a memory foam strip. It had made sleeping on the sand bearable. Light rain beat against the canvas as Mudbug lay nestled against Odette's head.

Though winter in Louisiana, the weather never exactly got cold on Oyster Island. A good thing because Odette only had a small pillow and a down throw, both of which fit into her knapsack nicely and provided her with all the comfort and warmth she needed.

The blue throw draped Odette, Mudbug cuddling against her when a noise outside the tent began disturbing her sleep. Covering Mudbug with the throw, Odette unzipped the tent's door and peeked outside.

A full moon, partially illuminating the beach, poked through the clouds. Something significant was moving about, although Odette couldn't see it. Grabbing the pink Afghan Paula Boutet had knitted for her, she draped it around her shoulders and crept outside on her hands and knees.

Crouching on the sand, Odette looked around, hoping to see what was causing the disturbance. She heard it again—the whinny of a horse. Though Odette couldn't see the animal, she heard it. Wheeling around, she looked in vain for the animal that sounded very close to her. When she glanced up, she saw why.

The horse was thirty feet in the air. Odette moved toward it with outstretched arms, her mouth open as she stared at a white stallion. The beautiful horse not only had wings, but also a spiraling horn protruding from its forehead. Odette pinched her arm to see if she was dreaming as she watched the white stallion float to a landing on the beach.

"Come here, big boy," she said.

The beautiful animal remained in place as Odette approached. Seeing how big it was, she stood on her tiptoes to touch the horn protruding from the stunning equine's forehead. When she did, the horny protuberance began glowing like a fluorescent bulb.

"You're a unicorn," she said, stroking the beast's flowing mane.

The great white steed trotted away down the beach. Stopping in the surf, it waited for Odette to follow. When she ran toward the beautiful animal, it moved away. Odette stopped when she finally tired of chasing it.

The storm had passed over the island, raising the humidity and leaving only the gentle lapping of waves against the beach. The disturbance had ended as quickly as it had begun, only dampening the sand pushing up through the toes of Odette's bare feet.

The moon, prominent amid puffy clouds left by the rain, lighted Odette's way as she began walking in the opposite direction. A shooting star disappeared into the distant darkness. Sensing the unicorn was following her, she halted, smiling when the beautiful animal nudged her shoulder with its cold nose.

"Quit teasing me," she said.

The unicorn hadn't finished playing. Backing away from Odette, it stayed just out of her reach. She crossed her arms and stamped her bare foot against the sand, thankful for the warm Afghan as her only other clothing was her skimpy white nightie. Even wrapped in the Afghan, goosebumps had risen on her arms from the chill breeze blowing across the island.

The unicorn finally moved away from the beach and walked toward the Majestic, the regal Prohibition-era hotel and casino sitting on stilts over Oyster Bay. Too late to worry about the weather, Odette followed it.

"Where are you going?" Odette called. "Come back here."

The unicorn paid no attention to Odette as it pranced in the direction of the Majestic,

4

occasionally stopping to munch on tuffs of sea sedge growing in the sand. Worrying about Mudbug, Odette gazed at her tent in the distance. Though thinking she should return to the shelter, she decided instead to continue chasing the unicorn. Upon reaching the board walkway to the Majestic Hotel and Casino, Odette found the creature had already moved past it. The fast walk had warmed her, and she didn't notice Paula's Afghan slipping off her shoulders.

The large wooden structure of the Majestic encompassed three stories and almost one-hundred thousand square feet. Prohibition-era mobsters owned the casino and ensured the wealthy visitors had plenty of illegal alcohol to drink.

The Majestic featured gambling, world-class restaurants, and amenities for those who could afford the luxury. The resort had a dark side: rum runners and prostitution. Now, only ghosts occupied the regal rooms. Odette had little time to reflect on the magnificent structure as she hurried after the unicorn, soon reaching the base of Chief's hill.

Oyster Island's only two permanent inhabitants were lighthouse keeper Jack Wiesinski and Atakapa Indian Gordon 'Chief' la Tortue. Though both about the same age, their physical appearances differed wildly. Jack was short, no taller than five feet eight inches, while Chief was closer to six nine.

Jack lived in a small house at the base of the Oyster Island lighthouse, while Chief's teepee sat perched atop the island's highest hill. At this morning's hour, Jack and Chief were asleep, unaware some supernatural creature was prancing across the sand.

Though Odette had lived on Oyster Island for

more than a month, she'd never explored the area north of Chief's property. Having little time to think about it, she followed the beautiful horse into a rolling ground fog.

The cold mist chilled Odette's bare neck, causing her to cross her arms, shivering as she hurried across the sand. When the fog grew so thick she could barely see her own hands, Odette lost sight of the magnificent animal.

Her words echoed when she called out, "Where are you?"

Confused by the lack of visibility, Odette soon lost her sense of direction. She knew she was lost when she bumped into a rock ledge jutting out of the sand.

"Oh, shit!" she said.

Boulders littered the ground around the sheer ledge Odette had bumped into and proved one of many. It concerned her because she knew no such rock formations existed in south Louisiana. It made her wonder why neither Chief nor Jack had ever told her about them.

Odette became more confused when she plowed into another rock ledge. Having lost sight of the unicorn, she knew she needed to find her way out of the mist and return to her tent on the beach. She started back to where she had come. At least, she thought. Odette began hearing escaping steam as the mist grew warmer. After traversing a maze of boulders in her path, she located the source of the high-pitched whistle.

The mist had cleared enough for Odette to see a pool of water surrounded by more strange boulders. The water looked hot. Bubbles, accompanied by the odor of sulfur, rose to the heated surface. Odette yanked her finger back when she tested the temperature.

Putting her finger between her lips, she licked it with her tongue and said, "Dammit, that's hot!"

Except for the unicorn, Odette had seen no other living creature since entering the mist. The swirling steam, sulfur odor, and the strange boulders and ledges made everything seem like a dream sequence. When she pinched herself, she knew she wasn't dreaming.

The strange surroundings and unusual aural and tactile feelings Odette was experiencing increased her anxiety. The sudden sight of a creature she recognized alleviated her apprehension.

Chief's calico cat, Buttercup, wandered out of the mist and rubbed against her legs. Odette scooped the beautiful cat off the ground, hugged it to her neck, and began stroking it.

"Buttercup, what are you doing here?" she said.

Buttercup purred, rubbing her head against Odette's neck. Odette's apprehension returned when she put the cat on the sand and watched her walk away to the other side of the boiling pool.

"Don't leave me, baby," Odette said.

The three-colored cat disappeared into the mist, paying no attention to Odette's request. Thinking Buttercup might lead her back to someplace she recognized, Odette hurried after her.

The farther from the bubbling pool that Odette went, the more her visibility increased. Though losing sight of Buttercup, she followed her by the tracks she'd left in the sand. She found the cat at the base of a wall of rock.

"You almost lost me, Buttercup. Where are we, and how do we get out of here?"

The cat continued pacing in front of a sheer wall rising at least twenty feet above the sand. When Odette reached it, she saw the first signs that some human had preceded her into the mist.

7

Someone had drawn symbols on the rock wall. Odette had seen pictures of the drawings, though never in person. Petroglyphs covered the large rock wall that someone had probably drawn centuries ago. Odette knelt and called the cat to come to her.

"Here, kitty, kitty," she said.

Buttercup didn't respond. Odette blinked to insure she had seen what she thought she saw when the cat disappeared into the wall. Crawling on her hands and knees to the spot where the calico had disappeared, Odette touched the rock. Chief's cat had passed through solid rock as quickly as if it had been an open door.

When Odette touched the face of the wall, her fingers disappeared into it. Pulling back her hand, she was relieved that her digits were still attached. Putting her palm against the rock, her arm disappeared up to her elbow.

Disbelieving what had happened, she tried it again. This time, something grabbed her arm and yanked her bodily to the other side.

Chapter 2

The sun was popping up on the eastern horizon when Grogan 'Chief' la Tortue exited his teepee on top of la Tortue Mountain.

There are no real mountains in Louisiana though Chief thought of the top of his scenic hill as a mountain. He returned from his privy when he saw his cat Buttercup sneaking up the path to the teepee. Chief grabbed the cat and picked it up.

"Just getting home from a night of tomcatting?" he asked. "I'm going to mount a camera on you one of these days and find out where you go at night."

When Chief released Buttercup, the calico cat went into the teepee to snuggle up against Coco and Old Joe. Old Joe, Chief's rescue German shepherd, was also an early riser. When he came out of the teepee, Chief filled his food bowl with dog food.

Chief had chickens, Mable, his setting hen, and the others beginning to exit their coop. While they ate, he checked the coop for eggs, finding a dozen for Jack Wiesinski. Mable came running when he pounded the metal feeding pan with a wooden spoon. Big Al, his red-headed bantam

9

rooster, was already up, crowing to greet the sun rising over the Gulf of Mexico.

Coco, a late sleeper, exited the teepee when Chief returned with the eggs. Always grumpy when he first awoke, the Chihuahua spurned Chief's attempt to rub his head. His demeanor changed when Chief fed him.

At the very top of la Tortue Mountain, the natural flow of artesian water had created a cobblestone pool. After feeding his dogs and chickens, Chief doffed his loincloth and bathed in the water he'd dubbed the Magic Fountain. When he returned to his teepee and dressed for the day, the sun was well up in the blue Gulf of Mexico sky. Jack Wiesinski was waiting in the doorway of his little house when Chief arrived with his two dogs and a dozen fresh eggs.

"Where you been?" he asked. "Sun's been up for over an hour."

"Who's counting?" Chief said.

"Not you, that's for sure?" Jack said.

"You have a time clock for me to punch now?" Chief asked.

Jack took the eggs from Chief and said, "You wouldn't punch it even if I did."

"Got grub in this place?" Chief asked, pushing past Jack.

"Don't I always?"

Chief took a chair at the plank table without being asked, the aroma in Jack's galley tempting the big man's appetite.

"Want rum in your coffee?" Jack asked.

"Never too early for a spot of rum," Chief said.

"Too bad the Rougarou smashed our stash of the hundred-year-old stuff," Jack said.

"The Rougarou is one less problem we have to worry about, thanks to Old Joe."

Hearing his name, the solid black German

shepherd walked to the table, his tail swaying as Chief rubbed his big head.

A Rougarou, a Cajun werewolf, had recently terrorized Oyster Island and was why Jack and Chief had acquired some big dogs from the animal shelter in Chalmette, Louisiana. The beast had met its demise when Old Joe knocked it into the water occupied by many hungry alligators.

The sound of a truck in front of the house disturbed their breakfast. When they looked up, John Pierre Saucier and his chocolate lab Lucky came bursting through the door. J.P. was a Chalmette Parish cop and a partner in the dog training facility.

"We didn't think you were coming until tomorrow," Jack said.

"Got no other place to go," J.P. said. "The captain fired me."

"You kidding?" Chief said. "I thought you were the best man on the force."

"Guess the captain had other ideas," J.P. said. "I've wanted to quit for a year now. Seems like a slap in the face, though, not to have the final choice."

"What are you going to do?" Jack asked.

"I already got another offer from the N.O.P.D.," J.P. said.

"You going to take it?" Jack asked.

J.P. removed his Stetson and shook his head. "I'm done with police work. I have about a year's savings, and I rented my house in Chalmette to a young couple. I'll concentrate on getting our training facility off the ground."

"It's going to be a while until we have our first graduate," Jack said. "We could all be belly up by then."

J.P. had wavy black hair, dark limpid eyes, and the bone structure of a Hollywood movie star. Most women couldn't resist his smile, and J.P.

knew it.

"Ain't that the truth?" he said.

Despite J.P.'s Cajun-inflected drawl, he had a degree in political science from Southeastern Louisiana University, where he'd played baseball under a full athletic scholarship. Upon graduating, he'd turned down an offer to pitch in the major league, serving instead as an infantry lieutenant in Iraq.

"I don't see how we can speed up the timeline," Jack said.

"I do," J.P. said.

"We're all ears," Chief said.

"First, maybe you better give me a mug of that grog you two are drinking."

Jack smiled as he filled a coffee mug with rum.

"Good thing we found a substitute for the real stuff," he said.

"It's easy to grow attached to rum worth sixty-grand a bottle," J.P. said.

"That's a fact," Jack said. "Now tell us your plan."

"Except for Old Joe, none of the other dogs you got from the Chalmette animal shelter are smart enough to be service dogs."

"We're not selling Old Joe," Chief said. "That option is off the table."

J.P. grinned. "He saved both of our lives. There's no way I'd ever let you sell him."

"Good," Chief said. "Then what's your plan?"

"Old Joe isn't the only smart dog in the world. Let's go to the shelter and find a young, trainable dog. If I start now, I could have the student fully trained and ready for work in a few months."

"Great idea," Chief said. "When do we leave?"

"No use getting antsy," J.P. said. "We have all day."

They turned around when someone at the open door said, "All day for what?"

It was Paula and Jimmie Boutet.

Former high school sweethearts Paula and Jimmie were of Cajun descent. Both had dark hair and eyes and seemed like a match made in heaven. Paula was a traiteur, a Cajun witch who knew things beyond her years. Jimmie owned a hardware store in Chalmette and was a dedicated sportsman. Paula and Jimmie were partners in the training facility and had arrived on Oyster Island to help out over the weekend.

Ready for work, Jimmie was wearing faded jeans, a blue cotton cowboy shirt, and a pair of steel-toed boots. Paula looked sleek, dressed in khaki shorts, expensive sandals, and a simple white tee shirt.

"J.P. got axed," Chief said. "We're going to the animal shelter and pick out a dog J.P. can train while Jack and I work on infrastructure."

Chief's comment miffed J.P. "You don't have to tell the world," he said.

"We're partners," Paula said. "We need to know."

"Maybe," J.P. said. "I'm not proud of being fired, and I'd like to keep it between us."

"Too little, too late," Jimmie said. "Everyone in Chalmette is talking about it, figuring out what you did to get fired."

"Damn!" J.P. said. "Good thing my parents moved to Breaux Bridge."

Jimmie grinned. "Won't take them long to hear the news on the Cajun grapevine. My guess is they already have."

"Damn!" J.P. said. "Guess my mom will be calling soon."

As if on cue, J.P.'s cell phone rang. He was frowning as he stepped outside for privacy while taking the call. Jimmie was grinning, Paula

13

wagging her finger at him.

J.P. nodded when he returned, and Jack said, "Your mom?"

"She still thinks I'm ten," he said.

"Your dad will take up for you," Paula said.

"He wants to take me to get a crewcut every time I visit."

"Nothing you can do will rectify the situation, so forget about it," Paula said.

"When are you heading for the animal shelter?" Jimmie asked.

"Hell!" J.P. said. "I'm afraid to show my face in Chalmette now."

"Suck it up," Chief said. "Let's go."

"I'll come with you," Jimmie said. "I'm a pretty good judge when it comes to dogs."

"Why not?" J.P. said. "Forget about me getting fired. I'm tired of thinking about it."

"Hey, me and Chief never worry about getting fired," Jack said. "Now, you don't either."

"Small blessings," J.P. said as he headed out the door.

Jack said, "How have you been, Paula?"

"Bored," she said. "Itching to get back to Oyster Island."

"It's where the action is," Jack said.

"Where's Odette?" Paula asked.

"Haven't seen her today. Must be sleeping late," Jack said. "Want some coffee?"

Paula didn't answer. "Odette isn't a late sleeper. I'm going to check on her."

"Not even a spot of rum before you go?" Jack said.

"Got a go cup?" Jack filled a red plastic cup with rum and handed it to her. "I'll be back," she said.

J.P., Chief, and Jimmie drove over the bridge to mainland Louisiana as Paula headed to Odette's tent on the beach. Jimmie sat in the front seat, Chief in the extended cab's backseat.

"I haven't been to the shelter since Millie Folsom quit and moved to New Mexico," J.P. said.

J.P. and Jimmie glanced behind them at Chief. Chief had developed an instant crush on the full-blooded Choctaw Indian woman. Their single date had resulted in Millie reassessing her life, quitting her job, and moving to Santa Fe.

"Millie had her reasons for moving," Chief said. "I was only the catalyst in her life-changing decision."

"We aren't casting aspersions," J.P. said.

"Then don't," Chief said.

"Then shut up about the captain firing me," J.P. said.

"Deal," Chief said.

J.P. and Chief turned their gazes to Jimmie. "You keep it zipped too," J.P. said, "or Chief and I will make up some wild story and tell Paula."

"She won't believe it," Jimmie said.

"Don't be so sure about that," J.P. said. "I was a St. Bernard cop for quite a while. I have it on good authority you got drunk on a hunting trip and visited Bernadine's."

Everyone in Chalmette had heard of Bernadine's whore house at a truck stop in rural St. Bernard Parish. Getting laid there was almost a right-of-passage.

"You wouldn't, would you?" Jimmie said.

"Never know what I might do unless you start keeping your big mouth shut," J.P. said.

"Uncle," Jimmie said. "Paula would have my nuts if she knew I'd visited a whore house."

"And I'd be handing her the dull knife," J.P. said. "We got a deal?"

Jimmie gave J.P. and Chief fist bumps. "Deal," he said.

"Good," J.P. said. "Tell us what you know about the person who took Millie's place."

"A new woman is the head of the shelter now," Jimmie said.

"What's her name?" Chief asked.

"Susie Larsen. She was head of a high-kill shelter in south Texas. Turned it into zero kill. She came to Chalmette with quite a reputation," Jimmie said. "She's a cowgirl and don't take no bullshit from nobody."

"Sounds like a mean one to me," J.P. said.

"You damn sure don't want to get on her bad side," Jimmie said. "At least that's what I hear."

"I like cowgirls," J.P. said. "We'll get along just fine."

"Don't be too sure about that," Jimmie said. "Word on the street is she don't like men. Don't mess with her, or she'll knock your ass out."

"She can't be that bad," J.P. said.

"You ever know a woman bull rider?" Jimmie asked. "She rode one on a dare at the Fort Worth rodeo."

J.P. said, "Anybody can get on a bull. Staying on it is the problem."

"She rode the bull for eight seconds and jumped off on her own."

"Damn!" J.P. said. "I never made eight seconds."

"Maybe you'd better let me do the talking," Chief said.

"Then we're in real trouble," J.P. said. "You're the one that almost cost us our deal with the shelter in the first place."

"I was strongly attracted to Millie Folsom," Chief said. "Sounds like we're not going to have that problem with Miss Susie Larsen."

"Not if she can arm wrestle a bear," J.P. said.

"Our intentions are good. Things will work out," Chief said.

"Have you met this woman?" J.P. asked.

"Never laid eyes on her. Sounds like she can

benchpress a Saints linebacker," Jimmie said.

"You are both too insensitive," Chief said. "Better let me do the talking.

"I'm not a chauvinist," J.P. said.

"Maybe not," Chief said, "though sometimes you come across as one. Hell, Jimmie doesn't even know what a Chauvinist is."

"Yes I do," Jimmie said. "Paula never lets me forget. I'm as tolerant as the next fellow."

Chief grinned. "That's not very tolerant."

J.P. parked the truck in front. "We can handle this," he said.

They found a young woman behind the counter when they entered the shelter. Curly blond hair draped her shoulders and framed enormous blue eyes. Her worn jeans were so tight they highlighted her slender legs and well-rounded ass. The young woman's yellow blouse was tied in a bow, revealing her taut stomach and dimpled belly button.

The drop-dead gorgeous woman smiled when she said, "What can I do for you?"

"We need to talk to Ms. Larsen," Chief said.

"Susie Larsen?" the pretty woman asked.

"That's her," J.P. said.

The young woman smiled and said, "You're looking at her."

Chapter 3

Chief, J.P., and Jimmie bellied up to the counter, J.P. looking shell-shocked as the young woman waited for someone to speak.

"We'd like to adopt some dogs," he finally said.

"All three of you?" the woman asked.

"We're together," J.P. said. "We have a specialty dog training facility over on Oyster Island."

"So you're a business?" she asked."

J.P. glanced at Chief and then back to the woman named Susie.

"Yes," he said.

"We don't adopt our dogs out to businesses," she said.

"Why not?" J.P. asked.

"Too much potential for abuse."

"How's that?" J.P. asked.

"Factory owners are notorious for chaining dogs or leaving them with minimal food and shelter on the grounds after hours," Susie said. "I'm afraid you'll have to go somewhere else."

"We adopted seven dogs when Millie Folsom was the administrator here," Chief said. "She checked out our operation on the island and found no such abuse."

"What's your name?" Susie asked.

"I'm Grogan la Tortue. This is J.P. Saucier and Jimmie Boutet."

"What's the name of your facility?" she asked.

"It doesn't have a name yet," J.P. said.

"You said you've already adopted seven dogs. What happened to them?" Susie said.

"They proved unsuitable as service dogs," Chief said.

"Maybe we better go to my office," Susie Larsen said. "Jason, can you watch the front for a while?"

A young man returning from the kennel removed his ear protection, smiled, and took the young woman's place behind the check-in counter.

"Please follow me," she said.

They followed Susie Larsen down a long hallway, J.P.'s eyes glued on the worn fabric of her tight jeans. Chief gave his arm a bump.

"This is important," he said beneath his breath. "Get your head out of your ass."

Susie's office was plain vanilla, a gray metal desk occupying much of the little room. Susie took a chair behind the desk and motioned them to sit as she fired up her computer.

"Now," she said. "What's become of the seven dogs you previously adopted?"

There were only two chairs in front of the desk. Chief and J.P. each took one. Jimmie stood behind them.

"We built kennels for them. They are well-fed and taken care of," Chief said.

"What do they do?" Susie asked.

"We had a little problem," J.P. said. "We used them for security."

"What problem?" Susie prompted.

19

"An intruder was stalking the island. The dogs are guard dogs. They protected us from the intruder."

"Why didn't you just call the police?" she asked.

"The intruder wasn't human," J.P. said.

Susie glanced up from her computer and said, "Pardon me?"

Chief stepped forward after motioning J.P. to shut up. "What Mr. Saucier means is the intruder was an animal."

"What sort of animal?" Susie said.

"A wolf," Chief said.

'There are no wolves in Louisiana," Susie said.

"Grey wolves moving up from Mexico," Chief said. "It's becoming an epidemic."

Susie shook her head. "You aren't a very good liar, Mr. la Tortue. Better tell me the real story, or be good enough to get out of here before I call the police."

"We had a Rougarou problem," Jimmie said.

"What the hell's a Rougarou?" Susie asked.

"A Cajun werewolf," Jimmie said.

Susie rubbed her hand through her curly hair. "I may be blond, Mr. Boutet, but I'm not stupid."

J.P. stepped forward. "I was a lieutenant with the St. Bernard Parish police until this morning. Call my former boss. He'll verify our story. I'll give you his number."

"I've had several conversations with Captain Comier and already have his number."

Susie dialed her cell phone, soon smiling as she engaged in a pleasant chat with someone she knew. She glared at J.P. when she returned her cell phone to the top of her desk.

"I'm from Texas, Mr. Saucier. I don't believe in fairy tales. Still, Captain Comier verifies your story." She showed J.P. a palm when he started to speak. "I live in Louisiana now and I'm prepared to give you the benefit of the doubt."

"Great," J.P. said with a smile. "Can we pick out our dogs?"

"You can have one dog. I choose which one it is," Susie said.

"But. . ."

"No buts, Mr. Saucier. Lady is a five-year-old Golden Retriever and possibly the smartest dog in this facility."

"We were looking for a younger dog," J.P. said.

"Well, that's too bad, Mr. Saucier. Lady is the only dog you're walking out of here with today. Take her or leave her."

Seeing the passion in Susie Larsen's eyes, J.P. said, "We'll take her."

"Fine," Susie said. "There are other stipulations."

"Such as?" J.P. said.

"I'll be checking on Lady's progress. If you have ulterior motives in this transaction, I'll prosecute you to the fullest extent of the law. Am I making myself clear, Mr. Saucier?"

"Yes, ma'am," he said.

"I'm Susie," she said. "You don't have to call me ma'am."

"You got it, Susie," J.P. said. "It's almost lunch, and Chico's is a little café on the south end of Montesquieu Street. They make the best gumbo in Chalmette."

"Chico's is a hole-in-the-wall," Susie said. "I love hole-in-the-walls. Let's do it."

"You like gumbo?" J.P. said.

"The only seafood I ever ate when I was growing up in Texas was fried catfish," Susie said.

"Gumbo is the nectar of the Gods. Nothing better on earth," J.P. said.

"Jason," Susie called before walking out the

door. "I'm going to lunch. You're in charge until I get back. And get Lady ready. We just adopted her out."

Chief and Jimmie climbed into the backseat of J.P.'s twin cab. When J.P. walked around to the front passenger seat to let Susie into the truck, he got a painful surprise. Reaching between the legs of his jeans, she grabbed him by the balls.

"I'm not sure what the name of the game you're playing is, J.P. Saucier, but if I find out you're anything other than on the up and up, I'm going to twist off your manhood. Got me?"

"Yes, ma'am," he said.

"My name is Susie, and I don't tolerate fools. I can get into the truck without your help."

"Yes, ma'am, Susie," he said as she released her grip.

Susie was all smiles as they drove the short distance to Chico's. They found the broken shell parking lot packed, and J.P. had to park a block away. Clifton Chenier's zydeco accordion blared from an old jukebox as they entered the tiny café.

"Looks like we might have to sit at the bar," J.P. said.

Before they could grab a stool, a smiling man exited the rear and grabbed Susie's arm.

"You don't have to sit there, Miss Susie," the man said. "I'll clear a table for you." The little bald man wearing a greasy apron ran off a table of regulars and cleared their table. "What are you drinking?"

"Lone Star for me, Isaac," Susie said. "Don't know what these gentlemen are drinking,"

"Abita Amber," Chief said.

"Coors," J.P. said.

Jimmie winked when Isaac said, "And you, Mr. Boutet?"

"Busch and a shot of whiskey," Jimmie said.

"You got it," Isaac said as he started through

the crowded little room.

"Seems you already knew about this place," J.P. said.

"Me and every other gumbo connoisseur in Chalmette," Susie said with a smile.

Susie's blue eyes shined when J.P. said, "You said you grew up eating fried catfish."

"New Orleans is one of my favorite places," she said. "I was a freshman in college when I first tasted gumbo. I'm a fan."

Diners filled every table in the tiny café, the din of conversation, rattling plates, and clack of pool balls heightening the ambiance. Jimmie and Chief were engaged in conversation. J.P. whistled when Susie bent over the table to grab a bottle of Louisiana hot sauce.

Susie smiled when J.P. said, "You got one nice ass on you."

"I ought to slap your face," she said.

"Why don't you?" J.P. said.

"I'm as hot over you as you are of me," she said. "Even intelligent women have lust in their souls."

"Then maybe we should do something about it," J.P. said.

"You like line dancing?" Susie said.

"Only a couple of things I like more," J.P. said.

J.P. realized how drop-dead gorgeous Susie was when she smiled and said, "Bet I know what your favorite is."

"Bet you're right, pretty woman," he said.

"My favorite, too," Susie said. "Been a while since I've ridden a bull."

"Are you suggesting what I think you're suggesting?" J.P. asked.

"Got a problem with it?" she asked.

"No problem at all," he said.

"When we return to the animal shelter, let

23

your friends take Lady back to the island. Stay with me. I'll give you a grand tour of the facility. When I get off work, we'll come back here, and you can challenge me to a game of pool. After I kick your ass, we'll go line dancing."

"Sounds like a plan to me," J.P. said. "Will I be staying the night?"

"If you don't get drunk and too obnoxious," Susie said.

Susie grinned when he said, "I'll do my best to stay sober. Sometimes I have a problem not being obnoxious. You want to place a little bet on that pool game?"

"I can't even remember the last time I lost at pool," Susie said. "You beat me, and I'll do anything you ask in bed tonight."

"And if I lose?" J.P. asked.

Susie could barely suppress her grin when she said, "Then we'll have some real fun."

"Think I'm getting scared," J.P. said.

"Don't," Susie said. "You might decide you like it."

"Sounds like I need to lose the game of pool on purpose," J.P. said.

Susie's lips lit a fire in J.P.'s loins when she kissed him.

"Don't do that," she said. "I like playing games, and I love it when somebody I trust calls the shots."

"You trust me?" J.P. asked.

Susie smiled and said, "Hell no. It doesn't stop me from being hot for you."

J.P.'s head was reeling. "You have a favorite place to go line dancing?"

"Boudreaux's Claws and Craws," she said. "On Lost Lagoon."

"One of my favorite places," J.P. said. "Hot as I'm feeling, maybe we should just go straight to your house."

24

Susie shook her head. "Not the way it works. You're a beautiful man, but nothing makes me hotter than working up a sweat while listening to a Cajun band and doing a little line dancing."

"I'm hip, pretty lady," J.P. said. "Let's do it."

A waitress in a flowing white dress appeared to take their orders.

"I'm Meika," she said. "The oyster po'boy is our special today, or you can order from our lunch menu."

Meika's dark hair flowed over her shoulders. Though she looked eighteen, J.P. realized she was older, maybe even thirty. Meika's eyes were also dark like her hair, and she was pretty enough to be a runway model. She wasn't smiling when she made eye contact with J.P. After Meika had delivered their food, J.P. noticed the smile on Susie's face.

"You know each other?" he asked.

"Meika's my roomie. Single girls sometimes have to split expenses to survive," Susie said.

J.P. didn't comment, and Susie added nothing further to her explanation. After eating, they paid their tab and hurried through the still crowded restaurant to the parking lot. Before exiting the door, J.P. turned to see Meika staring at them.

Jason brought Lady to Susie's office when they reached the Chalmette Animal Shelter.

"What a beautiful dog," J.P. said. Lady responded when he said, "Sit."

He'd soon put Lady through a half dozen commands. She responded positively to all of them.

"Impressed?" Susie asked.

"She's a dog trainer's dream," J.P. said, petting the Golden Retriever's big head.

When they'd finished filling out the paperwork, Chief said, "Maybe we'd better get on the road."

25

J.P. flipped the keys to Jimmie and said, "I'm not coming with you. When Susie gets off work, we're going dancing."

"I'll give him a ride back to the island," Susie said.

"Miss Susie and I have things to discuss. Treat Lady like a princess. She's going to be our first graduate."

Chief shot J.P. a glance and said, "Try to stay out of trouble."

Chapter 4

After seeing Chief's cat Buttercup disappear into what seemed a solid rock wall, Odette had put her hand on the rune-inscribed barrier. Something grabbed her arm, yanking her through the portal. She screamed when she saw what had hold of her arm.

A giant bear-like creature with glowing eyes and drool dripping from big fangs in its open maw had Odette in its grasp. Sharp talons left blood on her arm when she yanked it out of the beast's grasp and ran toward the rock wall.

The creature was like nothing Odette had ever seen. As big as a grizzly bear, the animal's head looked like a hyena. Whatever it was, it had convinced Odette it would make a meal of her unless she could escape. The beast backed away when large rocks began raining on it.

Someone had tossed the rocks, and Odette quickly learned who it was as she gazed at a powerfully-built man with blue eyes and blond hair reaching his bare shoulders. The man's chest was also naked, his only clothing an animal skin loincloth and skin boots. Grabbing Odette's hands, he pulled her to her feet.

"Can you run?" he asked.

The man didn't wait for her answer when the creature came bursting from the fog. Pushing Odette ahead of him, he followed her, the sound of snarls and growls directly behind them. When they reached a narrow path leading up the rock wall, he motioned her to start climbing.

Odette stumbled on the loose rock, slipping back into the man's grasp.

"It's too slippery," she said. "I can't make it."

The man grasped Odette's buttocks and lifted her upward.

"We'll either make it to the top or die here," he said. "This path is too narrow for the cave bear. It's the only chance we have."

Odette's bare feet were bleeding when they reached the top of the ledge. A blanket made of animal skins and a rock-tipped spear rested on the ground. The man grabbed both.

"Who are you?" Odette asked.

Though powerfully built, the man who'd saved Odette wasn't much taller than she was.

"Asger," he said. "The spear of God."

"I'm Odette. Though I don't recognize what language you speak, I understand your every word."

The creature had found another path up the rock ledge, and they could tell from the noise it would soon reach them.

"No time for conversation," Asger said. "The cave bear is close and too big to kill with my spear. Your feet are bleeding. Can you run?"

"Lead the way," she said.

Though in her new surroundings for only a moment, she quickly realized the temperature had dropped nearly twenty degrees.

That wasn't all. The lighting had changed, the dark sky becoming a color Odette had never seen. It sparkled with red, orange and yellow colors. The strange hues of Odette's new surroundings shook her sense of reality, and she wondered if she was dreaming.

Asger pulled Odette into a maze of shrubbery. Stunted shrubs she couldn't identify covered the sand. The beast had crested the ledge as they disappeared into the undergrowth. Odette and Asger soon outdistanced it.

Odette had never seen the Northern Lights. When she gazed skyward, she experienced them for the first time. The lights weren't the only thing in the sky: giant hairy bats circled above them, one coming so close that Odette could feel the beat of its wings. As the sky continued to darken, the temperature began rapidly dropping. She was near exhaustion when Asger found an opening in a rock wall.

"I'm freezing," Odette said.

Asger took the animal skin cloak and draped it around her shoulders.

"This will warm you," he said.

"What about you?" she asked.

"I'll use what magic I have left to shield myself from the cold," he said.

"This cloak is big enough for both of us. Come under with me," Odette said.

"It will slow us too much," he said. "I'm okay."

"The temperature is dropping," Odette said. "If you freeze, I'll die with you."

The sky had disappeared, the light hazy as snow began falling in large clumps. Wind whistling through the shrubs made it seem even colder.

"You have no boots," Asger said. "We must hurry before your feet turn to ice."

"Where?"

"Refuge in the distance that will provide us warmth."

"I hope it's a house with a roaring fire in the

fireplace," Odette said.

"A warm pool," Asger said. "We must reach it before the winter gods freeze our souls."

Odette's face became numb as Asger pulled her through the drifting snow. When they reached a steaming pool of water, he pulled Odette's nightie over her head. Removing his loincloth, he placed it beside the hot water pool and led Odette into it. Up to her neck in hot water, Odette began to revive.

"Where are we?" she asked.

"In a thermal pool of water," Asger said.

Asger shook his head when Odette asked, "Do you live here?"

"I doubt anyone could survive long in this place," he said.

Rock ledges surrounding the pool helped to break the wind. Steam rising from the clear water reeked of sulfur. Odette didn't care as she reclined in the shallow pool letting hot water cover every part of her body except for her nose and the top of her head.

"What were you doing out here wearing nothing but boots and a loincloth?" Odette asked.

When Asger smiled, Odette could see how handsome he was.

"I was hunting and wandered too far from where I live. I'm lost."

"Oh, shit! What are we going to do?" she asked.

"Stay in the pool until I come up with a plan," he said.

"It feels wonderful, but we'll soon be shrunken prunes," she said.

"What's a prune?" Asger asked.

"A plum shrank by dehydration," Odette said.

Asger grinned. "I understand your words, but not their meaning."

"Sorry," she said.

"Maybe I should leave you here in the pool," Asger said. "If I could find my people, I could return with furs to protect you from the cold."

"You said you were lost," Odette said.

"This isn't the place where I live," he said. "I somehow crossed over to another world. I've wandered in circles for days, finally returning to this spot."

"I'm also from another world. You saved my life, or it would have ended in a place I don't recognize. What are we going to do?"

"It is almost summer in Vinland, where I live," Asger said. "Here, the nights are unbearably cold."

"Not to mention some scary creatures," Odette said.

"It'll grow warmer when the sun comes up. We'll spend the night in the pool. Tomorrow, we'll try to find either my home or yours."

He smiled when Odette said, "If we aren't shrunken."

"Like prunes?" he said.

"I think I like you," Odette said.

The rock ledges around the thermal pool kept the heated air from dissipating. When Asger and Odette got out of the hot water and dried on the bank, Odette put on her nightie and Asger his loincloth. After draping the skin cloak around Odette's shoulders, he cut the tops of his knee-length boots with his knife and began crafting a pair of leather shoes for her. When he finished, he slipped them on her feet.

"Perfect," he said.

"Ooh! They feel so warm and wonderful. How did you do that?" Odette asked.

"In Vinland, you learn to survive or die very young," Asger said.

Odette kissed him and said, "Thank you."

"Today is my birthday," he said.

31

Using her best sultry voice, Odette began to sing happy birthday. When his smile turned to a frown, she said, "What is it?"

"A tiger stalks," he said. "Can you hear it?"

Odette had trouble hearing anything over the blowing wind.

"Tiger?" she said.

Asger said, "It has our scent."

"What'll we do?" she asked.

"Run," he said.

Pulling Odette to her feet, he led her out of the rock ledges encircling the hot water pool. Even with the skin cloak wrapped around her, she could feel the cold when they left their temporary shelter.

"Where are we going?" Odette asked.

"I don't know yet. Remain silent, or the tiger will hear us."

The snow grew progressively deeper, the winds howling. The animal skin cloak and the shoes Asger had crafted for her kept her warm though she wondered how he would survive dressed in only boots and loincloth. After they had traveled a kilometer, she pulled him under the skin cloak and put her arms around his waist.

"You're freezing," she said. "Stay under the cloak with me."

"Even with it, we'll die unless we find shelter. And that's if the tiger doesn't kill us first."

"I'm scared," Odette said.

Asger showed her the spear. "If we can't run, then we fight."

He nodded when she said, "Can you kill a tiger with only a spear?"

"I'll fight to the death," he said.

Odette squeezed his hand. "I'll help you. I'm one mean bitch when I get pissed."

He laughed. "If we die, we'll give the big cat

indigestion."

Odette wasn't so sure when she said, "We aren't going to die."

"The tiger is faster than we are, and he isn't far behind us. Can you hear him now?"

Odette was surprised that, having attuned to the surroundings and the huffing of the tracking beast, she could. Though unsure how Odette realized it had their scent and was closing in on the kill.

"We need a plan," Odette said

"This place is familiar to me. It's very close to where I crossed over from my world. There's a rock ledge ahead, a log stretching across a stream to the other side. If we cross the log, the cat can't follow us."

"Because?" Odette asked.

"It's too heavy. After we reach the other side, I'll push the log into the chasm," Asger said.

"The tiger is close," Odette said. "I can smell it. How much farther is this log?"

"Close," Asger said.

They followed a narrow path to the top of a ledge, the wind howling. The snow began falling harder, the cold almost unbearable. Odette wondered if they were going to survive. She gasped when Asger tripped, going to his knee in the snow. Odette had a tight grasp on the skin cloak to keep it from blowing away.

The tiger was close behind them when they reached the stream crossing. The log was no more than a foot wide and barely reached the other side of a chasm. The wind blew so strongly that it moved the log spanning the frightening gorge.

"I can't do it," Odette said. "I'm not a tightrope walker."

"The log, or the tiger," Asger said. "That's our choice."

Odette turned to see the giant cat for the first

33

time. It was twice as big as any lion or tiger she'd seen. It crouched as if to spring.

"You can do it, Odette," Asger said. "Get on the log."

"I can't," she said.

"You must. I can't carry you across. Spread your arms to help keep your balance."

Odette thought she was going to faint as she stepped on the log. If she lost her footing, she wouldn't survive the fall.

"I can't do it," Odette said.

"Then the tiger will kill us both," Asger said.

Odette glanced over her shoulder. Asger was crouched, his spear raised as he and the tiger eyed each other. She took one step forward and then another.

"I made it," she screamed. "Hurry!"

Asger lunged across the chasm, barely touching the log. The tiger, intent on sinking his teeth into fresh prey, followed him. Diving the final feet, Asger wheeled around, grabbed the end of the log, and pushed it off the precipice. Odette threw her arms around Asger's neck, refusing to let go until he pried her fingers loose.

"Did we cross over into your world?" she asked.

"This isn't my world or the one from where we just came."

"How do you know?" Odette asked.

"It's too dark, the weather colder. We must find shelter before we freeze. At least the tiger is gone," Asger said.

Odette's lips had turned blue when she said, "I don't see anything that looks like shelter."

Asger pulled her forward. The wind and blowing snow whipped through the canyon when Asger drew to a halt, ducking his head as he led them into a narrow opening proving to be the entrance to a small cave.

"Stay here until I return," he said.

"No," she said.

"We'll die without a fire," he said. "I won't be long."

Odette watched Asger disappear into the darkness, returning shortly with an armload of dry wood. He found a spot near the cave's rear and began distributing the wood. When he finished, he exited the cave again to gather another armload.

"How are you going to light it?" Odette asked when he returned.

A flame appeared from the muscular man's outstretched index finger.

"Magic," he said. "This will keep us warm."

Odette shivered and said, "Better hurry."

As the crackling fire began heating the cave, Asger drew himself and Odette beneath the skin cloak. She hugged him when he draped his big arms around her.

"Shouldn't you have built a fire at the entrance to the cave?" Odette asked.

"Where it's at is the best place," he said. "The flames will heat the entire cave, not just a few feet near the entrance."

As Asger had said, the fire warmed the cave, and the smoke swirled out the opening. Odette needn't have worried about the cave becoming too smoky. The weather outside was well below freezing, but the fire, skin cloak, and Asger's muscular arms kept her warm. She pressed closer to the heat from his body as the chill wind howled outside the cave.

Odette would have fallen asleep from exhaustion had a sound behind them not disturbed her and Asger. Asger threw off the skin cloak, grabbed his spear, and wheeled around to face the intruder. Odette's hand went to her mouth when she saw what it was.

35

Chapter 5

Odette awoke to someone outside her little tent calling her name.

"Odette, are you in there?"

Unzipping the door flap, she stared at the smiling face of her friend, Paula Boutet. The sun was high overhead, and Odette shielded her eyes as Mudbug hurried out of the tent to go to the bathroom.

"What time is it?" she asked.

"Way past the time you normally roll out of bed," Paula said. "What's up?"

"Let me visit the facilities. Tell you when I return," Odette said.

The beach where Odette camped had been public access during the time of the Majestic Hotel and Casino. The showers and toilets in the beach house were still operable, albeit without hot water. Though Odette had yet to grow used to the shower's tepid water, she stayed beneath the flow for ten minutes, ensuring she'd washed every last grain of sand from her hair.

Paula and Mudbug awaited patiently for Odette to return.

Paula grinned when she said, "We thought you must have fallen in."

"Sorry," Odette said. "My hair was a mess."

Odette was draped in a bath towel, a smaller one forming a turban around her damp hair. Paula had spread a beach towel on the sand in front of the tent, and Odette joined her.

"Well?" Paula said. "You were about to explain why you were sleeping so late."

"Something strange woke me last night," Odette said.

"Like what?"

"A white unicorn, a large beautiful animal. That's not all. It had wings and could fly."

"Sister," Paula said. "What were you smoking last night?"

"Nothing, I swear," Odette said.

"Did your unicorn up and fly away?" Paula asked.

"I'm not making this up," Odette said. "I followed it past the Majestic and beyond Chief's hill to a part of the island where I've never before been. The unicorn had disappeared, but I crossed paths with Chief's cat Buttercup."

"Are you making this up?" Paula asked.

"I promise I'm not," Odette said.

"Then I'm sorry I interrupted you. Please go on with your story."

A flock of seagulls flew over the tent on their way to the beach. Odette gave them a glance before continuing.

"This is where it starts getting strange," Odette said.

"Stranger than a flying unicorn?"

"You got it," Odette said. "There were huge boulders and rock ledges like I've never seen in Louisiana. Buttercup led me to a wall of rock covered with runes."

"You were having yourself quite a dream," Paula said.

"If it was a dream, it seemed as real as you

and I, right now."

"I'm listening. Go on with your story," Paula said.

"While I was looking at the runes, Buttercup walked into the rock wall, as if it were a door, and disappeared. When I put my hand on the rock, my right arm went into it up to my elbow."

"Must have freaked you out," Paula said.

"Not as much as what happened next," Odette said. "Something grabbed my arm and pulled me through the rock wall."

"This is starting to sound more like a nightmare," Paula said.

"It became one when I saw what had hold of my arm."

"What?" Paula said.

"A giant creature that looked like a cross between a bear and a hyena. It would have killed me if it weren't for Asger."

"Asger?" Paula said.

"A blond, blue-eyed Viking who seemed a body-building runway model. He was on the ledge behind me and dropped rocks on the beast until it let me go. It was snowing, the temperature below freezing. Asger rescued me from the beast."

"You had a dream, all right," Paula said. "A wet dream."

"You're laughing. It isn't funny to me," Odette said. "I've never had a dream that felt so real."

"Not even a lucid dream?" Paula asked.

They heard the creaking of the bridge to the island as J.P.'s truck crossed it. Its horn honked when it stopped in front of Jack's little house.

Odette grinned. "I've had lucid dreams so real I'd wake up swearing I'd just had the best sex of my life. Last night was more than a lucid dream."

Paula blushed. "Me too," she said.

"Love your sandals," Odette said. "Where'd you get them?"

"Riverwalk Marketplace," Paula said. "I love it. Get some clothes on. We should at least find a few hoofprints if you followed a unicorn across the island last night."

Odette exited the little tent dressed in khaki shorts and a white tee-shirt emblazoned with L.S.U. Logo. Looking so much alike, she and Paula could have passed as sisters.

Paula grinned when Odette said, "My sandals aren't as stylish as yours."

Paula said, "Then trade me," Flipping her sandals into the sand.

"You kidding?" Odette said.

"You're my best friend," Paula said. "It makes me happy to know you'll enjoy the sandals as much as I did. Besides, your pair isn't exactly chopped liver."

Odette smiled when she said, "You're the best, Paula."

Early spring, the weather was warm as Paula, Odette, and Mudbug set out toward the Majestic. They hadn't gone far before they found prints in the sand.

"See," Odette said.

"It rained last night," Paula said. "These could be hoofprints. Then again, they could be something else."

"What else?" Odette said.

"I'm not doubting you, baby," Paula said. "Just saying. . ."

As they approached the Majestic, Odette saw something in the sand in front of them. She ran to retrieve it and smiled when she showed it to Paula.

"The Afghan you made me. I must have dropped it last night."

"Something could have taken it from your tent," Paula said.

"No way," Odette said. "When I'm inside, the

flap is zipped to keep out mosquitos and other creepy-crawlies."

Paula took the Afghan and said, "We need Old Joe. If you were out last night, he'll be able to track your route."

"Great idea," Odette said. "Let's go get him."

"No need to do that, baby," Paula said. "I have a mental bond with Old Joe. If I concentrate, he'll come."

Paula dropped to her knees, lowered her head, and closed her eyes. Almost immediately, they heard a dog barking in the distance. When Odette glanced toward Jack's house, she saw a big dog running toward them. When the beautiful animal reached them, it went straight to Paula.

"You're not Old Joe," she said. "Who are you?"

Odette checked the tag on the collar of the beautiful Golden Retriever.

"Her name is Lady," she said.

"The boys went to the Chalmette Animal Shelter today to get a smart dog J.P. could train to get some quick money," Paula said.

"For what reason?" Odette said. "We have money for the project."

"The Chalmette Police canned J.P. today," Paula said. "Like most bachelors, he hasn't saved a penny."

"Why did Lady come and not Old Joe?" Odette asked.

Lady wagged her tail when Paula wrapped her arms around her neck.

"Because I feel I've known her forever," Paula said. "I've always wanted a Golden Retriever. Now I have one."

Paula frowned when Odette said, "Until J.P. trains and sells her."

Paula didn't respond to Odette's prediction as she let Lady smell the Afghan they'd found in the sand.

"Find the scent, Lady," Paula said.

Lady immediately put her nose to the sand and moved away from the Majestic. Paula and Odette followed close behind, passing Chief's hill as Lady led them to the island's backside.

Odette kept glancing around, looking for boulders and rock ledges. There were none, only lots of sand, sea sedge, and a grove of pine trees stunted by the salt air. Lady's nose came up from the sand, her circles ever-widening. The beautiful dog finally returned to Paula and lay in the sand for another order. Paula hugged her and rubbed her head.

"She's lost the scent," she said. "See anything you recognize?"

Odette shook her head. "Maybe it was just a dream," she said.

"It's okay if it was," Paula said. "Let's go to Jack's and get the scoop on this pretty dog. I missed lunch, and I know you did too."

Paula, Odette, and the two dogs headed back across the island to Jack's house at the foot of the Oyster Island lighthouse. Lady was no longer in the lead and seemed happy to stroll behind the two women and her new pal Mudbug. When they reached the house, they found Jack, Jimmie, and Chief erecting a wall at the site of the dog training facility.

"You missed breakfast and lunch," Jack said. "Where have you been?"

"Can't a girl sleep late occasionally?" Odette said.

"Why not?" Jack said with a smile. "I see you and Paula found our newest student."

Lady's tail wagged when Jack petted her.

"She's going to be a service dog?" Paula asked.

"That's the plan," Jack said. "J.P., Chief, and

Jimmie went to the shelter to get three dogs. Jimmie, Chief, and Lady returned without J.P."

What happened to him?" Odette asked.

Jimmie laid his hammer on a sawhorse and said, "A woman. What else would you think?"

"What woman?" Odette asked.

"Susie Larsen," Jimmie said. "The person who took Millie's place as head of the Chalmette Animal Shelter."

"You're kidding," Paula said. "I heard Ms. Larsen is a lesbian and lives with a woman."

"Meika, a waitress at Chico's," Jimmie said. "She didn't like it one little bit how Susie and J.P. were flirting and touching between bites of gumbo."

"What about Lady?" Paula asked. "I thought you said you wanted three dogs."

"Susie would only give us one, and that dog is Lady," Jimmie said.

"Then we'll have to get three dogs somewhere else," Paula said. "Lady and I are attached. She's staying with me and is my dog now."

"J.P.'s not going to like it," Jimmie said.

"Then he'll have to stuff it," Paula said. "I'm keeping Lady. Does anyone have a problem with that?"

Jimmie gave Chief and Jack a glance but declined to comment further. Knowing when to keep quiet, Chief and Jack did the same. Seeing trouble brewing, Odette changed the subject.

"I can't believe how much progress you've made on the training facility," she said.

Jimmie's dour expression changed into a smile. "Come see," he said.

Odette and Paula followed Jimmie down the hill a hundred feet to where the terrain had flattened. They had already poured the concrete slab, complete with plumbing fixtures, and erected some of the framings for the walls.

"I didn't realize how big it'll be," Paula said.

"Twenty-thousand square feet of office space and storage," Jimmie said. "Another twenty for kennels and training."

"We're debating whether to add a second story," Chief said.

"Do we need that much space?" Odette asked.

"Don't know yet," Jack said. "Depends on how successful we are. If it fails, it'll wind up going to waste."

"It's not going to fail," Paula said.

She gave Jimmie a go-to-hell look when he said, "Unless we can't get enough dogs to train."

"You want to sleep on the couch tonight?" Paula said.

"Just saying," he said.

"There are plenty of shelter dogs that need rescuing," Paula said. "Chief, what do you think?"

"Ms. Susie Larsen controls the Chalmette shelter with an iron fist," he said. "Let's hope J.P. makes a lasting impression on her when they go dancing tonight."

"And if he doesn't?" Odette asked.

"Could be bad for all of us," Jack said. "Too soon to worry about it. Let's call a halt for today and get something to eat. I have a new recipe I've wanted to try out."

"What?" Paula said.

"Grillades and grits," he said.

"That isn't new," Paula said.

"Maybe not to you. It is to a boy from Massachusetts," Jack said.

"Sounds wonderful," Odette said. "Paula and I will help you."

"Love it," Chief said. "It's time we broke out the rum."

"Amen to that," Jack said.

Jack and Jimmie played checkers as they

enjoyed the rum and Jack's strong coffee. The aroma of grillades and grits soon began wafting from Jack's galley, filling his house as the waning sun began dipping toward the western horizon. Distant thunder shook the rafters as a storm over the Gulf moved landward.

Chapter 6

When Jimmie and Chief disappeared down the road in his pickup, J.P. began having concerns.

"Where did your smile go, Cowboy?" Susie said. "We'll have fun tonight, though it's too early to start now."

"I hope so," J.P. said. "I rented my house here in Chalmette, and it's a long walk back to Oyster Island."

"Wipe that frown off your pretty face," Susie said. "Mama will take care of you."

"Last time I heard that I ended up in a Cancun hotel room with no pants or wallet."

"Relax. That's not going to happen," Susie said. "How about a facility tour until it's time to go dancing?"

"I'd love a tour," J.P. said, his smile returning.

Susie handed him a pair of ear protection. "You'll need this," she said. "The shelter is subdivided into offices, kennels for the big dogs, kennels for the small dogs, and pens for the cats."

They followed a concrete sidewalk into the area housing the small dogs. Chihuahuas were by far the number one breed of abandoned animals.

"Why do you have so many Chihuahuas?" J.P.

asked. "I would think they'd be the perfect pet."

"You, the puppy mills, and half the pet lovers in America. They aren't."

"Why not?" J.P. asked.

"They can be noisy, temperamental, headstrong, and stubborn. The little dogs often fail to form a strong bond with their owner. You can't imagine the returns we get, even after what seems like a successful adoption."

"Chief loves his Chihuahua," J.P. said.

"For people who understand how independent the little dogs are, they are wonderful pets. It's a case of one size doesn't always fit everybody."

"Seems to be a problem," J.P. said. "What do you intend to do about it?"

"I started a Chihuahua support group in Fort Worth. You couldn't adopt a Chihuahua until you'd completed a course."

She smiled when J.P. said, "Did it work?"

"Most people are wonderful, and education is the key. Once pet adopters know what they are dealing with, they are more likely to form a lasting bond with their adopted pet. We had almost no long-time Chihuahuas during my term in Fort Worth."

"Love it," J.P. said. "What about the other little dogs?"

"The full-blood dogs are adoptable unless they have special needs. Shelters have a problem placing animals that are blind, deaf, missing a limb, or simply old. Even in perfect health, mixed breeds are also hard to place," Susie said.

"Jimmie said you turned your shelter in Fort Worth from high kill to no-kill. How did you accomplish that?" J.P. asked.

"Education," Susie said. "I got involved with the community and local leaders. Different groups worked on different problems. We sponsored adoption fairs and made them fun for the whole family to attend. It took time, but the situation began turning around."

"What about the big dogs?" J.P. asked.

"Pitbulls are a problem because they have a bad, mostly undeserved reputation. Dogfighters and hunters adopt them. If they don't work out, they kill them."

"How do you handle that?" J.P. asked.

"Background checks, word-of-mouth, and old-fashioned common sense," Susie said.

"Dogfighting is a problem all over the south," J.P. said. "I busted many dog fighting rings when I was a cop."

"Maybe you better tell me why you aren't a police officer anymore," Susie said.

"Police work has a high burnout rate," J.P. said. "It's hard-working twenty or thirty years without developing PTSD or other mental problems. I've been on the edge of burnout for longer than I admit, and training dogs has always interested me."

"Sorry for prying," Susie said. "I needed to ask. I'm glad you quit while you still had your sanity."

J.P. grinned. "I had a little help making the decision. My boss recognized all the signs and didn't like what he saw. He fired me."

"I'm so sorry," Susie said.

"Glad he did," J.P. said. "When I woke up this morning, I felt better than I have in I can't remember when. Then it hit me; my stress was gone."

"Sometimes it takes a smack in the chops to realize where your priorities lie," Susie said.

"Enough about me," J.P. said. "What other problems do you have with your big dogs?"

"People won't adopt big black dogs," Susie said.

"Why is that?" J.P. asked.

"A multitude of reasons," Susie said. "Your friend Chief adopted a German Shepherd, Old Joe, who had been at this facility for quite a while."

"We'd take a hundred dogs like Old Joe," J.P. said. "He's the smartest dog I've ever been around."

"Thank God he found a home," Susie said.

"Then why won't you let us adopt more dogs like him?" J.P. asked.

"There are no other dogs like Old Joe," Susie said "At least full-blooded dogs."

"What's that supposed to mean?" J.P. asked.

"We have mixed breeds as smart as Old Joe at this facility."

"No one wants to pay twenty to fifty thousand dollars for a mixed breed dog," J.P. said.

"Even if they are the perfect service dog?" Susie asked.

"They wouldn't sell," J.P. said.

"Then you're marketing isn't working."

"It isn't marketing. It's perception," J.P. said. "No one wants to pay Ferrari prices for a Honda."

"Even if the Honda is twice as fast and posher?"

J.P. shook his head. "Who is going to believe that claim?"

"You're pissing me off," Susie said. "You're telling me you can't sell a superior product because of the packaging? Then change the packaging."

"What are you saying?" J.P. asked.

"I have three mixed-breed dogs that are smarter than Old Joe. Take them and make me proud, or you'll never get another animal from this shelter," Susie said.

Susie smiled when J.P. said, "Let's see these three super dogs."

On the intercom, she said, "Jason, will you, please bring Clipper, Chuckie, and Venus to the viewing room?"

Shelter worker Jason soon arrived with the three dogs Susie requested.

"Good-looking dogs," J.P. said.

"This is Clipper," Susie said. "We think he is part Border Collie and Standard Poodle.

J.P. knelt and rubbed Clipper's head. The dog barked when he said, "You even look smart."

Chuckie was big and black, a cross between a Labrador and a Rottweiler. Wagging his long tail, he licked J.P.'s mouth. Venus was primarily a German Shepherd and had a look in her eyes that instantly caught J.P.'s attention.

"They're all smart, though Venus is the most intelligent dog I've ever known," Susie said. "She survived life on the street until she was almost grown. She's just begging for someone to train her."

"What's her downside?" J.P. asked.

"She's never had a master and is fiercely independent," Susie said.

"The only way I can sell this is for these three mixed breeds to be smarter than their purebred counterparts," J.P. said.

"Training dogs takes a special person," Susie said. "I see that in you. Won't you give them a try?"

"It's going to be a hard sell," J.P. said.

"Mixed breeds are smarter than full-bloods," Susie said. "It's a proven fact. These three will make wonderful service dogs. Please, give them a try."

"You're very persuasive, pretty lady," J.P. said. "I don't have my truck. How will I get them to the island?"

"Mr. Redd, our truck driver, can deliver them tomorrow. Will you take them?"

"I'm convinced," J.P. said. "Let's fill out the paperwork."

Both J.P. and Susie looked satisfied an hour later as J.P. signed the last document.

"You won't be disappointed," Susie said.

"You're one hell of a salesman," J.P. said. "We may need to hire you as our marketing agent."

"If you can train dogs as good as your ass looks in those tight jeans, you'll have no problem," Susie said.

"Glad you like my ass because I'm in love with yours," J.P. said.

"Then let's go shake them," Susie said. "I'm hot, bothered, and you're the cause."

J.P. grinned when he said, "I like everything you're saying, girl. I can't help thinking you're playing me like a cheap fiddle. It doesn't matter because I love the hell out of it."

Susie held J.P.'s hand on the walk to the parking lot. She pointed to a sky blue Pontiac Firebird and motioned him to get in.

"I didn't know you like vintage cars," J.P. said.

"My granddad owned this car," Susie said. "Dad almost disowned me when he gave it to me instead of him."

"I can see why," J.P. said. "This is a creampuff."

Susie pulled over after driving a mile down the road. J.P. waited as Susie removed the T-top panels. He held on as she powered out of the parking lot.

"Want to drive?" she said.

"You bet," he said.

J.P. spun the tires and laughed when he said, "Glad I'm not a cop anymore. I'd have to arrest myself. This baby is powerful."

"And guzzles the gas," Susie said.

"Where to?" J.P. asked.

"Claws and Craws," she said. "We can watch

the sun go down and have a few drinks before the band kicks off."

"You like oysters?" J.P. asked.

"You have something in mind?" Susie said.

"I'm hoping you do too," he said.

"I like you, cowboy," she said. "I told you that."

"Doesn't matter," J.P. said. "I like hearing it."

The music was loud when they entered the bucolic restaurant abutting a picturesque bayou on the outskirts of Chalmette. The bartender with long dark hair and handlebar mustache smiled and nodded when he saw J.P. The sun had set when J.P. stepped out of the Firebird at Claws and Craws

"How you are?" he asked.

"Happier than a cat with two tails," J.P. said. "How about you, Rémy?

"Tolerable," Rémy said. "What are you drinking?"

"Wild Turkey straight with an Abita chaser," J.P. said.

"And you, ma'am?"

"Dry martini. Can you bring it to us on the deck?"

"You bet," Rémy said.

Susie and J.P. were the only customers on the deck and became locked in a passionate embrace when a waitress arrived with their drinks. Tight jeans accented the young woman's long legs, her raven hair tied in a ponytail beneath her cowboy hat.

"I'm Heather," the woman said. "I have your drinks."

Susie pinched J.P.'s ass before sitting in a plush deck chair. Japanese lanterns swaying in the cool breeze blowing up from the bayou cast shadows across the deck, sparkling in Heather's dark eyes. Her dour expression morphed into a smile when she recognized J.P.

"Is that you, John Pierre Saucier? I haven't seen you in a month of Sundays. Where you been?"

Heather didn't wait for him to answer, jumping into his arms as he sank back into a deck chair. Susie watched them exchange a moment of passion with an amused grin.

"Susie, this is Heather. Her daddy owns Claws and Craws."

Susie never missed a beat. "I like pretty girls, too. You can sit in my lap anytime."

Heather grinned. Most men would have blushed as Susie and Heather exchanged a passionate kiss. J.P. was enjoying it. When Heather broke the clinch and bent over in front of Susie to retrieve her cowboy hat, Susie pinched her.

"Nice ass, cowgirl," she said.

Heather winked at J.P. as she adjusted the cowboy hat on her head.

"I'll be back in a bit with more drinks."

Susie was still grinning when she said, "Please do." When Heather disappeared into the restaurant, Susie noticed J.P. giving her a look. "What?"

"Nothing," J.P. said.

"You like girls," Susie said. "So do I."

"No problem," J.P. said.

"I've never met a man yet that didn't like having two pretty girls in the same bed," Susie said.

"Heather has a steady," J.P. said.

"We can persuade her differently," Susie said.

"Will I be enough for you if she doesn't?" J.P. asked.

"Maybe," Susie said.

By ten o'clock, most of the people at the restaurant for the food and atmosphere had gone home. The club was far from empty as the nightclub crowd seeking live music began taking their place. When J.P. and Susie joined the crowd, a Cajun band called the St. Bernard Playboys was firing up inside, the dance floor already packed.

When the Playboy's finished its first set, J.P. and Susie were perspiring. The temperature in the large room had grown warm as the crush of people dancing to the band's catchy music became ever-more frenetic. Heather had staked a small table in the corner for them and made sure nobody took it while J.P. and Susie two-stepped on the dance floor.

Heather showed up at their table with fresh drinks, laughing aloud when Susie grabbed her hand and pulled her into her lap.

"How about coming home with J.P. and me?" she asked.

"I can't," Heather said.

"Why not?" Susie asked.

"My boyfriend would kill me. He works on a jack-up out in the Gulf; twenty-one days on, seven days off. He's coming home tomorrow night."

"You don't have to tell him, do you?" Susie said.

Heather hiccupped and said, "My mama didn't raise a liar."

"It's not lying if you never tell him," Susie said, handing her the dirty martini. "Have a drink. You might change your mind."

Chapter 7

Having grown up in south Louisiana, J.P. could handle his liquor. Still, he felt no pain when the Cajun fiddle, accordion, and steel guitar of the St. Bernard Playboys began beckoning the dancers back to the dance floor.

Susie grabbed J.P.'s hand and dragged him out of his chair.

"If we don't leave soon," he said, "I'm liable to fall asleep in the backseat of your car on the way to your house."

"Don't be like that," Susie said. "I'm having the time of my life and not ready to leave. Besides, my car doesn't have a backseat."

"What about our night of sexual bliss?" J.P. asked.

"Time for that later," Susie said. "Let's dance."

The dance floor became even more crowded as late-night partiers continued pouring in. When J.P. glanced over his shoulder, he saw someone he recognized. Meika, the dark-haired waitress from Chico's, stared at him and Susie. She wasn't smiling.

At the end of the second set, Susie tossed down her martini as she gazed around the room, looking for Heather.

"Our little waitress is one sexy girl," Susie said. "Hope you didn't scare her off."

J.P. slumped back into his chair. "I've had so much to drink already. I'm not sure I can handle one hot woman, much less two."

"You can always watch," Susie said.

"Not what I had in mind," J.P. said.

"You can't always get what you want," Susie said. "I have to go to the little girl's room. Order me another martini?"

"You got it, sexy lady," J.P. said.

The noise and humidity in the restaurant's ballroom had grown stifling, and J.P. made his way to the deck for a breath of fresh air. He found the deck deserted as he stared down at the bayou known as Lost Lagoon and took a deep breath to clear the smoke from his lungs. He jumped when someone tapped his shoulder. It was Heather.

"You okay?" she asked.

"I'm good," he said.

"I heard the news," she said. "So sorry to hear about you losing your job."

"Damn!" he said. "Is there anyone in Chalmette that doesn't know I got fired today?"

Heather's grin was telling. "I'm so sorry," she said.

J.P. brushed away a mosquito from his neck. "As I said, I'm good."

"You sure?" Heather said.

"Right now, I'm not sure about anything," J.P. said.

"You know Susie's a lesbian," Heather said.

"Then why is she stringing me along?" J.P. said.

"She's playing you for a fool," Heather said. "Her main squeeze Meika is here, and she isn't happy."

"What's the deal?" J.P. said.

"Word on the street is trouble in paradise between Meika and Susie. Meika may be seeing a younger version of Susie on the sly. She also has a boyfriend that doesn't yet know her sexual orientation. Susie is using you to make Meika jealous."

J.P. squeezed Heather's hand. "Is there anyone in Chalmette you don't know about?" he asked.

"When you're a waitress at Claws and Craws, you hear pretty much everything," she said.

"What should I do?" he asked.

"Get in your car and drive away," Heather said.

"Problem one," J.P. said. "I'm In Susie's car."

"What's problem two?" Heather asked.

"Me and some partners of mine have a dog training facility over on Oyster Island. We're getting our dogs from the Chalmette Animal Shelter. Susie runs the shelter." J.P. said.

"Then I have some advice for you," Heather said.

"Give it to me," J.P. said.

"Don't date people you work with," she said.

J.P. grinned. "Too late for that," he said. "What now?"

"You're never going to get into Susie's pants," Heather said. "Let the charade play out. Whatever you do, don't come between Susie and Meika."

Heather left J.P. alone on the deck to ponder her words. When he wandered back into the noise and racket of the dancehall, he found Susie sitting alone at the table. She didn't look happy.

"Where have you been?" she asked.

"Out on the deck for some air," he said.

The band had already fired up its third set, two-steppers crowding the dance floor. Fiddle and accordion music echoed from wall to wall.

"I don't like being left alone," she said.

J.P. gave her a grin and kissed her forehead. "I'm back now and ready to two-step. Are you already worn out?"

Susie's smile returned. "I'll dance you into the ground, cowboy," she said.

Halfway through the third set, a man dressed in Western apparel with a microphone appeared on stage and stopped the music.

"It's time, people, for our weekly two-step contest. The winners get their tabs comped and win a hundred bucks each. They'll share the title of best dancers in St. Bernard Parish."

"We have to win," Susie said.

"There are fifty couples on the dance floor," J.P. said. "Some of them pretty good."

"Not as good as you are," Susie said. "You could be a professional dancer."

"Don't know about that," J.P. said.

"I do," Susie said. "We're the best dancers on the floor. Haven't you noticed how everyone watches us?"

"Not really," he said.

The man on stage with the mike began speaking again. "When the Playboys start their next song, I'll wander through the crowd. If I tap your shoulder, stop dancing and step back from the stage. The contest will be between the last three couples standing. Your applause will decide who wins the title."

Susie squeezed J.P.'s hand in anticipation. When he glanced over his shoulder, he saw why. Meika was staring at them. Susie's little plan was working. She gave Meika a wink through the crowd, put her arms around J.P., and then kissed him.

"Well?" J.P. said.

"You help me win this dance contest," she said.

"And?"

"I'll do my best to ensure your dog training facility on Oyster Island is a success," she said.

"And if we don't?" he asked.

"Not an option," she said.

When the St. Bernard Playboys began their last set with a rousing rendition of Cotton Eye Joe, Susie grabbed J.P.'s hand, pulling him out on the dance floor. The announcer waded into the dancers, tapping a couple on their shoulders. Soon, only three couples remained on stage, J.P. and Susie among them.

"All right, folks," the announcer said. "We got our finalists." He put his hand on the shoulder of one of the dancers. "What are your names, and where are you from?"

"Raymond Berlioz," the man dressed in black, including his boots and hat, said.

"Cyndi Guillory," his pretty blue-eyed dancing partner said.

"And where are you from, Raymond and Cyndi?" the man with the mike asked.

"Metairie," Raymond said.

"Okay, Cyndi and Raymond. You're up. Give us your best moves."

When the Playboys fired up Cotton Eye Joe, the couple performed a half-dozen synched line dance moves to the crowd's applause.

"Great job, Cyndi and Raymond. Please wait on stage until we decide the final results of the contest."

The second couple wore identical western outfits, including flowered shirts, white hats, leather chaps, and boots with spurs.

"What's your name, and where are you from?" the announcer asked.

"Gil LaPierre and Janie Billings from New Orleans," the man said.

"Let's see what you got, Gil and Janie."

Applause began immediately as the couple did a sultry samba to the strains of Cotton Eye Joe.

"They're pros," Susie said. "Not fair."

The music stopped to the enthusiastic applause of an appreciative audience. Janie and Gil were smiling as they joined the other couple on stage.

Most of the people in the audience recognized J.P. and Susie. The smiles of the two couples onstage disappeared when they realized they were the crowd favorite.

"Give us your names and tell us where you're from," the announcer said.

"Susie Larsen and John Pierre Saucier," Susie said. "From Chalmette, America."

The crowd went wild with applause as the band started to play, and Susie and J.P. began to dance. Hoping Susie could follow him, J.P. twirled her in dizzying rotations and then grabbed her by both hands, sliding her between his legs.

An old girlfriend had taught J.P. the swing dance routine, Susie following as if they'd performed it together dozens of times. When they finished, it was apparent from the raucous applause they were the dance contest winners.

"Congratulations," the announcer said. "Here's a hundred bucks for each of you and a trophy you'll have to share.

He didn't need to prompt the audience to applaud as Susie and J.P. left the dance floor. Heather was waiting with fresh drinks when they returned to the table. So was Meika, her frown broadcasting she was less than happy. Susie decided it was time to rub it in. Getting out of her chair, she crawled into J.P.'s lap.

Excited by the music, most of the late-night crowd was drunk. No one seemed to notice—except Meika. When J.P. and Susie felt her cold stare and glanced up into her angry eyes, they knew something dramatic was about to happen.

Grabbing Susie's blouse, Meika yanked her to her feet and slapped her.

"How could you?" she said.

Pushing away, Susie said, "You are the one who wants to date other people. Did you forget?"

Tears appeared in Meika's eyes as her frown melted away.

"I'm sorry," she said.

"I didn't hear you," Susie said.

"I said I'm sorry. Please forgive me?"

Susie stood on her tiptoes and imparted a sensual kiss on Meika's lips.

"Baby, it's me who should be sorry. You've been spending so much time with other people I got jealous."

Meika turned to the big man in Western clothes standing beside her.

"He means nothing to me," she said. "It's you I love."

Susie smirked when she glanced into the eyes of Bruce, Meika's escort.

"Sure about that?" she asked.

"I'm sure," Meika said. "Let's go home."

The big cowboy named Bruce grabbed Meika's wrist. "Now, wait just a minute," he said. "You came with me. Remember?"

Susie slapped his hand away. "Don't you ever touch her again," she said.

J.P., Heather, and Bruce watched as Susie led Meika through the crowd and out the door.

"Damn it!" Bruce said.

"Sometimes you get the bear, and sometimes the bear gets you," J.P. said. "Sit down. I'll buy you a drink."

Bruce backed away into the crowd but not before saying, "Screw you!"

J.P. glanced at Heather and said, "Bruce doesn't know it but he never had a shot. Don't know why I'm laughing. That old bear's claw just raked me across the ass. Hell, Susie even took the trophy."

Heather crawled into J.P.'s lap, draping her long arms around his neck.

"You'd complain about a sharp stick in the eye," she said. "Where'd you learn to dance like that?"

"Long story," he said. "Looks like I've lost my transportation. Can you give me a ride back to Chalmette when you get off work?"

"I thought you rented your house?" Heather said.

"I did," J.P. said.

Heather hoisted Susie's martini and sipped it. "Where are you going to spend the night?"

"Not with Susie," J.P. said.

"I could have told you that when you walked in the door," Heather said.

"Then why didn't you?"

"You had fun," Heather said. "Free drinks, oysters, and the best gumbo in St. Bernard Parish. Not to mention you're a hundred bucks richer."

"Not me, you," J.P. said, stuffing the cash into Heather's shirt pocket.

"You had fun, didn't you?" Heather asked.

"Hell yes!" he said. "Nothing I like much better than dancing to a live Cajun band at Claws and Craws."

"And have the two prettiest girls in the place sit in your lap and rub their bodies all over you," Heather said.

"True that," J.P. said. "Give me a ride to Chalmette?"

"I've already tabbed out," Heather said. "Not only will I give you a ride to town, but you can also spend the night at my apartment."

Heather's old pickup was desperate for a fresh paint job, a new muffler, and replacement springs in the front seat. Happy to have a ride to Chalmette and a place to spend the night, J.P. didn't complain.

When they reached Heather's tiny apartment, she left J.P. in the living area, shutting the door behind her as she went into her bedroom. She returned carrying a pillow and blanket, handing them to J.P.

"My old couch isn't very comfortable. It's the best I can do. Sweet dreams," Heather said as the bedroom door closed behind her.

Chapter 8

John Pierre Saucier was one of those persons who woke up no later than six in the morning despite how late they'd partied the night before. The sun hadn't yet peeked through the only window in Heather Boudreaux's apartment when he opened his eyes and found Heather's cat asleep on his chest.

J.P. had once slept on a park bench during a rainstorm on a camping trip. The worn springs in Heather's old fake leather couch had been even more uncomfortable than the wood he remembered digging into his back. Heather's cat never awoke when he lifted her off his chest and laid her on the blanket.

"Don't know your name," he said beneath his breath, "but you kept me from sleeping alone."

J.P. found Heather's spare bathroom, feeling better when he exited it. Pouring a cup of day-old coffee, he heated it in the microwave. After washing the cup beneath the sink, he returned it to the cupboard before leaving the apartment and locking the door behind him.

Heather was a nighttime cocktail waitress and probably used to sleeping until noon. A morning chill was in the air as he walked up the road toward the Chalmette Animal Shelter. J.P. didn't go far as a Chalmette cop car stopped and rolled down the window. J.P. recognized the young police officer with a buzz cut and big smile who had recently joined the force.

"Is that you, Lieutenant Saucier?"

"It's me, Henry," J.P. said. "I'm not a lieutenant anymore, just J.P."

"Where you going?" Henry asked.

"The animal shelter. I have three dogs headed for Oyster Island this morning. I'm trying to get there before the driver leaves without me."

"Hop in," Henry said. "Heard you and Miss Larsen won the dance contest at Claws and Craws last night."

"Word travels fast," J.P. said. "We sort of had a home-court advantage."

"Don't matter," Henry said. "Where's your truck?"

"Long story," J.P. said. "Tell you about it next time we have a beer together."

Henry pulled the police cruiser around the back of the animal shelter. An older man whose once red hair and handlebar mustache had gone gray was loading three dogs into a yellow van emblazoned with the words Chalmette Animal Shelter.

The young police officer waved and drove away when J.P. said, "Thanks, Henry."

"How you doing, Red?" J.P. asked.

"Fat and sassy," the man named Red said.

"Sassy, maybe," J.P. said. "You've never been fat a day in your life."

"You're right about that," Red said. "What are you doing up before the sun, Officer Saucier," the older man asked.

"Hoping to catch a ride to Oyster Island with you."

"You're in luck. The dogs are loaded. Climb

in."

The inside of the van was neat and clean, the front seat comfortable, unlike the one in Heather's truck.

"What's your last name, Red?" J.P. asked. "Red's the only name I've ever heard you called."

"Michael Redd," he said. "Everyone always called me red because of my hair color. I'm pushing eighty, and that's long gone."

"Why the hell are you still working?" J.P. asked.

"Hell, I got nothing better to do, and I like it," Red said. "No nursing home for me."

"Amen to that," J.P. said.

"Heard you and Miss Susie won the dance contest last night."

"Damn!" J.P. said. "Glad I didn't murder someone. Everyone in town would have known I did it before making it out of the parish."

"You know what they say about small towns," Red said.

"Chalmette isn't that small anymore," J.P. said.

"Got that right," Red said.

J.P. saw a building he recognized up the road. "If you have time to stop at Portie's, I'll buy you breakfast."

"I was hoping you'd ask," Red said, his stoic expression almost becoming a smile.

Portie's was a café on the side of the road to Oyster Island. It stood alone in the center of a tiny broken shell parking lot usually filled with cars and pickups. The wood-framed structure perched atop concrete blocks crying out for a new coat of white paint. The little café bustled with customers as Red and J.P. entered the front door.

"Come in this place," a woman with gray hair and a blue apron said.

When he hugged the older woman, J.P. smiled

65

and followed her to a table barely big enough for him and Red. Without asking if they wanted any, she poured each of them a cup of coffee.

"How you been, Miss Lily?"

"Better now that I seen your pretty face," the woman named Lily said.

"How's Harold?"

"In the kitchen cooking, just like always," Lily said. "Heard you won the two-step contest last night at Claws and Craws."

"Dammit! The Cajun grapevine is working overtime. What else did you hear?" J.P. asked.

Lily had a missing front tooth, the gap in her gums prominent when she laughed.

"That the little girl you went dancing with left you for another woman. Heather Boudreaux took you home. Her boyfriend is looking to kick your ass when he comes in from working offshore tonight."

"Hell, Lily!" J.P. said. "I slept on Heather's couch. I have a sore back to prove it."

"Tell that to Basil Doles," Lily said.

"Heather's boyfriend is Basil Doles?"

"All-star linebacker at L.S.U. before he tore up his knee." Lily cackled and nodded.

"And the oldest son of wealthy cattleman Basil Doles, Sr., the second richest person in St. Bernard Parish," Red added. "Not to mention the most powerful senator in Louisiana."

Red and Lily laughed when J.P. said, "I knew I got up on the wrong side of the bed. I didn't realize I'd stepped off into a knee-deep pile of cow manure."

Customers came in the door, and Lily said, "Got to get back to work. What are you boys eating?"

"Ham and eggs, grits and gravy," Red said.

"Tomato, avocado, and cream cheese omelet," J.P. said. "And don't forget the grits."

"Biscuits or toast?" Lily said.

"Toast with some of your homemade mayhaw jelly," J.P. said.

Red was grinning as Lily hurried away to wait on the table of new customers.

"Lots of people in town think Heather and young Basil are the perfect couple," he said. "The boy's finishing his degree. His daddy is planning a career in politics for him, beginning with a run for school board."

"I never touched the girl," J.P. said.

"Good luck with that argument," Red said.

Though she was grinning, Lily didn't speak when she dropped off their food and winked at J.P.

"I have bigger problems than Basil Doles," he said.

"Such as?"

"Since I'm no longer gainfully employed, I need dogs to train to get ahead of the game until we get our dog training facility up and running."

"You got three heading that way now," Red said.

"Mixed breeds. No matter how well I train them, no one will take a chance buying them," J.P. said.

"Why do you say that?" Red said. "Lots of people buy generic drugs instead of name brands."

"Because generics are cheaper," J.P. said. "That's my point. I'll have to sell the service dogs at a cut-rate price."

"Then why did you take them instead of full-bloods? We have plenty of both at the shelter," Red said.

"Susie Larsen," J.P. said.

Red nodded. "I hear that," he said. "Her way or the highway."

"At least she gave me one good dog to train,"

J.P. said. "A Golden Retriever that's amazingly smart. She's already on the island, and I'll train her first."

Red and J.P. finished eating and were soon again on their way to Oyster Island. After nine, Red pulled the van to a stop by Jack's house and began unloading the three rescue dogs. Jimmie didn't look happy when Red led them into the house on leashes.

"What the hell, J.P.?" he said. "Did you pick those dogs up off the road?"

"They're our new trainees," J.P. said.

"You have to be kidding?" Jimmie said. "My customers want dogs with a pedigree."

"I know," J.P. said.

"Then why the hell did you take them?" Jimmie asked.

"Ms. Larsen gave me no choice. Either take these dogs now or never get another from the Chalmette Animal Shelter." Jimmie's expression changed again when J.P. added, "At least I have Lady to train."

"Sounds like you boys have a family squabble," Red said. "Got to get back to Chalmette. See you later."

Chief, Jack, and Jimmie stared at J.P. with blank expressions as Red walked out the door.

"You might want to talk to Paula about Lady," Chief said.

"What about Paula and Lady?" J.P. said.

"Paula seems to think Lady is her dog now," Jack said.

"Well, she isn't," J.P. said. "She belongs to the Oyster Island Dog Training Facility. We all own a piece of her." Jimmie's head was hanging as he glanced away from J.P.'s stare. "Am I right, Jimmie?"

"You know Paula as well as me," Jimmie said. "She's one hard-headed woman with this crazy idea that Lady is hers."

"And?" J.P. said.

"I'm married to her," Jimmie said. "If someone wants to advise her differently about Lady, have at it. Paula would have my nuts, and it's not going to be me doing it."

J.P. glanced at Jack and Chief. "What do you think about this?"

"Though I'm unsure how it happened, Paula and Lady bonded," Chief said. "I feel your pain. Doesn't matter because it isn't going to be me who says anything about it."

Jack turned away when J.P. said, "Am I the only person who thinks Lady belongs to the group and not Paula?" When no one answered his question, he said, "I need a mug of rum."

J.P. sat in a chair at the plank table, his head in his hands, when one of the rescue dogs offered him a paw. J.P. patted the mutt's head after shaking its paw.

"That's one smart dog," Jack said

"He's smart, all right," J.P. said. "Susie Larsen told me these three were the most intelligent dogs at the animal shelter."

"Then why can't you train them?" Chief asked.

"I can train them and turn them into the best service dogs in the country, but who will buy them?" J.P. asked.

"Who wouldn't buy the best product available?" Chief asked. "It's Marketing 101."

"Seems I've heard that already," J.P. said. "Jimmie thinks differently."

All eyes were on Jimmie when he said, "People want the best there is to offer. Guess we need to make them believe these three mutts are the cream of the crop."

"Can you do that?" J.P. asked.

"It'll be a lot easier if they are the best,"

Jimmie said.

Chief grabbed a fresh bottle of rum, opened it, and poured them a full mug.

"Maybe we hit on something," he said.

"Like what?" J.P. asked.

"Every training facility in the country offers quality dogs," Chief said. "What the Oyster Island Training Facility offers is the best of the best."

Jack sat beside J.P. at the plank table. "The mixed-breed mutt I had growing up was the smartest dog I ever knew. I'm betting that many potential customers have had similar experiences."

"Jimmie," J.P. said. "I'd say you owe me one because of Lady. Can you market these three hounds and get us some serious money for them?"

Jimmie slugged his mug of rum and motioned Jack to pour him some more.

"Don't know about the marketing idea of the century. I'll do my best," he said.

Chapter 9

Well past noon, the sun was still ablaze over Oyster Island as Paula, Odette, and their two dogs frolicked in the surf. Lady, Paula's Golden Retriever, shook the water from her back after fetching Paula's red rubber throw into the waves breaking on the beach. Odette began stripping off her shorts and tee shirt.

"Lady and Mudbug are having too much fun. I'm joining them. What about you?" she said.

"It's broad daylight," Paula said. "The water's cold, and someone might see us."

"You won't freeze, and there's no one near us," Odette said. "Take off your clothes and come swimming with me."

"You're crazy, but I love it," Paula said as she stripped off her shorts and tee-shirt and ran into the surf.

Paula and Odette soon had mile-wide grins as they swam in the whitecaps kicking up from the Gulf of Mexico. A large wave swept over Paula. She was coughing up saltwater when her head popped out of the surf.

"I'm done," she said, climbing out of the waves and lying on the damp sand.

Lady lay down beside her. Mudbug soon joined them.

"Wus," Odette said.

"Don't you ever get tired?" Paula asked.

"Not yet," Odette said, disappearing beneath the waves.

When Odette didn't immediately return to the surface, Paula sat in the sand.

"Odette," she said. "Where the hell are you?"

Paula's heart beat faster as she prepared to dive into the surf. Before she did, Odette's head popped out of the water.

"Oh, my God! You're not going to believe it," she said.

"What? Did something attack you?" Paula asked, grabbing Odette and hugging her when she came dripping out of the water.

"Look what I found," Odette said.

Odette opened her hand, showing Paula a gold doubloon.

"Is it gold?" Paula asked.

"Solid Gold," Odette said. "Feel it if you don't believe me."

Paula took the doubloon from Odette and hefted it in her hand.

"Where did you find it?" she asked.

"In the surf," Odette said. "There's a sunken Spanish treasure ship out there somewhere."

"What's this thing worth?" Paula said.

"Thirty grand, maybe," Odette said. "Hell, I don't know."

"What are you going to do with it?" Paula asked.

"I have no idea. Let's go to Jack's and see if he's cooking. I'm starving."

"Me too," Paula said.

Paula and Odette grabbed their clothes and headed for Odette's tent. They were almost dry when they put on their shorts and tee shirts.

Mudbug and Lady led the way as they set out across the sand to Jack's little house. They found Jack and Jimmie in a spirited debate.

"That's no way to cook redfish," Jimmie said. "You need to blacken it."

"What's going on?" Paula asked.

"I took the skiff out beyond the breakers and caught two good-sized redfish," Jimmie said. "I filleted them up. Jack wants to bake it with lemon and butter."

"Might be good," Paula said.

"Redfish needs to be blackened," Jimmie said.

"The fillets are beautiful," Jack said. "I have no idea how to blacken anything."

"I do," Odette said. "Want to learn how?"

"You bet," Jack said. "Do I have the ingredients you need?"

"I'm sure you do. If not, we'll suffice with what you have," Odette said.

"I'll make the sides," Paula said. "Creole coleslaw and creamy rice pilaf. Got any cabbage and rice?"

"There's rice in the pantry and cabbage ready for harvesting in my winter garden out back," Jack said.

"You're my kind of cook," Paula said.

Jack blushed when Paula kissed his forehead. "What spices do we need?"

"Paprika, cayenne, garlic and onion powder, black pepper, oregano, basil, and salt," Odette said.

"Got all of those," Jack said.

"Now we're talking," Jimmie said with a smile.

J.P. and Chief were playing spades on the plank table, J.P. looking as if he had a caterpillar on his tongue. Everyone was drinking rum, and Jack poured mugs for Odette and Paula.

73

"Does your stove have an exhaust?" Odette asked. "If not, we'll have to blacken the fish outside to handle the smoke."

"No problem," Jack said. "My little galley has all the bells and whistles as a commercial restaurant."

"Great," Odette said. She and Jack soon had a bowl of Cajun blackening powder prepared along with clarified butter. "The cast-iron skillet needs to get hot; ten minutes on an open flame."

The aroma of Paula's savory rice had filled the house, Chief bouncing in his chair in anticipation.

"What now?" Jack asked.

"Dip the fillets in the butter and then rake them through the seasoning to form a crust on both sides," Odette said.

"Now what?" Jack said.

The clarified butter was smoking and rose into the exhaust fan above the stove.

"Stick a fillet in the skillet," Odette said. "A minute or so on both sides is all you need."

Jack was a master cook, and the blackened redfish fillets were perfect when he pulled them from the skillet and began setting them on a bed of the rice pilaf Paula had made.

"Oh, my God!" Jack said as he took a bite. "This is wonderful."

"Best I've ever had," Chief and Jimmie both chimed.

Everyone seemed ecstatic about the meal. Everyone except J.P. Jack had a fire burning in the hearth. Lady was asleep, along with Mudbug, Oscar, Lucky, Coco, and Old Joe. Paula couldn't miss J.P.'s frown.

"Did I serve you a piece of bad fish?" Paula finally asked.

"Best redfish and sides I've ever had," J.P. said.

"Then what's wrong?" Paula asked.

"Nothing," J.P. said. "I know when I'm outvoted."

"Outvoted on what?" Paula said. "Am I missing something?"

"J.P. was planning on training Lady, selling her, and cutting a fat hog," Jimmie said. "He brought three mutts back from the animal shelter."

"I didn't plan to bond with Lady," Paula said. "It just happened. She's mine now."

"As I said, I know when I'm outvoted," J.P. said.

"How much could you have sold Lady for if you had trained her?" Odette asked.

"Twenty grand," J.P. said. "We won't get anywhere near that for the three half-breeds I got from the shelter."

Odette showed him the doubloon she'd found in the surf. "I have a new doubloon. My guess is it's worth thirty thousand or more. Take it," she said.

"For what?" J.P. asked.

"Lady. I'm buying her for Paula," Odette said. "I'll take the three mixed breeds and train them."

"Those three dogs are plenty smart, and I'd have no trouble training them," J.P. said. "We just won't be able to sell them."

"Why is that?" Odette asked.

J.P. nodded when Jimmie said, "No one wants to pay big bucks for a mixed breed dog."

"If the product is superior, what does it matter if it isn't in a premium package?" Odette said.

"J.P. and Jimmie may be right," Jack said. "No one will want to pay top dollar for a mixed breed dog."

Paula threw up her hands. "If you have a product you can't sell, it's either because it's inferior or the work of a piss poor salesman. My Jimmie can sell those three dogs. Can't you, Jimmie?"

"Don't know, honey babe," he said. "Probably not for as much as a full-blood dog."

Paula grinned when she said, "You sleep on the couch tonight."

Paula's change of expression lightened the mood for everyone.

J.P. tossed the doubloon back to Odette. "Keep the gold. I apologize for being such a crybaby. I wouldn't want anyone to take Lucky, so I know Paula's feelings about losing Lady. I'll train the new dogs."

"I'm going to sell the doubloon in New Orleans and donate the money to our project to use as we see fit," Odette said. "J.P. can draw a salary from it until our operation becomes profitable."

"You don't have to do that," J.P. said.

"Let's take a vote," Odette said. "Everyone in favor of J.P. drawing a salary until the operation gets on its feet, say aye."

"Aye," they said.

"The vote is unanimous. I'm available if you need help training the recruits," Odette said.

"Me too," Paula said.

"Thanks," J.P. said. "One more thing, though.

"What?" Jimmie asked.

"Though it'll be hard, we can't keep getting attached to our students. If we do, our training facility will go bust, and we'll have more dogs to feed than we can afford."

"It's hard not getting attached," Chief said.

"Trust me when I tell you they'll be well-treated and loved wherever they go," J.P. said. "Keep things professional, and everything will work out just fine."

76

"Let's look at the new dogs," Paula said.

Jimmie was on it, returning from the kennel with the three new dogs on leashes.

"Gorgeous animals," Paula said. "Do they have names?"

The dog wagged its tail when J.P. knelt and gave him a head rub. "Clipper is a Border Collie, Standard Poodle mix," he said.

Clipper was black and white with floppy ears and the size and tail of a border collie.

"Can you teach him something?" Chief asked.

J.P. had training treats in his left hand. Transferring a treat to his right hand, he held it near Clipper's nose until he lay on the floor.

"Yes," J.P. said, giving him a treat. "Once he learns when you want him to lie on the floor, you add the command 'stay.' With a bit of work, he'll stay on command and remain in that position until he has the 'yes' command."

Clipper learned the routine in record time to the amazement of everyone, including J.P. Clipper obeyed the command, staying in place as J.P. walked across the room. Clipper's tail wagged when J.P. said 'yes,' and he hurried across the floor to retrieve his treat.

"Damn!" Jimmie said. "That's one smart dog."

"We scored a winner with Clipper," J.P. said. "Won't take long to train him. He's going to make someone very happy."

"If he were only full-blood," Jack said.

"He's a full-blood Bordoodle," Odette said. "And he's beautiful."

"Then that's the way to market him," Jimmie said. "We won't have any trouble selling him. This next big boy might be a problem."

"This is Chuckie," J.P. said. "I'll put him through the same paces as Clipper."

Chuckie was a big boy, a cross between a Rottweiler and Labrador retriever. The dog with a big head and massive shoulders had the head of a Rottweiler and the floppy ears of a Labrador. He was also solid black. He learned the stay command quickly enough that everyone applauded.

"This one's going to be a problem," Jimmie said.

"Why is that?" Odette said. "He's brilliant."

"People have an aversion to big black dogs," Jimmie said.

"Because?" Chief asked.

"Because people perceive them as dangerous," Jimmie said.

"That's both racist and preposterous," Odette said.

"I agree," Jimmie said. "Doesn't matter because that's the reality of the situation. We might not be able to sell him."

"Don't know about that," J.P. said. "He'd make a hell of a police dog."

"I wouldn't want to mess with him if I was a criminal," Jack said.

"Venus is our newest female recruit," J.P. said.

"Susie seems to think she's the smartest dog in the universe," J.P. said.

"Susie?" Paula said.

"Susie Larsen, the new head administrator of the Chalmette Animal Shelter."

Odette and Paula exchanged a smiling glance as J.P. taught Venus to stay. Venus was smaller than a German shepherd though it was evident from where most of her DNA was derived. A brindle, Venus was brown with dark streaks.

"She's one intelligent dog," Chief said. "Maybe we should breed her with Old Joe before selling her."

"Is breeding all you men ever think of?" Paula asked.

"If she's half as smart as Susie thinks, Chief may have a great idea," J.P. said.

"She may not like Old Joe," Odette said. "Let's see what she thinks of the idea first."

Jack shook his head as he grabbed a bottle of rum from the pantry.

"We need to hire an administrator," he said. "We're arguing like a bunch of old ladies."

"Who's an old lady?" Paula asked.

Jack was grinning as he poured Paula a mug of rum. "I knew that would get your goat," he said.

A clap of thunder, signaling an unexpected rainstorm, shook Jack's little house.

"Rain's coming," Chief said. "We may as well break out the rum for everybody and settle in for a while."

Chapter 10

It was late when Odette left Jack's house and headed across the island to her tent, a golden moon peeking through the dark clouds remaining from the storm.

She pulled on her nightgown, tired and half drunk from Jack's rum. Much later, something interrupted her sleep. Unzipping the tent, she glanced outside. Odette was alone, Paula having asked if Mudbug could spend the night with Lady.

"Is it you making the noise?" she said.

The whinnying of a horse told Odette the unicorn had returned. As before, Itit was hovering ten feet above her. As she watched, it descended to the sand until it stood directly in front of her. The unicorn stayed put as she stood and hugged its big neck. Instead of moving away, it lowered its front legs, making it easier for her to climb on its back.

Odette could feel the large beast's rippling muscles when she straddled its shoulders. Instead of walking away across the island, the magnificent animal's wings began to beat. Odette was soon in the clouds, high above her tent.

"Where are you taking me?" she asked.

Odette held on tightly to its big neck as it powered away into the cloudy night.

Odette should have been frightened. She wasn't. The clouds were so thick she couldn't see the ground or more than ten feet in front of her. How the unicorn knew where he was going was beyond her comprehension. She was soon aware the temperature had decreased dramatically. When the big animal returned to earth, she saw someone she recognized.

Asger helped Odette off the unicorn's back and wrapped her in his fur throw. "I awoke, and you were gone. I sent Pegasus to search for you," he said.

"Your unicorn is named Pegasus?" Odette said.

"Do you find that strange?" Asger asked.

"Pegasus is one of the most recognized creatures in Greek mythology," Odette said. "You're not Greek, are you?"

"I do not know what a Greek is," Asger said.

"Where are you from?"

"The summer solstice approaches. Festivities will soon begin," Asger said. "I'm hoping we can find our way out of here."

"You have never been here?"

Asger petted the big unicorn. "Only in my dreams," he said.

"It can't be summer," Odette said. "It's freezing."

"Even winter is never this hard where I live," Asger said.

"Then we should go there," Odette said.

"We must return to the cave or freeze out in the cold. Tomorrow, we will search for Spiro."

"What about Pegasus?" Odette said. "He won't fit in the cave."

"Pegasus is magical," Asger said. "The cold doesn't affect him."

Asger smiled when Odette said, "Magical? You like spells and sorcery?"

"The greater the magic one practices dictates their standing in society. The greatest magicians are our spiritual advisors," Asger said.

Asger's fire lighted the inside of the cave. "It feels so much better in here," Odette said. "What are all the markings on the wall?"

"The ancients drew the pictures. Some of them are animals which no longer exist," Asger said. "I'm sorry, I have nothing for you to eat."

"It's okay," Odette said. "Let's crawl under the fur blanket."

Odette wrapped her arms around Asger. Though he smelled of stale sweat, she didn't care as she caressed his rippling muscles. When he put his big arms around her, she felt safer than she ever had in her life.

Dim light filtered through the cave door when Odette realized she was alone beneath the skin blanket. Asger was crouched beside her, his spear pointing at something or someone standing in the mouth of the cave. Her hand went to her mouth when she realized what it was.

A tiny man, no taller than three feet, stood looking at them, a fur cloak draping his spindly arms and legs. He had a crooked cane in his hand raised over his head in answer to Asger's spear. Odette put her hand on Asger's wrist until he lowered the spear. Before he could react further, she stepped in front of him.

"We mean you no harm," she said. "Who are you?"

"Noni," the tiny man answered in a reedy voice. "Who are you, and what are you doing here?"

"It was freezing outside when we found this

cave last night," Odette said. "We didn't know it belonged to someone. Is this your home?"

Noni lowered his cane. "Like you, I sought the cave's shelter to escape the weather."

When Noni let the fur throw fall off his shoulders, she and Asger could see how spindly his arms and legs were. He was also hairless, having no eyebrows or any hair on his body Odette could see.

"Your fire feels good," he said. "I was caught out in the blizzard. I thought I was going to blow away."

The fire had waned, only coals burning hot still heating the cave.

"I'll get more wood for the fire," Asger said. "Will you be all right while I'm gone?"

"I'm small, but I doubt Noni could beat me in an arm-wrestling contest," she said.

"I won't be long," Asger said.

Noni crouched by the embers of the fire without waiting to be asked. Odette joined him.

"You aren't afraid of me?" she asked.

"You don't live into your twenties around here without knowing whom to trust," he said. "You and Asger are human."

"Yes. Aren't you?"

"I haven't seen a human in years. When they were around, they called me an Ozomute," Noni said.

"What the hell is that?" Odette said.

"Someone who isn't normal," Noni said.

"Hell, Noni, if that's the case, then I'm not human," Odette said.

Noni smiled. "I like you," he said.

Asger appeared from the swirling fog outside the cave door with an armload of wood. Flames crackled as he added the bundle to the embers in the fire pit.

"Your fire is wonderful," Noni said. "Thank

you for sharing."

"I'm so sorry we have no food or drink to offer you," Asger said.

"I have water," Noni said, handing a bota bag to Asger. "Drink," he said.

Asger put the bag to his lips. "The only water we found was in the pools created by the geysers. It tasted like salt and sulfur. Where did you get this?"

"From a nearby spring," Noni said, passing the bag to Odette. "Are you thirsty?"

"You can't imagine," she said. "This is the best water I've ever tasted."

"I don't have much else, though I have lots of water," Noni said.

"Can you take us to it?" Asger asked.

"Not until the storm outside ends," Noni said. "We wouldn't last long."

"I need to use the bathroom," Odette said.

Noni motioned to the back of the cave. "This cavern was home to generations of primitives. They ate lots of corn because cobs are littering much of it. There are petroglyphs drawn on the walls. The cave extends into the mountain. There's a portion of the cave the primitives used as a privy. It's still functional.

Odette was smiling when she returned. "Kind of creepy."

"Hungry?" Noni asked.

"I can't remember the last time I ate," Asger said."

"You?" Noni said.

"My stomach is starting to growl," Odette said.

Noni reached into his bag and handed them each a small can. Though Asger had no idea what it was, Odette did. After popping the top of the can, she put her finger into the concoction and then licked it.

"Potted meat," she said. "The label's still on it. Where did you get this?"

"From the great expanse of land where people who used to live here disposed of things they no longer wanted," Noni said.

"Even uneaten cans of food?" Odette asked.

"You can't imagine all I have found there," Noni said.

Odette watched as he consumed its contents.

Asger grinned when Noni said, "Like it?"

"I've eaten worse," he said. "Though not much."

"Can you take us to where you found it?" Odette said.

"After the storm abates," Noni said.

"How long will it last?" Asger asked.

"Sometimes for days," Noni said.

"We may starve before that happens," Asger said.

"It will subside. When it does, and we reach my home, there will be plenty for us to eat," Noni said.

Odette and Asger were asleep again when Noni shook their shoulders and awakened them. A cloudy mist continued wafting outside the cave door. The howl of the wind had ended.

"How long did you let us sleep?" Odette asked.

The question seemed to puzzle Noni, and he shook his head without answering.

"We must go now," he said.

The temperature outside the cavern was still freezing. The frozen terrain began to roll. Rounded hills, some rising hundreds of feet in the air, came into view.

"Is it always this cold here?" Odette asked.

"Always," Noni said.

"There are no seasons?" Asger asked.

"This is all there ever is," Noni said. "The humans called it nuclear winter."

Abandoned bulldozers with broken tracks, rusted dump trucks, rotting tires, and various broken pieces of discarded humanity lay strewn everywhere. Flames, lapping from holes in the bare earth, lighted the dimness with hypnotic, flickering motion. Flying insects, cockroaches, and giant rats were sticking their heads out of holes.

"My God!" Odette said. "I've never seen rats and cockroaches so big."

"Survivors, like me," Noni said. "There are also worms, fleas, and other parasites.

"And the flames?" Asger said.

They jumped when flames burst from the ground in front of them.

"Burning methane formed from buried organic waste," Noni said. "Step carefully."

"It's beautiful," Odette said. "In a weird kind of way. Are there ghosts here?"

"The whole place is haunted," Noni said. "My home is just beyond the next hill."

The color of the sky was pink and green. There was no sun, but it wasn't dark either.

"What are the metal things littering the landscape?" Asger asked.

"Ancient rusted and abandoned vehicles the humans used to tend this place," Noni said

"What's a vehicle?" Asger asked.

"A machine that carries things moves dirt or has some other function," Odette said.

She smiled when Asger said, "What's a machine?"

"It's complicated," she said. "Humans created them to help them do things."

"Like what?" Asger asked.

"As I said, it's complicated," Odette said. "I'll try to explain it to you some time. Right now, I'm at a loss for words."

"My home is near the foot of the next hill," Noni said.

Large creatures with leathery wings soared among the strange clouds. Noni ducked when one of them dive-bombed the ground, swooping skyward after catching a rat scurrying across the terrain.

"Are they dangerous?" Odette asked.

"If you're as small as I am, they are," he said. "I almost made a meal for one of them, but I beat it with my cane until it dropped me."

Odette and Asger glanced skyward before hurrying after Noni as the wings flapping grew louder. The entrance to his home was a dark hole barely discernible until they were almost on top of it. Ancient timbers shored the opening only about two feet in height.

"I am little, and the entrance is tight," Noni said. "We'll have to crawl on all fours for about a hundred yards. It'll be pitch black until we reach the end of the tunnel. Can you make it?"

"I'm game," Odette said.

"Then I'll go first," Noni said. "The darkness is almost unbearable. Don't let it take control of your senses, or it will drive you mad."

"You're scaring me," Odette said.

Noni smiled. "Keep moving, and don't forget to breathe. Stay strong. Once we enter there'll be no room to turn around. There's a light at the end of the tunnel."

Chapter 11

The tunnel was so small and tight Odette wondered if she would make it. She could hear Noni in front and Asger behind her.

"I can go no further," she said. "Back out before we all get stuck."

"You can't go back, only forward," Noni said. "Don't stop."

Suddenly overcome by the darkness and claustrophobia, Odette wanted to scream. Afraid of panicking Asger, she didn't. Asger nudged her from behind. Noni kept up a continuous banter, trying to encourage her.

"Go forward."

"I can't," she said.

"Yes, you can," Asger said. "I'm bigger than you, and there's room enough for me."

Disoriented by her paranoia, Odette inched forward. Dirt crumbling from the tunnel's roof dropped into her hair, eyes, and nose. She could smell Noni in front of her and Asger behind her. Strangely, their odors were comforting. A memory flashed through her anxious brain.

Odette remembered as a child falling off of her bicycle and skinning her knee. Her father, hot and sweaty from working in the yard, had held her in his big arms until she had stopped crying.

"Let's get you in the house and get that knee cleaned up," he had said. "You'll be okay, baby,"

Odette stopped crying when she heard Asger's voice behind her.

"Keep moving. Everything is okay," he said.

Odette did scream from joy and not paranoia as Noni exited the tunnel. A burst of light flooded her beleaguered brain. Noni was also smiling.

"You're going to wake the dead," he said.

Overcome with relief, Odette hugged him and Asger when he exited the tunnel behind her. When she glanced upward, she saw why. The darkness was gone, and a brilliant light flooded the giant chamber.

The underground room extended as far as the eye could see, a concave roof of hazy glass capping an area twice the size of a football field. The light through the octagonal panes cast ghostly reflections. Asger gazed in awe at the unbelievable scene.

The distance from the roof to the floor was at least three hundred feet, the tops of giant trees almost touching the glass roof. The trees weren't the only vegetation. Vines and multicolored flowers covered plots of the lush green grass growing on the ground. The sound of running water greeted their ears. Odette drew a lungful of humidified air.

"It's like the Garden of Eden," she said.

"The humans who created this place called this the Biowomb," Noni said. "Many species of animals live here among thousands of different plants."

The warble of a bird caught Odette's attention. A beautiful thrush sat perched on the limb of a tree. Waves of swallows chasing insects darkened the area beneath the glass roof.

"Where is the light coming from?" Asger said.

"It can't all be through the roof."

"I'll show you," Noni said.

The journey from the cave through the frigid weather had tired Noni, and he leaned on his cane as he led Odette and Asger down a cobbled pathway. Steel beams formed a framework supporting the walls and glass ceiling. They soon reached another human creation: a small city constructed of glass and steel rising to the top of the dome.

"This is an engineering masterpiece," Odette said. "I've never seen anything like it. Where are the people who created it?"

"All ghosts," Noni said as he entered the abandoned city through an open portal.

What they found inside the steel walls was a replica of a rustic Swiss village, complete with shops, narrow streets, sidewalk cafes, and a working fountain in the town square. The village sat empty of all occupants.

"Beautiful though kind of creepy," Odette said. "Did people live here?"

"It must have thrived for a while," Noni said.

"Are there cemeteries?" she asked.

Noni shook his head. "I've searched every square foot of this giant subterranean world, and I haven't found a single human bone."

Noni shook his head again when Odette said, "Not even one? What happened to them?"

"I don't know and don't suppose anyone else does either," Noni said.

"There are lights," Odette said. "Where is it coming from, and who supplies it?"

Odette and Asger followed Noni to a large building. Like the rest of the village, the structure was devoid of human habitation, though rows of file cabinets, desks, and computers occupied the rooms they passed through as if the last person had just gone home for the night. Noni showed them a large room alive with the roar of a giant machine.

"What is it?" Odette asked.

"The heart of the Biowomb," Noni said. "The machine generates light and energy and powers everything."

Noni smiled when Odette asked, "How does it work?"

"Methane gas created by the waste tossed away by generations of human life," Noni said. "Probably the reason they located this cavernous world here."

"Do you run these machines?" Odette asked.

Noni smiled again and shook his head. "They are self-sustaining and perpetual."

"Nothing is perpetual," Odette said.

Noni disagreed. "These machines are."

"How long have they been running?" Odette said.

"Who knows?" Noni said. "There's much more to see."

"How many people lived here?" Asger asked.

"Hundreds," Noni said. There are rows of apartments stacked upon each other. Families occupied the flats.

"I'd like to see," Odette said.

Their trip through the village led to a wall of apartments reminding Odette of jail cells. Each small apartment had a living area, a kitchen, a bathroom, and two bedrooms. Furniture, personal possessions, and a few pictures remained as if the owners had only just left. Odette gazed at a grainy black and white revealing a mom, a dad, and two children in clothes of some era she didn't recognize.

"So strange. Who are these people?" Asger said.

"Occupants of the Biowomb," Noni said.

"I find it hard to believe none of them

survived," Odette asked.

Noni nodded. "All ghosts."

"Maybe not," Asger said. "If there are no bones, perhaps they moved somewhere else."

"But where?" Odette asked.

"Except for the Nether World, there is no place else to go," Noni said.

He shook his head when Odette asked, "Do you live in one of these apartments?"

"Ghosts haunt these rooms," Noni said. "I'll show you where I live. Though the village occupies a small portion of the Biowomb, there is no indication the occupants ever strayed far from its sterile walls."

"Then where did the trees, birds, and other vegetation come from?" Odette asked.

"All part of the massive landfill created over decades," Noni said. "Seeds waiting to sprout and eggs ready to hatch required no human intervention."

They followed a cobblestone path into the forest to a gypsy wagon painted in vibrant reds, yellows, and blues. The wagon sat in a grove of trees beside a babbling brook. Odette and Asger froze when an enormous dog emerged from beneath the wagon to greet Noni.

"Oh, my God!" Odette said. "I have never in my life seen a dog that big."

The brown dog with a thick coat of bristly fur stood taller at its shoulders than Noni.

"Don't be frightened," Noni said. "Duchess won't harm you."

"Sure about that?" Odette said. "She doesn't look pleased."

"Her puppies," Noni said.

Noni returned from the wagon with three puppies that looked like miniatures of Duchess.

"They're adorable," Odette said. "Where is the father?"

"Duchess hunts outside the Biowomb every night. Many strange and dangerous creatures roam the Nether World. She may have a mate out there though she has never brought him here," Noni said.

"Probably a good thing she hasn't," Odette said.

While Odette and Noni were talking, Asger wandered down the hill to the brook and filled his bota bag. When he returned, he shared it with Odette.

"Tastes better than Jack and Chief's rum," she said.

"Who are Jack and Chief?" Asger asked.

"People I knew in another lifetime," Odette said.

"Are you hungry?" Noni asked. "Plenty of fruits, melons, tubers and vine vegetables grow in the Biowomb. I also have a treat I've been saving."

The temperature inside the Biowomb was perfect. No need for a fire. Noni started one anyway in his pit beside the wagon. Asger and Odette reclined on Noni's colorful gypsy rugs in a circle around the fire pit.

"Where did you get the wagon?" Odette asked.

"As I said, you can find almost anything buried in the landfill. Let me take the pups back to the wagon.

Noni returned with a canned ham. After opening the can, he plopped the ham on a plate. They soon feasted on watermelon, cantaloupe, ham, bread, and butter.

Asger speared a bite of ham with the knife Noni provided him.

"This must be magic," he said.

"You got the canned ham from the Nether World," Odette said. "Was the diet of the people who lived here mostly fruits and vegetables?

Where did the bread and butter come from?"

"The people raised fish in ponds. That was their only meat. Everything else they had brought with them. They stored their food in lockers and freezers."

"Maybe the people ran out of food and left to find more," Odette said.

Noni licked his lips. "There's enough in storage to last my lifetime. That's not the reason they are gone."

"No dairy cows?" Odette asked.

"I don't know what a cow is," Noni said.

"The animals that create the butter," Odette said.

"There are no cows, and I only eat butter on special occasions. Tonight is one of those occasions."

"This place is like the Garden of Eden," Odette said. "Yet, you continue to wander into the dangers of the Nether World. Why do you do it?"

"I like the danger and the unknown," Noni said. "I also like the adventure it brings to explore such a place."

"Are there more people like you in the Nether World?"

"There must be," Noni said. "Unfortunately, I don't have the leg strength to do much exploring."

Hearing something profoundly sad in Noni's voice, Odette grasped his spindly hand.

"You must be very lonely," she said.

"I have Duchess and the puppies," he said.

"Thank God for that," Odette said.

"Right now, I am tired," Noni said. "I'm going to bed inside the wagon. There is room enough for the three of us."

The lights generated by the control room of the Biowomb had dimmed. Night birds sang in the trees, and the soothing sound of the brook at the bottom of the hill relaxed them.

"This rug is comfortable. I'll sleep here," Asger said.

"Me too," Odette said. "Sweet dreams, Noni."

The night sounds of the Biowomb included frogs and crickets. Odette closed her eyes as Asger held her in his arms. The temperature was too mild for the fur throw, so they spread it over the rug and lay on it.

"What do you think of this place?" Asger asked.

"Like sleeping in a cemetery," Odette said. "It gives me the creeps."

"You should see Vinland," he said. "There's a real sky complete with moon and stars. The land goes on forever."

"I can't wait," Odette said. "How will we ever find it?"

"The sky," he said.

"What do you mean?" she asked.

"We came here from different places," he said. "We are caught in a maze connected to your world and mine. In my world, the sky is blue."

"Mine too," Odette said. "What about Noni?"

"This is a place for the dead, not the living. We'll take Noni and the dogs with us."

"What if he doesn't want to go?" Odette asked.

Asger didn't answer her question. "I can't imagine spending my life here."

"Me either," Odette said. "Though anyplace with you is better than anywhere I've ever been."

Still uneasy, Asger dozed off, listening to night sounds and Odette's gentle breathing. A wet nose awoke him.

Chapter 12

Odette awoke in her tent alone, worrying about Mudbug, when she remembered the little dog had spent the night at Paula's. She felt a twang of loneliness as she returned from the public bathroom. Something else was worrying her: the dream about riding bareback atop a white unicorn named Pegasus.

Paula had assured her that Asger, her Viking warrior, and the beautiful, winged unicorn were part of a dream fantasy. Odette wasn't sure as she walked across the beach toward the Oyster Island lighthouse. The lighthouse and Jack's place sat on a slight rise above most of the island. She could see the crew in the distance. She also heard the motor of a distant helicopter approaching the island.

After a rainy night of eating and drinking rum, Oyster Island was awash in activity. Jimmy, Jack, and Chief were erecting the framing for a wall, Paula helping J.P. as he put one of the new dogs through her paces.

"Susie Larsen ran me through the wringer, but she was right about one thing," he said.

Paula, dressed in khaki shorts displaying her tanned legs, a purple and gold L.S.U. tee-shirt accenting her buff arms and black ankle-high boots matching her dark hair and eyes looked svelte.

"I'll bite," she said. "What was Susie right about?"

J.P. was sitting on a bucket, his cell phone in the pocket of his blue work shirt. He tipped back his Stetson and rested the phone on the knee of his worn jeans.

"She told me Venus was the smartest dog in the Chalmette Animal Shelter. If she isn't, I want to see the one that is."

"We've been at this for less than an hour. Venus has already caught on to everything you've taught her," Paula said.

Venus nuzzled J.P.'s hand when he rubbed her German Shepherd ears and gave her a training treat.

Venus ran to Jack's covered porch when he said, "Take a break, girl,"

After rubbing noses with Lucky, J.P.'s Labrador, Old Joe, Coco, Oscar, Lady, and Mudbug, she joined them beneath the shady overhang.

"Are you still mad at me?" Paula asked.

"I'm getting over it. When you love dogs, it's not hard to grow attached," J.P. said.

"We have an audience watching you train Venus," Paula said.

"They're probably picking up the commands along with her. I wouldn't be surprised if Old Joe could teach the course himself."

"Please don't be mad at Chief and me," Paula said. "The training facility will turn a big profit even without Lady and Old Joe."

J.P. returned his cell phone to his shirt pocket and Stetson to his head after giving Paula a wink and a thumbs up.

"I felt sorry for myself, what with being rejected by Susie and all."

"Rejected, hell!" Paula said. "From the word on the street, you could dance professionally on Broadway if you wanted. Who taught you those moves?"

"My mom and an old girlfriend," J.P. said.

"Which old girlfriend?" Paula asked.

"Don't remember," he said.

"Oh yes, you do," Paula said.

The rotor noise of an approaching helicopter interrupted their conversation. Jack came running out of the house.

"It's Frankie Castellano, the owner of the Majestic," he said. "We've done enough for today. Let's knock off and start back tomorrow."

Odette walked up the rise to meet them as the jet helicopter landed in the sandy field near the Majestic Hotel and Casino. Jimmie and Chief were shirtless, sweating, and ready for a break. They both made a beeline to the metal cooler for a drink of water.

Odette grinned when Paula said, "Sleeping late again? Girl, we're going to have to dock your pay."

"I'm shaking in my boots," Odette said. "Who is that in the sexy chopper?"

"Frankie Castellano," Jack said. "He's the owner of the Majestic and bringing his new partner in the venture. The man who will live here while he restores it and prepares it for service again after all these years. I'm taking the ATV to pick them up."

"Want me to drive?" Odette asked.

"Why not?" Jack said, tossing her the key and moving into the passenger seat.

Odette powered the ATV down the gentle rise to the clearing where the sleek jet helicopter awaited. Three people exited the chopper when Odette parked the ATV and stepped out to watch.

The first person out of the helicopter was about ten years old. A man dressed in expensive shoes with no socks, dark dress pants, and a baby blue silk shirt open to the waist revealing his ample chest hair, followed. The third person out of the chopper had a look of apprehension on his handsome face. Jack shook the older man's hand when he reached the ATV.

"Welcome to the island, Mr. Castellano. This is Odette Mouton. Odette, I'm pleased to introduce you to Mr. Castellano."

"Just Frankie," the man said with a smile as he shook Odette's hand.

Frankie was probably fifties or early sixties. Though he hadn't stopped smiling, his bulldog features warned her he probably wasn't someone with whom to trifle.

The boy smiled when Odette said, "Who is this handsome man?"

"My grandson Jojo," Frankie said. Jojo smiled as he shook Odette's hand. "The man behind me is Eddie Toledo."

When Odette made eye contact with Eddie, she knew he was trouble. Like J.P., he was just a little bit too handsome. She knew it from the look in his eyes and his slight smile. She quickly made a mental note to avoid any involvement with him.

Eddie was dressed in wingtips, dark pants and a starched white shirt. Though he held Odette's hand a brief moment longer than he probably should, he smiled and nodded.

"Glad to meet you, Eddie," Jack said. "Frankie tells me you're my new boss."

"I'm just here to have a look," Eddie said. "Frankie hasn't convinced me yet that I'm the man for the task."

Frankie gazed at the Majestic Hotel languishing in Oyster Bay, devoid for decades of yachts and sailboats.

"She's as beautiful as I remember her," Frankie said. "Can you give us a tour, Jack? Eddie needs convincing, and I believe you're the man to do it."

"I'll give it my best shot," Jack said.

Odette hadn't been in the Majestic since the night she and Paula had, with the help of Paula's magic, defeated most of the ghouls living there and the ghosts of two vampires, Christopher and Laurel. With bright sunlight on her shoulders, she took Jojo's hand and followed Jack along the floating walkway to the Majestic's entrance.

The old building sat a hundred feet from shore, the walkway the only way to reach it. The ring of keys Jack kept on his belt rattled as he opened the three locks securing the gate of the covered walkway.

"Watch your step," he said. "Some of the old boards need replacing."

"We'll follow you," Frankie said with a smile.

Buoyed by rusting oil barrels, the walkway swayed beneath them. The paint was faded, and everything dusty as hell. The grandeur of the old restaurant far exceeded expectations.

"This place must have been like a palace back in the day," Eddie said.

"People came from everywhere to have their pictures made here. It was quite the showplace."

It was dark the last time Odette had visited the Majestic. Now, even in diffused light, she could see the ballroom highlighted by the most beautifully carved wood bar she'd ever seen. The room was huge, the ceilings high and ornate. The building was regal even in its present state of dust and disarray. Jack pointed to the large bar.

"Carved by Italian artisans from giant cypress

trees cut in a swamp near here."

"A significant work of art," Frankie said. "It's one of the many things that drew me to this old beauty."

"Impressive," Eddie said.

"Needs lots of T.L.C. and fresh paint," Jack said. "The Majestic was abandoned for seventy years."

"What do you think, Jojo?" Eddie asked.

"Mama would have this place up and running in a heartbeat," he said.

"My daughter Josie, Jojo's mom is a world-class interior decorator, among other things," Frankie said.

Odette couldn't help but notice Eddie's solemn reaction when Josie's name was mentioned.

"There's lots more to see," Jack said. "An interesting level up these stairs. This deck has a history unique to the Prohibition Era."

A circular tier comprised of tiny rooms overlooked the bar and ballroom area. Tattered curtains covered the openings to the rooms. Jack pulled open a curtain, showing Frankie and Eddie inside one of the empty cubicles.

"During Prohibition, this place was both a casino and speakeasy. Mobsters brought their mistresses here for drinks and dinner. No one knew who was up here except the waiters and waitresses who served them."

"Must have been quite a scene," Eddie said.

"I can only imagine," Jack said.

He led them up a staircase to an even higher level of the old structure. They exited to an observation deck overlooking the bay.

"Great view of the Gulf," Eddie said.

Jack handed him a pair of binoculars. "You can see ships and offshore rigs if you use these."

Through the powerful lenses of the

binoculars, the Gulf came alive. Gulls soared high above the water, floating in and out of the dark clouds. It seemed like a living diorama.

"Gorgeous," Eddie said, handing the binoculars to Frankie.

"Barrier islands protect this cove," Jack said. "Centuries ago, it was a haven for pirates. Local legend says a fortune in gold is buried someplace on this island."

"I wouldn't doubt it," Eddie said. "It's so secluded and pristine. It's hard to believe this place is even inhabited."

"There's more to see," Jack said. "It's starting to sprinkle. Let's go inside before the bottom falls out."

Up the stairs, windows afforded a three-hundred-sixty-degree view. Polished teak and mahogany paneling evoked the look and feel of the bridge of a ship.

"You like it, Jojo?"

"Yes," Jojo said.

"The original owner must have liked to play sea captain," Eddie said.

"A retired sea captain," Jack said. "He escaped the crowds when he came up here."

"This will be part of your suite," Frankie said. "The electricity is working, and Jack has stocked the fridge for you."

Eddie remained noncommital. "You can almost see Biloxi from up here," he said.

"Except for the lighthouse, there's no better view on Oyster Island," Jack said. "Want to see the living quarters?"

The deck below the bridge housed a large apartment with a galley, primary bedroom, living area, pot-bellied stove, and bathrooms. Dust covers protected the original furniture still in place.

"Everything a man could need," Jack said.

"Cozy," Eddie said. "Anything else?"

"This old building has dozens of nooks, crannies, and secret passageways in the walls. You could spend a month here and not see everything there is to see."

"Secret passageways?" Eddie said.

"And the building is haunted."

"Sounds sinister," Eddie said. "Where are all the boats?"

"Only two remain," Jack said. "A sloop and a trawler. Both are seaworthy and have traveled more than once from here to islands in the Caribbean."

"Pleasure trips?" Odette asked.

"Business," Jack said. "They were both rum runners. Even during Prohibition, patrons to Oyster Island could sample the best scotch, rum, or Canadian whiskey, courtesy of those two vessels."

"Are they still operable?" Eddie asked.

"You bet," Jack said. You could sail from here to the Bahamas tomorrow in either of them if you wanted to."

"If I could sail or knew how to operate a boat," Eddie said.

"I'll teach you," Jack said.

"What do you think, JoJo?" Frankie asked.

"I love it," Jojo said.

"Maybe Eddie will invite us down for the weekend when he gets the place up and running," Frankie said. "What else, Jack?"

"You hungry?"

"I could eat something." Frankie said. "Jojo?"

"Maybe," the boy said.

Jojo's eyes lit up when Jack said, "I have all the ingredients for a chocolate cake. A big slice with a scoop of vanilla ice cream will go great after a plate of mac and cheese and beanie weenies."

"We better hurry," Odette said. "The thunder shaking the roof means an approaching storm." Jojo smiled again when she said, "You play checkers?"

Chapter 13

The sprinkle of rain had turned into a downpour when the ATV reached Jack's front door. Paula and Jimmie had gone to their camping trailer to clean up and change clothes. Chief, Coco, and Old Joe had returned to his hill to feed his chickens. The only person at Jack's was J.P.

Frankie was on his cell phone, stowing it in his back pocket after a short conversation. J.P. stood up from the plank table to shake his hand.

"J.P., this is Frankie Castellano and his grandson Jojo."

"Happy to meet you, Jojo," J.P. said as he shook the boy's hand. "Frankie and I know each other."

Frankie was smiling when Jack cast him a worried glance.

"Lieutenant Saucier ran me in once," he said.

"Sorry," J.P. said. "Just doing my job."

"No problem," Frankie said. "My lawyers had me released soon as we reached the jail. I heard you got canned recently."

"Is there anyone in Louisiana who hasn't heard that piece of news?" J.P. said. "Surely you can't still be mad at me for something that happened ten years ago."

"You know what they say," Frankie said. "Keep your friends close, your enemies closer."

"Hell, Frankie, I'm not your enemy. I'm just a lowly dog trainer."

"You got a set of balls on you. I'll give you that," Frankie said. "Need a real job? I can always use someone like you in my organization."

J.P. grinned and said, "Thanks, Frankie. I'm done with stress and danger in my life. Training dogs suits me just fine."

Jojo was on his knees, his arms around Venus's neck.

"And I can see you're good at it," Frankie said.

"What's her name?" Jojo asked.

"Venus," J.P. said.

"I love her," Jojo said.

"I see from the way her tail's wagging that the feeling is mutual," J.P. said.

"That was my pilot on the phone," Frankie said. "She was afraid to leave the chopper on the ground, so I told her to take it back to the pad. Looks like Jojo and me are going to be here a while."

"My Airstream is parked outside the door," J.P. said. "You and Jojo can sleep there tonight. I'm used to Jack's couch."

"Can Venus spend the night with us, Papaw?"

"You'll have to ask J.P.," Frankie said.

"You bet she can," J.P. said.

Jojo put his arms around Venus and smiled at J.P. "Thank you," he said.

"My pleasure," J.P. said. "You'll have to stay close to her. Venus gets a little scared when she's in a storm."

"She'll be safe with me," Jojo said.

"I'll bet she will," J.P. said.

After dropping off Frankie and JoJo at the

house, Odette was still outside, showing Eddie everything they had built so far for the dog training facility. They were both wet when they burst through the door.

"J.P.," Jack said. "This is Eddie Toledo. He's the new owner of the Majestic. If he takes Frankie's offer."

J.P. rushed to help with the bags, smiling and pumping Eddie's hand once they had his luggage situated in a corner."

"Eddie, you dog. Where the hell have you been keeping yourself?"

"A little bit of everywhere," Eddie said. "You heard the D.A.'s office in New Orleans canned me?"

"Welcome to the club," J.P. said.

"Are you staying on the island now?" Eddie asked.

"I rented my house in Chalmette and live in my Airstream outside the door."

"What are you doing for a job?" Eddie asked.

"I'm part of the dog training facility Odette was showing you," J.P. said. "Venus, here is my first pupil."

"You two know each other?" Odette asked.

"Drinking buddies from way back," Eddie said. "When I was an assistant Federal D.A., the St. Bernard Parish cops aided us on a case. I worked with J.P. almost every day for more than a year."

J.P. and Eddie grinned when Jack said, "Sounds like trouble to me."

"Got that right," J.P. said. "Eddie has gotten me in more messes with women than you can imagine."

Seeing the frown forming on Frankie's bulldog face, Eddie raised a palm.

"I was engaged to Frankie's daughter and Jojo's mom Josie. I jilted her at the altar. Frankie decided to give me another chance," Eddie said. "I'm doing my best to get back into his good graces, and maybe Josie's someday."

"Good luck," J.P. said.

Thunder shook the walls of Jack's house, causing the lights to flicker. When they came back on, Frankie's frown was gone.

"You said you're training Venus to sell her. I'll buy her from you," he said. "Every boy needs a dog. I can write you a check right now for a thousand bucks." Seeing J.P.'s frown, Frankie said, "Is something wrong?"

"Only the smartest dogs become service animals," J.P. said. "They sell for considerably more than a thousand dollars."

"How much more?" Frankie said.

"Upwards of twenty-five grand," J.P. said.

"You got to be kidding," Frankie said.

"Venus is the smartest dog in south Louisiana," J.P. said. "I just began training her this morning, and she is soaking up everything like a sponge."

"You're saying you want twenty-five grand for her?" he said.

"I didn't say that," J.P. said.

"What did you say?"

"Venus will bring fifty-thousand dollars when she's fully trained," J.P. said.

J.P. didn't flinch when Frankie began staring a hole through him. Frankie's gaze turned to his grandson Jojo whose arms were still around Venus's neck.

"I've bought thoroughbred race horses that didn't cost me fifty grand," Frankie said.

"She's not for sale now, anyway," J.P. said. "She's still in training."

Frankie's smile returned when Jojo jumped to his feet and hugged him.

"It's okay, Papaw," he said. "You don't have to

buy Venus for me."

The front door opened as a clap of thunder rocked the house again. Paula and Jimmie rushed inside. Both were smiling.

"Paula and Jimmie, this is Frankie Castellano and his grandson Jojo."

Jimmie pumped Frankie's hand. Frankie nodded when he asked, "Was that your chopper that landed? You got one hell of a pilot. Paula and I thought the wind was going to blow it away."

"She's the best," Frankie said. "Jennifer Kuhl flew combat missions in Afghanistan."

"Jennifer?" Paula said.

"There are women combat pilots now," Frankie said. "We call her Cool Jenny."

"Don't know about Afghanistan," Paula said. "She knows how to fly in a Louisiana storm. What's happening?"

"This is Eddie Toledo. I've offered him an ownership position in the Majestic. Though he hasn't accepted my offer, I'm still working on him.

"Frankie and Jojo are spending the night," Jack said.

"Good call," Jimmie said. "It's not a fit night out for man nor beast, so make yourself comfortable. Something to drink?"

"Scotch, if you have it," Frankie said.

"Make that two," Eddie said.

"You must try a mug of Jack's rum," Paula said.

"It's to die for," Odette said.

Frankie joined Odette and Paula at the plank table, smiling when he sipped the mug of rum.

"Best rum I've ever tasted," he said. "Must be expensive."

"Ten bucks a bottle," Jack said.

"For premium Dominican Rum?" Frankie said. "You gotta be kidding me. How can that be?"

"Chief and I found a crate of Prohibition-era

rum under the bridge after a rainstorm."

"Chief?" Frankie said.

"Grogan la Tortue," Jack said. "One of our partners in the dog training facility. Everyone calls him Chief."

"I know who you're talking about," Frankie said. "The crazy Indian who claims to own Oyster Island and everything on it."

"I wouldn't call him crazy to his face," Jack said. "He's at least six-foot-six and pretty much all muscle."

Seeing Paula and Odette's frowns and crossed arms, Frankie said, "I apologize. Sometimes my chauvinism and racial biases bubble to the surface. If Adele were here, she would have corrected me."

"Adele?" Paula said.

"My wife, and the best woman on the face of the earth. I do my best to live up to her expectations. Sometimes I slip up. Please forgive me."

As if on cue, Chief and his two dogs burst through the door.

"Can I borrow a towel?" he said. "We got drenched on our way here."

When Chief returned from the bathroom, Frankie met him with an extended hand.

"I'm Frankie Castellano. I want to apologize to you."

"For what?" Chief asked.

Chief almost smiled when Frankie said, "In anger, I called you an Indian."

"So what?" Chief said. "I am an Indian."

"You don't find the term derogatory?" Frankie asked.

Chief scoffed. "My parents and grandparents were Indians. That's what they were called all their lives. Why do you think the term is offensive?"

"Then should I have called you a heathen?"

Realizing Frankie was joking, Chief said. "Only if you want me to scalp you."

"You're joking, right?" Frankie said.

"I have a grievance with you about this island. Tonight isn't the time to discuss it," Chief said. "Is this your grandson?"

"This is Jojo, the love of my life," Frankie said.

Chief was smiling when he reached down and shook JoJo's hand.

"Are you a real chief?" Jojo asked.

"You bet I am," Chief said. "Want me to teach you how to shoot a bow and arrow?"

"Would you?" Jojo said.

"We'll have to go to the back of the island and find a sapling to craft a bow for you," Chief said. "If it's okay with your grandfather."

"Papaw?" Jojo said.

"Of course, you can," Frankie said. "Grab a mug of rum, Chief, and join me on the couch. I'm dying to hear your story about this rum I'm drinking."

Jack had stoked the fireplace. Mudbug was in Odette's lap, and the other dogs were lying in front of the licking flame. Rain pounded the roof, lightning flashing through the windows.

"Oyster Island is like no other place on earth," Chief said. "I was chasing a rougarou the night we found the rum?"

"A rougarou?" Frankie said.

"A Cajun werewolf," Chief said.

"You're kidding me," Frankie said.

"I kid you not," Chief said. "The beast was a head taller than me and supernatural. He had one little problem."

"What?" Frankie asked.

"He was afraid of dogs, even little Coco, my Chihuahua," Chief said. "We found the crate of

Dominican rum under the bridge the first night the rougarou terrorized the island."

"What did you do with it?" Frankie asked.

"Sold some on Canal Street and drank most of it. The rougarou destroyed the last three bottles we had," Chief said.

"This rum is wonderful, Where did it come from?" Frankie asked.

"The old distillery had sat dormant for decades. A company recently bought it and is making rum using the local water and the original recipe," Chief said. "They have no clue how good the rum they're selling is?"

Jack gave Chief a dirty look when Frankie asked, "What's the name of this distillery?"

"Maybe I shouldn't have opened my big mouth," Chief said.

"If I buy the distillery, I'll cut you guys in," Frankie said. "I'm not a heartless bastard."

"Is there a sunken rum runner near the island someplace?" Eddie asked.

Chief eyed Jack and didn't answer. Jack said, "Almost anything is possible."

"What's your best guess?" Eddie asked.

"We're uncomfortable talking about it with people we just met," Jack said.

Lightning flashed outside the window as thunder shook the roof.

"Damn!" Frankie said. "I need more rum."

"What we need is food," Jack said. "Are you hungry, Jojo?"

Jojo had a big grin when Odette asked, "How about a corndog?"

The aroma of boiled shrimp began permeating Jack's galley. Paula tossed pasta, and Odette prepared scampi sauce. They were soon dining on French bread and shrimp scampi. Frankie's expression had turned into an eternal smile as the rain had abated.

"This is all too wonderful," he said. "Jojo, Venus, and I had better make a run for the Airstream."

"Sleep tight," Odette said.

"I can't remember having such a great time," Frankie said. "I'd like to repay the hospitality."

"We're open to suggestions," Paula said.

"I have a casino and resort located on an abandoned jack-up rig in the Gulf of Mexico," Frankie said. "It's called Stilts, and I'd love to treat every one of you to some world-class hospitality for a few days."

"When are you talking about going to your resort?" Paula asked.

"My helicopter will be back to the island tomorrow," Frankie said. "We could leave from here."

"Most of our clothes are in Chalmette," Paula said. "Guess we'll have to pass."

"Nonsense," Frankie said. "There are shops of all sorts at the offshore resort. I'll outfit everyone. No need to pack a bag."

Paula glanced at Odette. "Does sound inviting," she said.

"All I need is my bikini," Odette said.

"You'll have a dozen more before you leave the resort. I'll even spot each one of you a thousand bucks to gamble away at the casino," Frankie said.

"I'm in," Odette said. "All I need is someone to care for Mudbug while I'm gone."

"My international guests all have pets," Frankie said. "They can come with us and will be well taken care of."

"Jimmie doesn't do the day-to-day managing at our hardware store," Paula said. "We've been thinking about a vacation, and now is as good a time as any to take it."

"There's no one to care for the rest of the

dogs or the lighthouse," Jack said.

Catching the conversation as he came in through the backdoor, J.P. said, "I'll stay and keep the animals fed and the hearth burning. Eddie and I have lots to catch up on, and he'll need help getting situated."

"If Chief goes, I'll go," Jack said.

"Go where?" Chief said, coming through the backdoor.

"Frankie's resort," Jack said.

"I can't leave," Chief said. "There's no one to feed Buttercup and my chickens. Besides, we still have a genuine dispute about who owns this island."

"I'll feed your cat and chickens," J.P. said. "Just leave me the keys to the ATV."

"Come with us, Chief," Frankie said. "I'm a reasonable man," "If you have a legitimate claim to the island, I'll honor it."

"Sure about that?" Chief said.

"Not just sure," Frankie said. "I'm positive."

"Go to Frankie's resort and have the time of your lives," J.P. said. "The island will still be here when you return."

"What?" Jimmie said when he returned from a trip to the bathroom.

"We're going on vacation," Paula said.

The storm on Oyster Island had passed sometime during the night. When Frankie, Jojo, and Venus returned to Jack's, the aroma of homemade biscuits and sausage gravy filled the room.

"Jojo looks like we left the party early," Frankie said.

J.P. and Jimmie were feeding the dogs in Jack's backyard, and Venus disappeared through the doggie door to get her share. Odette and

Paula were flipping hotcakes on the grill, Jojo grinning when Paula placed a buttered short stack on the plank table in front of him.

"Blackstrap molasses or chocolate sauce?" she asked.

"Can I have both?" Jojo asked.

"Why not?" Paula said.

Eddie Toledo had still not indicated if he would accept Frankie's offer and become a co-owner and managing partner of the Majestic. The sound of a helicopter landing put Eddie on the spot.

"Well," Frankie said. "Are you going to make me a happy man and take the reins of the Majestic or leave me standing at the altar?"

Despite Frankie's painful innuendo, Eddie couldn't help but smile. "The Majestic will take months of work and sap all the energy from the person who takes on the task."

"Well?" Frankie said.

Eddie extended his hand. "I'm your man. Hope I don't disappoint you."

"You got it," Frankie said. "Come with us to the resort, and we'll celebrate your decision in style."

"Let's wait until the Majestic is up and running and we have something to celebrate. Can I catch a ride back to New Orleans?"

"Suit yourself," Frankie said.

"When will you return?" J.P. asked.

"I have a few loose ends I need to tie," Eddie said. "I'll be back the day after tomorrow at the latest.

By noon, most of the inhabitants of Oyster Island, along with Eddie, were in Frankie Castellano's helicopter on their way to his resort in the Gulf of Mexico and then on to New Orleans. John Pierre Saucier watched them lift off and then disappear into the clouds.

Chapter 14

When Odette worked on the Gulf of Mexico jack-ups, she'd ridden in a helicopter more times than she could count. The other occupants of the chopper couldn't say as much.

"Please relax and enjoy the view," the pilot said as they lifted off the sandy beach.

As Paula and Jimmie settled into their seats, the big chopper turned south, over the Gulf of Mexico. Jack and Chief had flown in planes but never in a helicopter. The sensation crossed between a riding lawn mower and a hot air balloon. When Jack glanced at Chief, he saw he was grimacing.

"You okay?" he asked.

"Nothing some rum wouldn't fix," Chief said.

Frankie handed him a bottle of scotch from the chopper's liquor larder.

"I have none of your wonderful rum," he said, "This will help."

"Thanks," Jack said, returning his attention to the vista below. "It's beautiful."

"The Gulf is beautiful," Frankie said. "Relax. Choppers are as safe as they come."

"Where are we headed?" Jack asked.

"Out of state," Frankie said.

"What are all those objects below us?" Paula asked.

"Offshore platforms. Some are jack-up drilling rigs, others permanent production facilities. Choppers like this one and crew boats supply them."

"I had no idea how much activity goes on out here," Paula said.

"Me either," Jimmie said. "I've lived in Louisiana all my life and never imagined there were so many wells in the Gulf."

"Then you are about to visit a place you've only experienced in your wildest dreams," Frankie said.

Most passengers had fallen asleep, awakening when the chopper began a steep descent. Dense fog covered the water below. Feeling as if they were in a falling elevator, they braced for a crash that never came. Seeing their discomfort, Frankie grinned.

"Relax. We're descending for a landing," Frankie said.

When the chopper emerged from the clouds, Odette saw a giant offshore complex. It looked like a drilling platform, except there were no draw works or drill pipes. The chopper touched down on a bull's eye near the top of the complex. When the door opened, a man in a helmet appeared. Lights in hand, he motioned them out of the chopper.

"I'm Louis," the man in the helmet said. "Welcome to the far end of the earth."

"This way," Frankie said. "Tamela's waiting for our arrival and will get you situated in your rooms. Jojo and I will see you again after you settle."

Frankie, Jojo, and Venus disappeared into the opening door of a bank of elevators. Jojo waved as the door closed. Someone spoke.

"I'm Tamela," the young black woman who had walked up behind them said.

Tamela looked sharp in her khaki shorts and Tulane tee shirt, a red scarf tying her dark hair into a ponytail. After following her up a flight of metal stairs, Paula realized why she seemed so happy.

They were on a deck high above the Gulf of Mexico, a warm though persistent breeze blowing in their faces. The sky was still cloudy but a shade of blue she'd never seen. So was the water around them.

"I'm Mr. Castellano's recreation director," Tamela said. "We have a suite of rooms reserved for you. Please come with me."

The group followed Tamela out of the elevator into a wide hallway. She opened a door with a plastic entry card. The curtains opened revealing a wall to wall, floor to ceiling window gazing out over the Gulf of Mexico. Odette's mouth dropped when she saw the inside of the suite.

"Breathtaking," Paula said.

"This suite has four bedrooms connecting to the central congregating area," Tamela said. "Occupant names are on the doors. Room service is available twenty-four hours a day. You are on Mr. Castellano's account so feel free to order anything you want, anytime you want."

Paula squeezed Jimmie's hand and said, "Oh, baby, this is like heaven."

"When everyone is ready," Tamela said. "I'll take you on a tour of this resort known as Stilts. After that, you're free to enjoy all the amenities, including the casino."

Tamela left five entry keys on a coffee table, smiling as she left the crew to check out their rooms. The four bedrooms sat in a circle around the large living area. Chief went directly to a small refrigerator.

"It's stocked with beer, wine, and snacks," he said. "Even our favorite brand of rum."

"You're kidding," Jack said.

"Frankie must have called someone while we were in the helicopter," Odette said.

"Abita, anyone?" Chief said.

He tossed an icy can to Jimmie when he said, "Me, daddy."

Jack, Chief, and Jimmie were sitting on a couch, drinking Abita and gazing at a lone crew boat when Paula came out of one of the bedrooms. A light blue crochet mini dress covered her new red bikini.

"The closets are full of clothes for me and Jimmie. Everything I tried on fits," she said.

"How are the bedrooms?" Jack asked.

"To die for," Paula said. "If this suite indicates the rest of Stilts, then I never want to leave."

Odette appeared from her room in a bikini, so skimpy Paula put her hands over Jimmie's eyes.

"This swimsuit is so suggestive. It's better than going naked," Odette said.

"You're my bestie," Paula said. "But if you don't put something over that piece of nothing, I'm going to have to punch either you, Jimmie or maybe both of you,"

"No problem," Odette said. She returned from her room dressed in a yellow sun dress. "Is this better?"

"Not much. The more I think about it, you should parade around the room naked more often," Paula said. "Jimmie will be so hot he'll perform as if he were still eighteen tonight."

"You know I love no one but you, honey babe," Jimmie said.

"Is that why your dick is poking a hole in your shorts?" Paula said.

Jimmie's grin turned silly as his hands went to his crotch. Jack and Chief had left the comfort of the couch and were staring out the window.

"Better put a chastity belt on him," Jack said. "My guess is the pool is full of half-naked ladies."

"My kind of place," Odette said.

Two waiters in white tuxedo tops appeared when Chief opened the door.

"Mr. Castellano ordered some food for you," one of the waiters said.

The group soon tore into shrimp, oyster, and crawfish po'boys, along with every imaginable side dish.

"Damn!" Jack said. "Is there a good reason for leaving the room?"

The door opened, Tamela smiling when she appeared. "I heard that. If you think this room is nice, wait till you see the rest of the resort."

"I'm ready," Odette said.

Paula had found a sundress matching Odette's, and the two looked almost like sisters.

"Me too," she said. "Let's go, Jimmie."

"These catwalks are normally used only by the resort's employees," Tamela said, hurrying along a gangplank overlooking the Gulf.

Chief glanced at the angry clouds bearing the threat of thunder, lightning, and lots of rain.

"I don't see land in any direction," Paula said. "How far from shore are we?"

"About a hundred miles south of the Louisiana coast," Tamela said.

"Is this a drilling platform?" Jack asked.

"More accurately, a production platform. This complex of raised structures overlies a once giant oilfield."

They were only a stone's throw, or so it seemed, from another large platform the size of a football field sitting high above the water on massive metal stilts. Futuristic buildings made of metal and glass topped the structures. A complex system of ramps, runways, and catwalks connected the structures. A flock of gulls circled overhead.

"Those buildings don't look like any offshore platform I've ever seen," Odette said.

"When the old company abandoned the field, the entire facility was stripped. Boston architects designed the buildings replacing them. There are three more ramps you can't see from here."

"I've been on every ocean in many different vessels," Jack said. "This complex seems like something out of a sci-fi movie,"

"We get that a lot," Tamela said. "The design accentuates the stark beauty surrounding us and is robust enough to withstand a hurricane's direct hit."

"It's a long way down to the water," Chief said. "How high up are we?"

"A hundred feet," Tamela said. "It can get rough fast out here in a storm."

"I bet," Jimmie said. "How is this thing anchored?"

"We're in a part of the Gulf known as the Flower Garden Banks," Tamela said. "The old oil field overlies a seamount."

"What's that?" Chief asked.

"A high spot caused when a salt dome pushes everything up. The water is only about sixty-five feet deep here. There's a coral reef beneath this complex."

"How deep is the rest of the Gulf?" Paula asked.

"Very deep," Tamela said.

"Two hundred feet?" Jack said.

"Some parts are as deep as fourteen-thousand feet."

"No way."

Tamela nodded. "The Gulf of Mexico is the ninth largest geographic body on earth. Some people call the Sigsbee Deep the Grand Canyon under the Sea. It's almost three miles straight down."

"I had no idea," Paula said.

"Most people don't. Here is where the Gulfstream originates, one of the most powerful currents on earth."

Odette glanced up at a flock of migratory birds flying overhead. "You're quite the tour guide. How do you know so much?"

"My degree in marine biology from Texas A & M. I've trained for this job all my life."

A large boat emerged from the fog, beginning to cover the water.

"Damn!" Jack said. "That thing looks like a little destroyer."

"Our security boat," Tamela said. "It circles Stilts continuously."

Jack did a double-take. "With a cannon and machine guns?" he said. Looks like it's ready for a major naval battle."

"Never know what might happen out here in the middle of the Gulf. We're in open water, far beyond continental waters of the U.S. We are responsible for our security."

"But . . ."

She stopped Jack with a wave of her palm. "Pirates and ne'er-do-wells reign out here. Our responsibility is to our guests. Our security measures are iron tight."

"Pirates?" Paula said.

"I promise you this is the safest place on earth.

"How do people get here?" Paula asked.

"Our guests are wealthy. They come here from all over the world on yachts, service boats, and helicopters," Tamela said. "The resort features diving, deep-sea fishing, gambling, and world-class entertainment."

"Such as?" Paula said.

"Other than probably Vegas, tourists would have a hard time matching the dining experiences and entertainment available to them. The theater screens all the latest movies. Our Performing Arts Center hosts world-class acts and musical groups. And, there's the Aqua Room even Vegas doesn't have."

Tamela led them through another winding pathway of corridors, stairs, and hidden passages, their ears popping as they rode in an elevator.

"Good God!" Jack said. "Did we just descend to the bottom of the ocean?"

The room's four walls were glass, the only thing separating them from the sea life swimming on the other side.

"Wow!" Odette said.

"We're surrounded by the reef's abundant plants and fishes. It's like a bathysphere at the bottom of the Gulf," Tamela said.

"Is that a whale?" Paula asked.

"A big one," Tamela said.

"It can't get through the glass, can it?" Jimmie asked.

"The walls are strong enough to prevent almost anything, even a large hurricane, from breaching it," Tamela said.

A shark swam toward Paula, bumping the glass with its nose. The beast stared at her with steely eyes before swimming away.

"The reef is a virtual paradise for creatures of the Gulf. Turtles, whales, sharks, manta rays, exotic fish, and other species beyond imagination. You'll see them all if you stay here long enough," Tamela said.

"It's magical," Odette said. "I feel like a passenger in Captain Nemo's submarine."

Tamela nodded, "Sponges, star, boulder, and brain coral. That's how the banks got its name. Commercial fishermen noticed the bright colors years ago. There's more."

They followed Tamela through a steel-encased corridor to another viewing room at a different part of the reef.

"You can return later and spend as much time as you like. We have the rest of the resort to see right now," Tamela said.

Chapter 15

The last stop on Tamela's tour was the Grand Casino. She gave them a plastic identification card to hang around their necks.

"Your I.D. cards have one-thousand dollars loaded on each of them, compliments of the casino and Mr. Castellano. This is where I leave you," she said. "If you need me, call my cell phone. Have fun."

There were no windows or clocks. Hundreds of people filled the ample room. Diamond chandeliers draped from the ceiling high above them, the buzz of active humanity palpable though probably dampened by acoustical engineering.

The casino had no dress code, casino goers dressed in everything from ball gowns and tuxedos to bikinis and flip flops. Paula spotted someone she recognized at one of the many blackjack tables.

"Oh my God!" she said. "It's Chad Drake. Jimmie and I saw his new movie last weekend."

"You sure?" Odette said. "He looks like a beach bum to me."

"It's him," Jimmie said. "He wore that same

outfit in the movie."

"Looks like he hasn't combed his hair in a week," Jack said. "Maybe he isn't as successful as the entertainment magazines say."

"Those are thousand-dollar chips in front of him," Jimmie said. "You can tell by their color."

"How would you know that?" Paula asked.

"I read," Jimmie said.

"That better be why you know the color of a thousand-dollar chip," Paula said.

"Don't be that way, honey babe," Jimmie said.

The dealer was blond, buxom, and attractive enough to act in the movies. Dressed like a beachbum as Jack had said, the handsome movie star sat alone at the blackjack table. Her smile and rapt attention indicated Chad Drake was winning and rewarding her with a big tip every time he did.

"There's more than one movie star here," Odette said. "Guy Nova's at the roulette wheel with a gorgeous Asian woman."

"That can't be Guy Nova," Paula said. "He's too short, old, and fat."

"It's him," Odette said.

The red-flocked wallpaper seemed as outlandish as the extravagant fountains, marble statues of satyrs, other naked mythological creatures, and scantily-clad cocktail waitresses.

"Looks like a French whorehouse in here," Chief said.

"I like it," Jack said. "Let's drink and gamble away some of this free money."

Chief flagged a smiling waitress dressed in red satin shorts, red shoes with three-inch heels, and a gold lame jacket over her white silk blouse.

"I'm Ava," she said with an engaging smile. "I see by your I.D. cards you are special guests—no need to tip. You're on the house tonight. What are you drinking?"

Once Ava had delivered their drinks, Jack asked, "Where are the craps tables?"

"Down that hallway and through the arch," she said. "Good luck."

When he attempted to give Ava a tip, she shook her head. "Trust me when I tell you my gratuity is more than covered. Everyone will be dying to serve you."

"Thanks, pretty lady," Jack said.

"You coming?" Jimmie said.

"I'm going to play the slots," Paula said. "Go with Jack and Chief and have the time of your life. I'll see you back in the room."

"Wow!" Odette said as they watched him disappear into the crowd of gamblers. "You're more of a trusting soul than I gave you credit for."

Paula's grin told the absolute truth. "Let him get into trouble," she said. "It always makes the bedroom more interesting when he does."

Odette glanced around to see if anyone was listening.

"Double wow!" she said.

Paula wasn't done, "I wouldn't mind a little trouble myself."

"Right," Odette said.

"You think I'm incapable?" Paula asked.

"You're as straight as an arrow."

"Sometimes arrows veer off course," Paula said. "Let's try out our plastic."

The room filled with slot machines was even more frantic than the other parts of the casino, the sound of loud bells, whistles, and repetitive music finally becoming obnoxious.

"Let's find a quiet bar and get out of this madhouse," Odette said.

"Great idea. My head's about to explode, and we're not winning anything," Paula said.

The noise subsided a bit when they left the

127

large room devoted to the slots. Odette spotted the smiling waitress that had served them their first drinks.

"That's Ava, the girl who first waited on us," she said.

"Hard to those long legs and red satin shorts," Paula said.

Odette tapped the smiling woman's shoulder. "Ava, remember us?"

"You bet I do," Ava said. "Ready for drinks?"

"We're ready to find a quiet bar and take a break from the noise for a while," Paula said.

Ava's long blond hair waved when she shook her head. "I hear that. I spend my breaks as far away from the bells and whistles as possible. Come with me, and I'll take you to Oz."

"Why do they call it that?" Paula asked.

"Because it's a world of fantasy," Ava said.

Ava laughed when Odette asked, "Should we be frightened?"

"You'll be fine. You can be who you are."

Odette didn't have a chance to ask Ava what she meant because they reached a darkened hallway.

"It's at the end of the hall," Ava said. "Have fun."

Odette and Paula watched the pretty woman meld back into the crowded casino.

"Kind of creepy," Odette said.

Things changed when Paula and Odette stepped into the hallway, and it became awash in ephemeral radiance, a prism of flickering colors lighting their way. White vapor with the distinctive aroma of a flower garden rose through slots in the floor, chilling their bare legs. Music of a sitar replaced the cacophony disappearing behind them. The floors and walls were worn bricks giving Odette the impression they were on the inside of a New Orleans crypt. The color of the floor was yellow.

"Follow the yellow brick road," Paula said.

The exotic music grew louder as they followed the winding hallway to a lighted opening. A young woman with flowing hair who looked like a Greek goddess in a diaphanous gown greeted them when they entered the room.

"Welcome to Oz," she said. "There's a place waiting for you."

Though brighter than the hall, only dim lights illuminated the bar named Oz. Colorful Oriental rugs covered much of the yellow brick floor. The woman led them to a purple pallet occupied by many lush pillows of different colors.

"Make yourselves comfortable," the woman said. "I'm Aphrodite, and I'll be waiting on you."

Paula winked at Odette as they reclined on the purple pallet. "I'll have a Beefeater's martini," she said.

"Make it two," Odette said.

As Aphrodite walked away through the vapor wafting up through the floor, Paula and Odette could see that nothing other than the flowing translucent fabric draped over her shoulder covered her voluptuous body.

Odette's grin had turned wanton as she sank into the plush velvet palette.

"I love it," she said. "Maybe we should strip off our clothes and get into the swing of things."

"We aren't the only people here, and I'd have to have more than a couple of martinis before the clothes come off this girl."

"Spoilsport," Odette said.

There were no tables or chairs in the place, only Oriental rugs and plush purple mattresses such as the one on which Paula and Odette were reclining. Through the vapor, they could see a group of fellow visitors to Oz. Six exotically dressed people circled a hookah. Smoke arose from the multiple hoses emanating from the large hookah. A pungent odor replacing the aroma of rose petals filled the room.

"Hashish," Odette said.

"How do you know?" Paula said.

"Tried it once. Nothing else in the world smells quite like hash. I can't believe someone's smoking it in a public bar."

"Remember what Tamela said. "We're a hundred miles from shore. Oz isn't a public bar, and there are no laws except the ones Frankie Castellano makes."

The group smoking hashish looked as though they'd stepped out of the pages of a Thousand and One Nights, the man who seemed to be the center of attention dressed in a turban and flowing pants. Everyone else reclined in a circle around him.

"I'm getting high from the vapors," Odette said.

"Me too," Paula said. "It's kind of relaxing."

Aphrodite returned carrying a goatskin jug and two gold goblets. After handing goblets to Paula and Odette, she filled them with red wine from the goatskin container.

Aphrodite smiled when Paula said, "What about our martinis?"

"Only blood-red wine is served in Oz. Try it. I think you'll like it."

Paula took a sip and smiled. "What about the hashish those people are smoking?"

"I'll bring you a hookah if you like," Aphrodite said.

"Why not?" Odette said. "I'd like a puff."

"This wine has something in it," Paula said when Aphrodite had left the table."

"It's intoxicating, whatever it is," Odette said. "Here comes our hookah."

It wasn't Aphrodite who delivered the

hookah. Instead, it was a muscular young man. He was completely naked, and his appearance caused Paula and Odette's eyes to pop.

"Who are you?" Odette asked.

"Adonis," the man said.

"Are you a god?" Odette asked.

The young man smiled. "Some people think so. How is the wine?"

"Wonderful," Odette said. "My head is spinning."

"Wait till you take a puff of the hash," Adonis said.

"Will you stay and smoke some with us?" Odette asked.

"Sorry," Adonis said. "I'm working."

The scent of raw hashish, roses, and haunting sitar music filled the room as the naked man returned to the bar.

"I don't know what's in this wine, but it's making me want to rip off my panties and hump that hookah hose," Paula said.

"Calm down, girl. You aren't wearing panties. We just got here, and Jimmie will be waiting for you no matter when you get back to the room."

"You think?"

"Get a load of that group with the other hookah," Odette said. "The center of attention looks like the Sultan of Arabie, the girl with her arms around his neck gorgeous enough to appear in movies. The other three beautiful women must be his harem."

"Get out of here!" Paula said.

"Am I wrong?"

"Maybe not," Paula said. "Are you going to try the hash?"

"Why not?"

Odette put one of the hoses into her mouth and took a puff. Breathing in too much, she began to cough.

Paula pounded her between the shoulder blades until her lungs cleared.

"You okay, baby?"

"I'll let you know when my eyes uncross," Odette said.

"Have you noticed something unusual about the sultan and his harem?" Paula said.

"They are all beautiful."

"What else?" Paula said.

"Hell, my eyes are still crossed. I can't see anything but a blur. What are you talking about?"

"Their fangs," Paula said. "They all have fangs. Big fangs."

"You're crazy, girlfriend," Odette said.

"You're about to find out," Paula said. "The sultan is on his way over here."

Paula gulped for air when the man In the turban arrived at their pallet.

She hadn't realized how big and muscular he was from a distance. Seeing Paula was eyeing him, he smiled and flexed his muscles.

"Are you two alone?" he said.

"No one is with us if that's what you mean," Paula said.

"You are beautiful, and I love beautiful women. Will you join us?" the man said.

"We don't even know your name," Odette said.

"Lobo," he said.

Lobo smiled when Paula said, "Are you, vampires?"

"Wolves," he said, showing her his mouthful of large teeth.

"We just got here," Odette said. "We may join you later. We have a few personal things to discuss first."

Lobo's grin was wolfish. "I'll check again later," he said as he returned to his harem.

"What do you think?" Odette said.

Paula was staring at the door. "We should cut our losses and get out of here before we regret it."

"Lobo's kind of cute," Odette said.

"He's a sexist pig," Paula said.

"I thought you were ready for fun," Odette said.

"I'm a witch. I have a witch's intuition. Right now, my alarm whistles are blaring in my head," Paula said.

"It's the hash," Odette said.

"I don't think so. Let's get the hell out of here."

"Take another puff of hash," Odette said. "You're overreacting."

Aphrodite had brought Lobo and his harem a steaming silver platter. She opened it to expose a very rare and massive cut of meat. The room filled with howls as Lobo and the women saw the bloody meat.

Paula took a puff and said, "I'm not overreacting. We're going to get killed."

"This is Frankie's bar," Odette said. "He wouldn't allow anything crazy to happen."

Lobo and the females tore into the hunk of meat, snarling at each other as they vied for their share. Lobo forced the women away from the last morsel and consumed it in one gulp.

"Hope you're right, girlfriend," Paula said. "They're looking at us like pieces of bloody meat."

Aphrodite appeared through the darkness, her lengthy hair billowing over her bare shoulders.

"More wine?" she said.

Paula was shaking her head. "Better bring us our tab."

"You don't have a tab," she said.

"Then we're leaving," Paula said.

"You can't leave," Aphrodite said. "Lobo and

his ladies are coming to join you."

"Exactly the reason we're leaving," Paula said.

Before Paula and Odette could stand, Lobo and the women surrounded them.

"Not going anywhere, are you?" he said.

"Sorry," Paula said. "It's past our bedtimes."

"Don't be rude," Lobo said.

"We're guests of Frankie Castellano," Odette said.

"Is that supposed to mean something to me?" Lobo asked.

"Mr. Castellano owns this resort. We're his guests," Paula said.

"You're in the Fantasy Room of the Oz Lounge," Lobo said. "Not a resort."

Lobo smiled when Odette said, "We're on a converted jack-up oil platform in the Gulf of Mexico. A resort called Stilts."

Lobo's laugh drew into a snarl, his features suddenly grotesque. The female's fangs and features had also changed, fur beginning to cover their faces and bare arms. Lobo and his harem weren't the only occupants of Oz transforming. Aphrodite and Adonis were still naked though no longer human. With the nightclub awash in howls, snarls, and throaty growls, Odette clutched Paula, both shrinking from the pack of wolves closing around them.

Things appeared hopeless when an explosion rocked the room, a plume of white smoke rising to the rafters. When the smoke cleared, Paula and Odette were no longer alone in the circle's center. A young man they both recognized had joined them.

"Christopher," Paula said. "Is that you?"

Christopher was short, colorful tattoos covering his shoulders and bare back. At least the portion of his broad back not attached to giant beating angel's wings. Christopher's clear blue eyes flashed a warning to the pack of snarling wolves surrounding them, his sword holding them at bay.

"It's me," he said.

Christopher's stoic expression morphed into a smile when Odette said, "You're an angel."

"Your guardian angel," he said.

The growls and snarls of Lobo's pack rattling the crystal chandeliers grew silent as Christopher began to grow. When he dropped the sword, grabbed Paula and Odette in each of his arms, and began levitating toward the ceiling. The roof disappeared when another explosion rocked the room.

Chapter 16

Odette gasped when she glanced at the water thousands of feet below her. Paula, held firmly in Christopher's other arm, was undergoing a similar reaction. The sky afire with starlight had never looked so brilliant.

"I won't drop you," Christopher said.

He laughed when Paula asked, "Are you taking us to heaven?"

"It's not your time," he said.

"Did you just save us from a pack of wolves, or was the hash making us think so?" Odette asked.

"I'm a benevolent supernatural entity and not your personal adviser. Figure it out for yourself," Christopher said. "I'll leave you something to make you feel better. Now, no more questions."

"Where is Laurel?" Paula asked.

"I said, no more questions. I'll be gone in a moment, and you won't remember this flight."

Laurel was the other half of the vampire couple Odette and Paula had freed from the Majestic Hotel using a witch's spell. Their flight was the first time Paula and Odette had seen Laurel or Christopher since their rise toward the sky following the ceremony. They reflexively closed their eyes when they heard a pop. When they opened them, they were in the living area of their suite of rooms at the Stilt's Resort. Christopher was gone.

"What the hell just happened?" Paula said.

"Don't know," Odette said. "I'm still loopy from all the hash we smoked."

Paula peered around the large room. "How did we get to our suite?"

Odette's eyes were closed as she rested her forehead in her hand. "Haven't a clue. I need more hash, a mug of rum, or ten hours of sleep. Maybe all three."

Paula picked up a jar from the coffee table. "

"At least someone left us a bottle of aspirin."

"I'll take a handful," Odette said.

Paula gave Odette two aspirins and took some herself. Within minutes, the physical effects of the hash and alcohol became a faded memory.

"It's not even midnight, and we're the only ones here," she said. "I feel better, and there's a chilled magnum of champagne in a bucket of ice on the cabinet. I'll get it."

Paula opened the bottle of champagne, smiling when the cork popped and flew across the room.

"I don't see any glasses," Paula said.

"To hell with glasses," Odette said. "Hand me the bottle."

"You're a wild woman," Paula said.

Odette drank straight from the bottle. "Don't know what was in those aspirins, but my headache is gone."

"Mine too," Paula said. "Let's do some exploring."

"Bring the bottle," Odette said. "That's good shit, man!"

Paula took the bottle, drinking until the champagne ran down her neck.

137

"This is wonderful," she said.

"I haven't felt this good in forever," Odette said. "Bring the aspirins. I may need another."

"Why not?" Paula said.

Their suite was on the highest floor of the resort, the hallway deserted.

"Frankie must have reserved this suite of rooms, especially for us," Paula said.

"There's a door with an exit sign," Odette said. "Hope it's not locked."

The door led them to a deck overlooking the Gulf of Mexico, an infinity pool extending over the deck.

"I think I just died and went to heaven," Odette said. "Let's go swimming."

"I don't have anything under this yellow sundress," Paula said.

"There's no one here but us."

Paula drank from the champagne bottle and let the little sundress fall off her shoulders and drop to the cement. Odette beat her into the water, swimming to the pool's edge.

"Oh my God! I can't believe this wonderful pool. It's like swimming in the sky."

"The water's so clear. You can see the boats below us."

Paula dived to the bottom of the pool, smiling when she surfaced and squeezed the water from her dark hair.

"It's almost like flying," she said.

"Creepy," Odette said. "Feels like we've done this already tonight."

"Have more champagne, girlfriend," Paula said.

Odette got out of the pool, drinking more champagne and taking another aspirin.

"This aspirin is like a mood enhancer," she said. "I can't remember ever feeling this good."

"Me either," Paula said, joining her. "The rig

lights flickering on the horizon are magical. I feel like dancing."

"A witches dance?"

"Why not?" Paula said.

Paula began moving slowly, weaving a sensual tribute to the hazy moon. Odette joined her.

"Are we casting a spell?" Odette asked.

"Dancing for the sheer joy of it," Paula said. "How better to celebrate the Moon Goddess?"

They both jumped when someone behind them cleared his throat. Frankie Castellano was smiling as he sat in an elevated spa above them.

"I'm enjoying your dance though didn't want you to think I'm a voyeur."

Paula grabbed the champagne and aspirins and followed Odette up the steps to a steaming pool of water they had somehow overlooked.

"May we join you?" Paula asked.

"I've been here a while and was just leaving," Frankie said.

"Don't go," Paula said, stepping into the hot water.

"We thought we were alone," Odette said, dipping her toe into the water.

"I relax here almost every night before I go to bed," Frankie said. "A little slice of heaven. What are you drinking?"

"Someone left us a magnum of champagne in our suite," Paula said, sliding beside him.

Odette joined them. "The aspirin is better than the champagne. Have a headache?"

"No," Frankie said.

"Then this will keep you from getting one," Odette said.

Paula plopped two aspirins into Frankie's mouth, giving him the champagne to wash them down.

"Good stuff," he said. "Your host is looking

out for you."

Frankie pulled himself out of the water and sat on the edge of the spa.

He grinned when Odette said, "Take off you're bathing suit. You can't let Paula and me be the only ones naked in your spa."

"I'm modest," he said.

"Bullshit!" Paula said, grabbing his trunks and pulling them down around his knees.

"Help me, girlfriend," she said. "Frankie doesn't need a bathing suit when you and I are naked."

Odette helped Paula pull the bathing suit down over Frankie's ankles. They were all laughing when Odette tossed it into the Gulf of Mexico. Odette scooted closer.

"More aspirin?"

Frankie took another, chasing it with a shot of champagne.

"I've never had aspirin that made me feel this good," he said. Where you girls been?"

"In one of your nightclubs in the casino," Paula said.

"Which one?"

"Oz," Odette said.

"There's no club in the casino called Oz," he said.

"Yes, there is," Odette said. "Aphrodite was barely dressed, and the waiter Adonis was naked."

Frankie laughed. "Sounds like Vegas to me. None of my employees wait tables naked. Who were the other customers?"

"He laughed again when Paula said, "A pack of hash-smoking wolves."

"I think you had one too many. There are no illegal drugs on Stilts, at least none I condone."

"Maybe I was dreaming. Hope this isn't a dream," Odette said.

"Seems like a dream to me," Frankie said. "What could make it better?"

He grinned when Paula said, "A table dance from Odette."

"I haven't given anyone a table dance in months," Odette said. "I used to charge a hundred bucks."

"Put it on my tab," Frankie said.

"There's no music."

Frankie fumbled for a remote control on the deck behind him, music instantly surrounding them.

"Something slower and more sultry," Odette said.

The music quickly changed into a suggestive, seventies rock anthem. "Seems like this was the song playing last time someone gave me a table dance," Frankie said.

Odette straddled Frankie and began gyrating to the music, her movements slow and sexy.

"Help me, girlfriend," Odette said. "Frankie deserves two gorgeous ladies dancing for him."

Paula was all smiles as she joined Odette. So enraptured by the song and naked bodies, neither Frankie nor Paula, and Odette were aware someone was watching.

When someone said, "Frankie, how could you?" they noticed.

Recognizing the voice, Frankie bolted to his feet, found the bath towel behind him, and wrapped himself in it.

"Baby, I can explain," he said.

The woman stalked off, not turning around when Frankie rushed after her. Paula and Odette slid back into the spa.

"Was that Frankie's wife?" Paula asked.

"Sounds like a good guess to me," Odette said. "What now?"

Despite the altercation, the aspirin continued

to lighten Odette's mood. She lifted the bottle of champagne with both hands and drank.

"Maybe Frankie will convince her to join us, and we can slip her an aspirin," she said.

"Yeah, and maybe hell will freeze over," Paula said. "Let's get out of here before Frankie comes back. He didn't look happy, and we don't want him to take it out on us."

Paula laughed when Odette said, "It wasn't our fault."

"I feel like we're drinking the last of Frankie's champagne."

Odette said, "You think? Maybe we should follow them and try to explain the situation."

"What are you going to tell her? We drugged your husband?" Paula asked.

"Well, we did," Odette said.

"He didn't exactly fight us off," Paula said.

"We weren't exactly making love, either," Odette said. "Frankie wasn't cheating."

"Try to convince his wife of that," Paula said.

"You forgave Jimmie when he went to Pauline's," Odette said.

"Because he doesn't know I know. It's not the same thing."

When Frankie returned, Odette and Paula pulled on their yellow sundresses, preparing to leave the deck. He wasn't smiling though he didn't seem mad at Paula and Odette either.

He nodded when Odette asked, "Was that your wife? I'm so sorry."

"I have only myself to blame," Frankie said.

"She'll forgive you," Paula said.

"I don't think so. Adele's first husband was an asshole and treated her poorly."

"You aren't that kind of man," Odette said.

"We weren't having sex," Paula said. "Surely, you can explain."

"What if it had been Jimmie instead of Adele.

Would he have forgiven us?"

"He wouldn't have been happy about it," Paula said. "Please don't tell him."

"I don't tell secrets," Frankie said.

"Thank you," Paula said. "Where did Adele go?"

"Took the helicopter back to New Orleans. She'll probably be packing her things once she gets home."

"Is there anyone there you can call?" Odette asked.

"For what?" Frankie asked.

"Explain what happened, and to run interference for you. Meantime, fill the house with roses and write a heartfelt apology."

"My daughter Josie, Jojo's mom, lives with us."

"Does she have any pull with Adele?" Odette asked.

"They are thick as thieves," Frankie said. "She's going to hate me as much as Adele does."

"Daughters are forgiving," Odette said. "I worked offshore in the summers with my dad. I went drinking with him one night at a Morgan City bar. He drank too much and spent most of the night making out with a drunk woman he picked up in the bar."

"Did he go home with her?" Frankie asked.

"No, but only because I kicked him in the nuts so hard, the bartender called the cops. By the time the police left, he and the woman had lost interest."

"And you never told your mom?" Frankie asked.

Odette shook her head. "I thought about it more than once, though I never did."

"Would your mom have left him if she'd found out?"

Odette smiled and shook her head again.

"Hell, she knows how men are and suspected Dad of playing around more than once."

Frankie groaned when Paula said, "Problem is, your wife caught you red-handed, or at least thought she did. Send the roses like Odette said and have your daughter Josie tell her you have an excuse."

"What excuse?" Frankie asked.

"Your gonads," Paula said with a grin.

Chapter 17

The first thing Asger felt when he opened his eyes was the warm nose of Noni's giant dog Duchess touching his forehead. Unable to suppress his surprise, he jerked his head away. Duchess didn't move. Realizing she meant no harm, he wrapped his arms around her large neck.

"What's the matter, girl?" he asked.

Duchess walked away, returning after going no further than ten feet. She repeated the process twice before Asger realized she wanted him to follow her. Odette was sleeping soundly on the fur throw, and he didn't disturb her.

"You want me to go with you?" he said.

Duchess responded by moving away from the rugs. Asger grabbed his spear and followed. Asger could easily see the opening to the Biowomb was too small to accommodate Duchess.

"Are you trying to go outside?" Asger said.

Duchess led him into the darkness, away from the artificial light created by long-missing human beings. Noni had told him she hunts every night in the Nether World. Since she was too large to go through the tunnel from which they had entered the Biowomb, she must know another exit.

Asger followed Duchess into the mouth of a small cavern. She led him along a rocky path, continuing until they'd exited Noni's Biowomb and had entered the dark and surreal landscape of the Nether World. Duchess raised her large head and emitted a bloodcurdling howl such as Asger had never heard. Far in the distance, another creature responded with a plaintiff wail.

Duchess glanced at Asger and then sprinted toward the distant howling. He began running, not knowing if he could keep up with the beautiful beast. Asger caught Duchess when she slowed at the top of a rise. Below them was a giant dog, bigger than Duchess, crouched on its haunches, his fangs bared at a creature at least three times his size.

Behind the dog were a half-dozen people the size of Noni, their spears awaiting the creature's attack if the big dog failed to hold it off. Duchess didn't wait. Springing forward, she dived into the furry chest of the giant were-beast. Asger raced toward the beast, his spear in attack mode.

Spurred on by the presence of Duchess, the big dog, along with the tiny people, attacked the creature's throat. Asger launched himself on the creature's back, holding on with one hand and using the spear to stab the beast with the other. He finally found the creature's jugular vein, and it began spouting red blood from the wound in its neck. When it dropped dead to the ground, the people started to cheer.

A tiny man who looked a lot like Noni said, "You saved us. We are forever in your debt. I've never seen anything or anyone kill one. You are a god."

"Like you, just a man," Asger said.

"You saved us," the man said.

"We saved each other," Asger said. "You were

all engaged in the fight. I am Asger. Who are you?"

"Bobbis. This is my wife Trysta and her sister, Alice. The three youngsters are our son and two daughters."

"And the dog?" Asger said.

"His name is Greatfall. He has been our salvation," Bobbis said.

Greatfall and Duchess were a couple, Duchess licking the blood from the larger dog's fur.

"Where do you live?" Asger said.

"Close by," Trysta said. "It's too dangerous to travel far from shelter."

"Are there more were-bears around?" Asger asked.

"Many horrible creatures haunt the Nether World," Alice said.

"And your people?" Asger asked.

"We haven't seen another person in quite some time," Bobbis said.

"Come with me," Asger said. "I'll lead you to a safer place with a bounty of food."

Trysta shook her head when Bobbis glanced at her.

"Our home is the Nether World," she said. "Where do you come from?"

"Vinland," he said. "A place of sun and plenty."

"What is the sun?" Trysta asked.

"A giant glowing ball in the sky that provides warmth and serenity," Asger said.

"Surely, you jest," Alice said. "There is no such place, except maybe in our imaginations."

"Come with me," Asger said. "I can show you a better place not far from here."

"Are you hungry?" Bobbis said

Alice and Trysta laughed when Asger said, "I stay hungry."

"The were-bear's fur will provide protection from the elements, and I need to skin it," Bobbis said. "Go with Alice and Trysta to our camp, and they will feed you."

The two big dogs raced ahead, Trysta, Alice, and Asger following behind. Exo, the boy, and his sisters Tis and Blossom took turns riding on Asger's broad shoulders. A wall of rock, hollowed in the middle, projected out of the landfill. It provided a fort-like shelter for the group's fur tent. A fire burning in a stone pit reflected heat from the rock wall into the tent.

"There's no wood in the fire," Asger said. "What is the fuel you use?"

"Methane from the landfill," Trysta said. "It burns continuously."

Asger sat in front of the fire, holding his hands close to the flame to warm them. The children continued to wrestle with him as Alice brought him a gourd filled with water.

"Good," he said with a smile. "Where do you get your water?"

"From a seep near here," Alice said. "We were getting water when the were-bear attacked us."

"I imagine a freshwater seep attracts lots of animals," Asger said.

"Yes," Alice said. "We must use care because there are often animals, some dangerous, gathered there."

"Is it always dark here?" Asger asked.

"Sometimes the electricity in the air sets the sky aflame in color," Trysta said. "When that happens, it isn't so dark."

A prism of colors danced across the sky above them as she spoke.

"Beautiful," he said. "I've never seen anything like it. The sound it made was almost like thunder. Does it ever rain here?"

Both women shook their heads. "What is

rain?" Trysta asked.

"Water that falls from the sky," Asger said.

Trysta and Alice looked as if he had concocted a fictitious explanation. Asger didn't pursue the subject. Exo's eyes grew large when Asger handed him a rubber ball from his leather pouch.

"What is it?" Exo asked.

"A ball. Watch." Asger tossed the ball into the air and caught it. "Catch," he said, throwing it to the boy.

Tis and Blossom weren't happy as Asger engaged Exo in a game of catch. Asger handed Tis a smaller pouch containing five polished stones and a smaller ball.

"What are they?" Tis asked.

"A game called ball and jacks," Asger said. "The polished green stones are the jacks. You need to find a flat surface."

Exo was soon practicing his toss with the ball as Tis and Blossom played jacks on a flat rock. Asger, Trysta, and Alice relaxed before the fire sipping water from the gourd.

"I'll get you something to eat," Trysta said.

The two large dogs were lying by the fire. Their heads perked up simultaneously as if they'd both heard something. Squeezing through the opening into the encampment, they disappeared into the darkness.

Asger shook his head and rose to his feet. "Bobbis is taking too long. The bear fur will be heavy, and I'm going to help him."

Grabbing his spear and fur throw, Asger followed the two dogs into the flickering dimness of the Nether World. The bizarre landscape and colorful light show filled him with a sense of awe and danger. He broke into a trot to keep up with the dogs rapidly disappearing from his view.

There were no stars, horizons, or landmarks

to guide him. He only knew he wasn't far from where he had killed the were-bear. The dogs were barking. When he reached them, he found out why.

A half-dozen hyena-like creatures had surrounded Bobbis and the were-bear carcass. Having skinned the beast, Bobbis stood behind it, brandishing his club. The Hyenas crouched and snarled as they circled ever closer. Asger and the approaching dogs proved the game-changer.

The hyenas didn't run away when the dogs chased after them, only backing away, waiting for them to abandon the Were-bear carcass.

"Thank you for returning," Bobbis said. "I didn't expect the creatures to smell the blood and show up so quickly."

"They're as thirsty and hungry as we are," Asger said. "Where is the freshwater seep?"

"Behind the stone boulder," Bobbis said.

The wind had carved out a fortress similar to where Bobbis lived. A pool of water bubbled to the surface near the center of the rock enclosure.

"Why didn't you put your camp here instead of in the distance?" Asger asked. "You wouldn't have to journey to fetch your water."

"Too many animals come here for their water. We didn't want to fend off wild creatures constantly."

Asger nodded and began filling his water bag. Bobbis's knife was made of bone. Asger tossed him his steel blade.

"Cut us off a few steaks," he said. "We'll have to leave the rest to the hyenas. I'll bring the hide."

Bobbis smiled as he snatched the sharp blade out of the air and began carving slabs of meat from the dead beast. The dogs held the hyenas at bay until Asger and Bobbis finished the task and had cleared the premises. They were barely away from the carcass when the hyenas moved in, snarling and growling as they tore off slabs of meat and began devouring it.

Bobbis had cut off two large slabs of meat for Duchess and Greatfall. The dogs and hyenas were in a feeding frenzy, forgetting about protecting their territory as they filled their bellies. A hundred yards from the seep, the dogs had still not joined them.

"How do you find your way around?" Asger said. "There are no points of reference."

"Only small ones," Bobbis said. "We never stray far from home for fear of becoming lost."

"Good thing I have Duchess with me. Otherwise, I'd be stuck out here."

"And you would freeze to death once darkness comes," Bobbis said.

"It's always dark," Asger said. "What do you mean?"

"When nightfall arrives, darkness dominates, and there is not a hint of light," Bobbis said. "With the darkness comes the wind and bone-chilling temperatures."

"Trysta told me it never rains here. How then can it snow?"

"I don't know what rain is though it snows here almost every night. I have no idea why."

The sky was beginning to darken as Asger glanced upward. "Then we'd better hurry," he said.

Trysta greeted Bobbis with smiles and a heartfelt hug when he and Asger appeared through the opening to their encampment. Blossom took the cuts of meat and began roasting them on the open flame. They were soon drinking spring water and feasting on rare were-bear steaks. The sky had become dark, snow falling as they finished their meal.

"When Duchess gets here, I must leave," Asger said. "Someone is waiting for me and will be frightened if I'm not there when she awakens."

Greatfall returned alone and reclined on the thick furs on the ground outside the tent. Bobbis placed his hand on Asger's wrist and shook his head.

"Without the dog, you'll never find your way back to your camp. Stay the night with us. You'll be safe, and tomorrow you can return to where you came."

Chapter 18

O dette didn't remember where she was when she awoke. It didn't take her long to remember. When Duchess showed up alone, Odette almost panicked. Noni came out of his wagon and calmed her down.

"Asger isn't here," Odette said.

"Maybe he went outside with Duchess to do some exploring," he said. "He'll be back."

"I'm scared," Odette said. "What if something killed him?"

"Asger is a warrior. Warriors don't die easily."

"Not normally, they don't," Odette said. "Nothing about the Nether World is normal. We have to look for him."

"Asger is big and strong. There's no way I can move as fast as him or you."

"Then I'll go alone," Odette said.

"That would be a mistake," Noni said. "You'd soon be lost yourself."

"I have to do something," she said.

Noni rubbed his forehead. "I may have an idea."

"Tell me," Odette said.

"Do you know what a truck is?" he asked.

"Of course I do," she said.

"Then come with me."

Odette went with Noni as he followed the pathway to the abandoned city. He led her to a room where there was a truck that looked brand new. It was a Ford, though a body style Odette didn't recognize.

Noni didn't answer when she asked, "Does it run on gasoline?"

"It's electrical," he said. "I believe it's fully charged and ready to run."

"You've never driven it?" she asked.

"I don't know how," he said.

Odette opened the door and looked at the controls. "There's no steering wheel, brake pedal, or throttle," she said. "I don't know how to drive it either. There is a key."

"A key?"

"The device used to start vehicles. It's in the ignition."

"Use it," Noni said. "See if it starts."

When Odette turned the key, a screen appeared where the steering wheel should be. From it, she could see the wall in front of the truck. A voice began to talk.

"I am Mona. Where do you want to go?"

"I have no idea," Odette said. "How do I drive you?"

"I'm responsive to your commands," the female voice said.

"How do I apply the brakes?"

"You don't. I am a self-driving vehicle."

"I don't know how to program you," Odette said.

"I don't need to be programmed. I read your thoughts and respond accordingly," Mona said.

"Get out of here!" Odette said.

"Do you want Noni to accompany you?"

"How do you know Noni?"

"I can read his mind as I can yours. He wants

to accompany you."

Odette got out of the truck and helped Noni into the front passenger seat. The vehicle had a large backseat.

"Is there a door big enough for you to exit into the Nether World?"

Both doors shut, and Odette and Noni could feel the pulse of a large electric engine. The truck sat on an elevator and began lowering them through the floor into a darkened tunnel. Incandescent lighting illuminated the tunnel once the elevator reached the bottom. The truck started forward for about a mile. When it halted, another elevator lifted them to the surface of the Nether World. The light was dim though Noni and Odette could see something running toward them. It was Duchess.

"Duchess knows every foot of the Nether World," Noni said. "She will lead us to Asger."

Mona took off after the galloping dog before Odette could respond. Odette and Noni watched as Duchess disappeared on the backside of a large rock formation. Mona followed, coming to a halt at the entrance to Bobbis's fortress. The trip was short; less than five miles.

"I'll wait here for you," Mona said.

"What do you think?" Odette asked.

"Duchess wouldn't have entered if it weren't safe," he said. "Want me to go first?"

"Please," Odette said.

A surprise awaited Noni when he entered the encampment. Bobbis jumped up from the fire and grabbed his spear.

"It's okay, Bobbis," Asger said. "I know this man."

Bobbis relaxed as Odette followed behind Noni. Seeing Asger, she hurried into his awaiting arms.

"Asger, I've been so worried."

"Duchess left without me. Without her help, I couldn't find my way back to the Biowomb. How did Noni manage to walk this far?"

Excited by the appearance of strangers and a human female such as they had never seen, Exo, Blossom, and Tis tugged at her legs.

"Who are these cuties?" Odette said, lifting Exo into her arms.

"I'm Exo," the boy said. "Who are you?"

"Odette."

"I've never seen a woman as big as you are," Exo said.

"At just under five feet tall, no one has ever called me a big woman," she said with a smile.

Odette put the squirming boy back on the ground and hoisted the two little girls into her arms.

"You are so pretty," she said. "What are your names?"

"I'm Tis. My sister's name is Blossom. Asger gave us ball and jacks. Will you play with us?"

"You bet," Odette said. "First, I'd like to meet your parents.

Everyone was all smiles during introductions. It was instantly apparent Noni was taken by Alice. She wasn't so forthcoming, disappearing into the tent after barely speaking.

"Is it something I said?" Noni asked.

"Alice is shy," Trysta said. "Are you hungry? Bobbis and Asger killed a were-bear and managed to save a few steaks for us before the hyenas moved in on the carcass."

"You killed a were-bear?" Noni said.

"Asger did the killing. The dogs and I were backing him up," Bobbis said.

"I'm impressed," Noni said.

"The steaks are wonderful," Trysta said. "We ate some last night."

Odette tried her best not to make a face.

"Sounds yummy," she said.

Noni and Asger ate their steaks with relish. Though Odette's steak wasn't half bad, the thought of eating a giant predator didn't sit well with her stomach. No one noticed when she passed her mostly uneaten meal to Asger. After eating, they sat around the fire, conversing like old friends.

"How did you get here?" Trysta asked. "Did you walk?"

"There's an operable vehicle in the Biowomb where Noni lives," Odette said. "It drives itself using voice commands. It's armored and mostly protected from the dangers of the Nether World."

"It's parked outside," Noni said. "Want to see it?"

Even Alice came out of the tent to see the shiny electric vehicle that could carry passengers using some strange power she didn't understand. Exo climbed up into the driver's seat.

"I love it," he said. "Can I drive?"

Odette glanced at Trysta and Bobbis. "I'll go with him," she said.

When Trysta smiled and nodded, Tis and Blossom said, "We want to go too."

The four of them were soon driving circles around the rock encampment, Exo, Tis, and Blossom having the times of their lives. They didn't want to leave the truck when Odette had Exo pull to a halt.

"Stay the night with us," Trysta said.

Odette glanced at Asger and said, "Why not?"

"I have to return to the Biowomb to feed the pups," Noni said.

"Pups?" Alice said, showing interest for the first time.

"Duchess and Greatfall's babies," Noni said.

"I'd love to see them," Alice said.

"Then come with me. The vehicle will return

157

automatically to the Biowomb. We can feed the pups, and I'll show you around."

"I don't know," Alice said.

"Please trust me," Noni said. "I wouldn't harm a hair on your beautiful head."

Alice blushed and said, "No one has ever called me beautiful."

"Sorry, Odette and Trysta. You, Alice, are the most beautiful woman I've ever seen."

Odette handed Noni the key to the truck. Asger helped Alice and Noni into the cab and then watched as they disappeared into the growing darkness.

"Come back into the fortress," Bobbis said. "Darkness is falling, and it will soon begin to snow."

A flame of methane burned inside the cozy and spacious tent. Asger spent the next hour playing catch with Exo while Odette taught the two girls how to play ball and jacks.

"Time for bed," Trysta finally said.

"Mom," Exo said, complaining.

"You can play again tomorrow. Right now, you need to get your rest so you can grow up big and strong like your father and Asger."

Despite their protests, the children soon slept peaceably beneath their fur throws. Outside, the wind had begun to howl.

"I hope Noni and Alice are okay," Trysta said.

"They're fine," Odette said.

"He's never driven the vehicle before now," Bobbis said.

"Noni will master it in no time," Odette said. "Is Alice your sister?"

"We found her living alone," Trysta said. "It took some convincing to persuade her to move in with us."

Trysta smiled when Odette said, "People need each other."

"There are tribes from where I come from," Asger said. "You are a tribe now."

"Tribes?" Bobbis said.

"Families and like-minded people who live together for the benefit of everyone," Asger said.

Asger nodded when Trysta asked, "Does your tribe have a name?"

"We are the Cahokias," he said.

"How many people are there in your tribe?" Bobbis asked.

"Thousands," Asger said. "We live on a hill overlooking a winding river. We occupy a fortress of wood surrounding the pyramids in which we live."

"What's a pyramid?" Trysta asked.

With a stick, Asger scribbled a picture of a pyramid on the part of the dirt floor not covered by rugs.

"How big are they?" Bobbis asked.

"Many times bigger than your tent," Asger said. "They are elevated about fifty feet off the ground."

"You aren't afraid of were-bears?" Bobbis asked.

"There are no were-bears in Vinland, where I live," Asger said.

Bobbis and Trysta soon said goodnight and climbed into their furs. Odette cuddled close to Asger as the wind continued blowing, occasional snowflakes wafting through the tent's flap.

"You called yourself a Cahokia," she said. "I thought you were a Viking."

"Cahokia," he said.

"Then where did you get your blue eyes and blond hair?"

"Your hair is the same color as mine," he said. "Are you a Viking?"

Odette grinned. "I'm a Cajun."

"What's a Cajun?" Asger asked.

"A person from south Louisiana who loves to eat crawfish," Odette said.

"What's a crawfish?" Asger asked.

"A tasty little creature that lives in shallow water. You probably know it by another name," she said.

"My people eat fish," he said.

"I can't wait to see where you live," Odette said. "Do you think we will ever see it?"

"We'll see it," he said.

"Sure about that?" Odette said.

"As sure as I know, I love you," he said.

"How can you love me? We just met?"

"Did you see the look in Noni and Alice's eyes? They are in love," Asger said.

When Odette laughed aloud, she glanced at the pallet of Trysta and Bobbis, hoping she hadn't awakened them.

"They are in lust. I don't know about love," she said.

Asger put his hand on Odette's breast and gently squeezed it. "They aren't the only ones in lust," he said.

Odette didn't move his hand away but said, "Don't get any ideas. I like you too, though I'm not making love with anyone while most of the occupants of the Nether World are within ten feet of us."

"Why not?" Asger said. "Trysta and Bobbis are doing it now."

"Get out of here," she said.

When she glanced across the dimly-lit room, she realized from the movement of the fur throw that Trysta and Bobbis weren't asleep and were making love.

"I'm noisy when I make love," Odette said.

"You don't have to be," Asger said.

Later, when Odette and Asger were beneath their fur throw, Asger put his hand over her mouth to suppress her moans of pleasure. Both had to muffle their laughter to keep from waking everyone in the tent.

Chapter 19

The nightly snowfall had ceased when Noni and Alice returned to the stony encampment in the electric truck. When they came through the tent door, they were holding hands.

"Look at you two," Trysta said. "From the smiles on your faces, you must have enjoyed yourselves."

"The Biowomb is amazing," Alice said. "I have never seen a place like it or dreamed such a place could exist."

"Tell us about it," Trysta said.

Alice motioned at the ceiling of the tent with her outstretched hand. "There is light and not the endless darkness of the Nether World."

"What else?" Bobbis asked.

Alice was beaming. "You have to see it for yourself. Meantime, I brought something for Exo, Blossom, and Tis."

"What is it?" Exo asked.

"Ice cream bars. Vanilla ice cream with a chocolate coating."

"What is chocolate?" Tis asked.

"Something you'll never get enough of," Alice said, handing each of them a bar.

"What do you do with it?" Exo asked.

"Eat it and tell me what you think."

The three youngsters unwrapped the treats and put them in their mouths.

"I love this," Tis said. "What did you call it?"

"Ice cream coated with chocolate. Noni thought you'd like it."

They were all smiles as they thanked Noni and then hurried to a corner of the tent to enjoy the rest of their treat. Noni and Alice joined the group by the fire.

"Greatfall and Duchess have three adorable puppies. Duchess stayed with them in the Biowomb."

"What is this place you call the Biowomb?" Bobbis asked.

"An underground city created by survivors of the Darkness," Noni said.

"Who are these survivors?" Trysta said.

"All gone, the Biowomb is? deserted except for me, Duchess and her pups, and lots of birds and small animals."

"What are birds?" Trysta asked.

"Feathered creatures that fly and live in trees," Noni said.

"Trees?"

"See for yourselves," Noni said. "There are far too many strange things to describe that you need to see to believe. I can take you there in the electric vehicle."

"Will you bring us back?" Bobbis asked.

"Of course."

"I'll gather some food to take with us," Trysta said.

"No need," Alice said. "There's plenty to eat in the Biowomb."

Still blown away by the big electric truck, Exo stood outside gazing at the sleek lines until Bobbis scooped him up and put him in the backseat.

"Please let me ride in front," he said.

"Take my place," Alice said, crawling into the backseat.

When Noni cranked the engine, Exo said, "I love all the controls and flashing lights."

"Would you like to drive?" Noni asked.

"You mean it?" Exo asked.

"The truck has a name," Noni said. "It's Mona. If you want Mona to go someplace, just tell her. Artificial intelligence controls it."

"What's that?" Exo asked.

"Mona has a brain and learns things, just like we do, and responds accordingly. Tell it where you want to go."

"Where are we going?" Exo asked.

"To the Biowomb," Noni said.

The truck's horn honked when Exo said, "Mona, can you hear me? Take us to the Biowomb."

Before they'd reached the entrance to the underground city, Tis and Blossom had crawled into the front seat beside Exo. They didn't want the trip to end when Mona reentered the corridor to its charging room.

"Exo, you are a wonderful driver," Noni said.

"I want to drive some more," Exo said.

"Tomorrow," Noni said. "Right now, I have so much to show you and your sisters. We'll get some more ice cream and then have some fun."

The first place Noni showed Bobbis and Trysta was his wildly painted Gypsy wagon. Duchess was outside, feeding her three pups on one of the plush mats. Odette and Asger laid beside them.

"I'm staying here to get some rest," Asger said.

"Me too," Odette said. "Have fun."

Long after Noni and the others were gone,

Asger and Odette remained silent, Asger holding Odette in his arms.

"Feels like we're stuck here forever," he finally said.

"Don't say that," Odette said. "Even if it's what you are thinking."

"For the first time in my life, I have no plan," Asger said.

"You're giving up?" Odette said.

"I'm out of ideas," he asked.

"You didn't quit when the tiger chased us."

"It was in the moment. I had no time to think about it," Asger said.

"There's a way out of here. We just haven't found it yet," Odette said.

"We're never going to find a way out here in the comforts of the Biowomb," Asger said. "We need to return to the Nether World. That's where our destiny lies."

"Maybe the people who once lived here had the same idea and returned to the Nether World and became the people Noni and the others now are."

"Perhaps," Asger said. "What do you think we should do?"

"Something proactive," Odette said. "Let's go to the city. The truck was a surprise. Maybe there are more surprises."

"I like lying here with you," Asger said.

Odette sprang to her feet. "Get up," she said.

"What's your hurry?" Asger said.

"I have a hunch. Do you believe in premonitions?"

"I believe in you," Asger said. "Lead, and I will follow."

Asger and Odette followed the trail to Dead City. Odette stood in the town square, glancing around for anything that might inspire her.

"Well?" Asger said.

Odette's blond hair moved when she shook her head. "I wish Paula was here. She'd know what to do."

"Who is Paula?" Asger asked.

"My best friend. She's a Cajun witch and knows things others don't."

"You have your powers," Asger said. "Use them."

Odette closed her eyes and concentrated. "Let's go this way," she said."

The path led to a building surrounded by a tall fence topped with barbwire. The gate opened, and Asger followed Odette to a building with no windows. Like the gate, they found the front door unlocked.

Dim lighting cast eerie shadows in the empty hallway leading to a metal door decorated with a skull and crossbones, and the words Prohibited Entry. Odette grasped the door handle and turned it.

Once commanding maximum security, the room and building were now unguarded and unlocked. Only a table and a single object atop the table occupied the space.

"What is it?" Asger asked.

"Looks like a brain under glass to me," Odette said. "It must be alive because it's wired up and pulsating."

Asger touched the glass, a light accompanied by electrical buzzing beginning when he did. Another light appeared, causing Odette to step backward, her hand at her mouth. A person stared back at them, at least the hologram of a person.

"Who are you?" Asger said.

"Albert Einstein. Who are you?"

"I'm Asger and this is Odette. Are you real?"

"Do you mean am I alive? My brain is alive. My body is dead and buried."

"You're a hologram," Odette said. "How are you responding to our questions? Are you some artificial intelligence?"

"The brain under glass is my brain," the hologram said. "When I died in 1955, the pathologist Thomas Harvey stole my brain and eyes. The brain they found several years later wasn't mine."

"What happened to it?" Odette asked.

"A powerful organization paid lots of money for it," Einstein said.

"To what purpose?" Odette said.

"Same old thing—money and power," Einstein said.

Einstein's hologram laughed when Odette asked, "Did they get what they paid for?"

"Horrid people put my brain under glass, wired to a computer and life-sustaining fluids. They expected a tremendous reward. I gave them nothing."

"Then you are actually Albert Einstein, and your brain is still alive?" Odette said.

"The only part of me that is," the hologram said. "The cretins who put me here are long gone."

"Then you got the last laugh," Odette said. "Can you tell me what year this is?"

"No idea," Einstein said. "The computer to which I'm attached hasn't been updated."

"How long did people live in this settlement?" Odette asked.

"Less than twenty-five years," Einstein said.

"What was your function?" Odette asked.

"I have a gift for numbers," Einstein said. "Mathematics provides the answer to every question." He chuckled again. "Except for personal problems. You probably need a rabbi or a priest for that."

"We don't need answers to personal

problems," Odette said. "We have other issues more pressing."

His interest suddenly piqued, Einstein's hologram said, "Such as?"

"Asger and I come from different worlds. We crossed time portals to get here. Can you help us? We want to go home."

"You help me, and maybe I can help you," the hologram said.

"What do you want from us?" Odette asked.

"Destroy the jar entrapping me," he said.

"You want us to kill you?" Odette asked.

"You can't kill someone who is not alive," the hologram of Einstein said.

"Your brain's alive," Odette said.

"It's my brain that is speaking to you. I want eternal peace. I can't have it when I'm locked in perpetual prison."

"There's a line I can't cross," Odette said. "I can't kill you."

"Death is an abstract term," Einstein said. "Life is energy which can neither be created nor destroyed. If my brain ceases to exist, its energy takes another form. My energy survives, and I will be free from the solitary cell I occupy."

"You're confusing me," Odette said. "Are you talking about reincarnation?"

Einstein's hologram shook its head. "Reincarnation is the wrong term. Renewal and rebirth is the correct explanation. Energy is infinite and immortal. My energy might return as a snail, or perhaps a tree. Release my energy from the jar and allow it to seek its next dominion."

"What about the Nether World and the Biowomb?" Asger said.

"What about them?" Einstein asked.

"Though I want to return home, I feel a certain responsibility with the people I've met here," Asger said.

"What about the pollution and radiation?" Odette asked. "The half-life of some radioactive elements can be thousands of years. Is there nothing we can do?"

"Radioactivity dissipates with time," Einstein said. "People and animals are living in the Nether World. The danger lessens with every passing day. The Nether World is experiencing renewal and rebirth as we speak."

"Asger and I were in the Nether World a few hours ago. It's pretty bleak out there," Odette said.

"You survived," Einstein said. "That should be all the proof you need that things are evolving."

"I can't help being doubtful," Odette said. "This world still has a long way to go."

"It will get there," Einstein said.

"But when?" Asger asked.

"Who knows?" Einstein said. "The last ice age lasted millions of years and only ended a few thousand years ago. A single heartbeat in the annals of geologic time."

"What about the people who live here now?" Asger said.

"They will survive, prosper, and evolve. Such is the way of the world."

"Can't we speed up the process?" Asger asked.

"To do that, you'd need Tesla's brain and not mine," Einstein's hologram said.

"I have no idea who Tesla is," Asger said.

"Why did you invoke Tesla's name?" Odette said. "Were you being sarcastic, or do you have an idea?"

"An idea? Yes. A way to implement it, I have no clue."

"What's your idea?" Odette asked.

"Tesla believed the earth and the universe

were an infinite source of cosmic power."

"What do you believe?" Odette asked.

"If it were true," Einstein said, "We could create an enormous amount of energy that could resculpt the world."

"Do you know how to do such a thing?" Odette asked.

"Maybe, with Tesla's help. The problem is Tesla's long dead. Even if he were here, I doubt he would work with me."

"If he were," Odette said, "could the two of you devise a plan to bring positive change to the Nether World?"

"Maybe," the hologram said.

Chapter 20

🦄

Two days had passed before Eddie returned to the island as a passenger in a pickup emblazoned with the words Roberts Body Shop. The driver helped Eddie unload three large suitcases from the truck's bed.

"What happened to your car?" J.P. said.

"Had a little fender bender outside of Chalmette. Mr. Roberts is fixing my car and was nice enough to give me a ride to the island."

"Glad you made it," J.P. said. "Everyone else is still at Frankie's resort in the Gulf. Maybe we should drive back to New Orleans and see what trouble we can get into."

"Must be someplace around here closer than New Orleans," Eddie said.

"Pauline's whore house," J.P. said.

Eddie grinned. "I haven't been to a whore house since I was a senior in college. I was afraid of getting thrown in jail, and my asshole was too puckered to have any fun."

"No worries at Pauline's," J.P. said. "The cops are complicit."

J.P. nodded when Eddie said, "You too?"

"I've never taken money under the table, but Pauline gives me a special discount."

"Same thing," Eddie said. "I'd have to prosecute you if I were still in office."

J.P. couldn't stop grinning. "You're such a damn hypocrite."

"Guilty as charged, your honor," Eddie said. "If you let me borrow the ATV, I'll stow my meager belongings in the Majestic."

"You're not going to stay in that hotel, are you?" J.P. asked.

"Why not?" Eddie asked.

"Paula and Odette swear it's haunted."

"I believe in ghosts," Eddie said. "You can't live in New Orleans as long as I have without seeing them. I'll deal with it."

"Then let's get you moved," J.P. said. "If you get too freaked out, I have an extra bedroom in my Airstream."

"Thanks, pal," Eddie said.

They were soon in the Majestic, toting Eddie's three suitcases up the narrow stairway.

"Know what I'm thinking?" J.P. said.

"Probably we need to install an elevator," Eddie said.

"Why did you pick a bedroom on the third floor?" J.P. asked.

"Because that's where all the bedrooms are," Eddie said.

"You better hope this damn building doesn't catch on fire," J.P. said.

They were out of breath when they reached Eddie's suite on the third floor of the Majestic. The suite featured a living area, a primary bedroom, a regal bathroom, and a little kitchen. A short flight of stairs led to the observation deck above them. They set down the suitcases and began removing the dust covers from the furniture.

"This place is posh," J.P. said as Eddie opened the refrigerator door.

"Frankie told me he'd had Jack stock the refrigerator and turn it on. Want an Abita?"

Eddie tossed a beer to J.P. as he glanced around the room.

"Where's the electricity coming from?"

"Underground line," Eddie said. "Same utility company that provides electricity for the lighthouse. Frankie had it activated."

"What about heat and air?" J.P. said.

"I have a window unit and a pot-bellied stove until I can get this place up and running." Eddie turned on the air conditioner. "Kind of stuffy in here," he said. "Guess I'm going to have to fend for myself for a while."

"You kidding?" J.P. said. "Jack never stops cooking, and he always has rum."

"What's the story on Odette?" Eddie asked. "She's one hot woman. Are you two a number?"

J.P. laughed. "She's Cajun and reminds me way too much of my mama."

"Seems intelligent," Eddie said.

"She worked on a degree in hotel and restaurant management at L.S.U. until her dad was killed on an offshore rig and had to drop out to help her mother. She did some stripping on Bourbon Street before hitchhiking to the island."

"Why did she come here?" Eddie asked.

"Jack and Chief visited the strip club and made the mistake of showing her a gold doubloon and a rare bottle of rum they'd found," J.P. said.

"So she's trying to take advantage of Jack and Chief?" Eddie asked.

There was no curtain on the picture window looking out over the Gulf of Mexico. J.P. glanced at the waves licking the shore.

"That's what I originally thought," he said.

"What do you think now?" Eddie asked.

"She's as good as gold and would give you the shirt off her back. She's part of our dog training group and has contributed to the cause as much as anyone. What's your deal with Frankie's daughter?"

"She's gorgeous, rich, and intelligent," Eddie said. "Even though she's Frankie Castellano's only heir, she sells millions in real estate every year."

"Then what's not to like?" J.P. said.

"I loved her, still do. When it came down to tying the knot, I couldn't do it," Eddie said. "Josie hates me now. Frankie and Adele still believe there's a chance to salvage the relationship."

"What do you think?" J.P. asked.

"I don't know. After losing my job with the Feds, I had no better choice than restoring the Majestic."

Eddie laughed when J.P. said, "What do you think now?"

"I like a challenge," he said. "If I can put this place back on the map, it'll be an accomplishment."

Someone was blowing a car horn outside the Majestic.

"Who the hell is that?" J.P. asked.

Eddie started up the stairs to the observation deck. "Let's go see," he said.

J.P. followed Eddie up the short flight of stairs to the observation deck over his suite of rooms. The top was off the sky-blue Pontiac Firebird parked in the sand below. Susie Larsen was behind the wheel, her elbow resting on the horn.

"Oh, shit!" J.P. said.

"You know who it is?" Eddie asked.

"Susie Larsen, the administrator of the Chalmette Animal Shelter."

Eddie followed J.P. down the stairs and back to the suite. J.P. kept going through the door and down the stairs.

"Why are you in such a hurry?" Eddie said as

he followed J.P.

"Susie's going to want to know where Venus is. She won't like it when she realizes she's not on the island."

"Explain to me how she has a dog in the fight," Eddie said.

"The animal shelter is our main source of talent to become students at the training facility."

"There are plenty of animal shelters. Just find another one."

"Sounds simple," J.P. said. "It's not."

Eddie was grinning when he saw Susie's pretty face. "Now, I think I understand."

Dressed in jean shorts, a red crop top, and a cowboy hat, Susie's blond, blue-eyed good looks embodied a California surfer girl.

"Where did you go the other night, cowboy?" she asked. "Meika and I were looking for you. You just disappeared."

"I'm calling bullshit on that one," J.P. said.

"I wouldn't lie to you. Meika and I were ready for a threesome."

"My ass!" J.P. said. "You left me stranded with no way to get back to Chalmette and no place to spend the night once I got there."

"You might have difficulty convincing Basil Doles, Heather's honey, of that."

"Basil Doles?" Eddie said.

"Who did you say is this gorgeous man you have with you?" Susie asked.

"I didn't say," J.P. said.

Eddie stepped forward with an extended hand. "Eddie Toledo," he said. "And what's your name, gorgeous lady?"

"I'm Susie. J.P. and I won the dance contest at Claws and Craws the other night. I dropped by to see if he wants to do more two-stepping tonight. If he doesn't, maybe you could take his place."

"Maybe so," Eddie said. "I'm not a dancer, but I could watch you move your wonderful body all night."

"You are naughty, Eddie Toledo. What are you doing on Oyster Island, and what's your claim to fame?"

"Eddie's a lawyer," J.P. said. "Valedictorian of his class at the University of Virginia and the most powerful assistant Federal District Attorney in the south until he got his pecker caught in the zipper of his pants."

Susie was grinning when she said, "Ouch!"

She opened the top of a red ice cooler on the passenger seat floor and flipped Eddie and J.P. cold cans of beer.

Eddie popped the top on the can and said, "What kind of beer is this?"

"Lone Star," Susie said. "My favorite."

"You don't have a local accent," Eddie said. "You're not from around here, are you?"

"You are one smart boy," Susie said. "I like Lone Star because I'm from Texas."

"Eddie is smart," J.P. said. "Except when he's around a pretty woman, and then he starts thinking with his dick."

"Nothing wrong with that," Susie said. "I like that in a man."

"Your law degree is useless around Susie," J.P. said. "You might as well strip off your britches, slip a gold ring through your nose and start drooling."

"I'm already drooling," Eddie said.

"Don't get too excited," J.P. said. "Susie has a better half. Sad as it might be, neither of us will ever get into her tight jeans."

"Maybe you ought to give Eddie a chance to find out for himself," Susie said.

"What the hell are you doing here, Susie?" J.P. said.

"Checking on Lady and Venus."

"They're doing well," J.P. said.

"Can I see them?" she asked.

"Lady is at Jack's house. Venus is spending a few days with a young lad who took a shine to her," J.P. said.

"You told me you were going to train her to be a service dog," Susie said,

"Her training has begun. As you said, she's the smartest dog in St. Bernard Parish," J.P. said.

"Then who took her, and where are they?"

"Frankie Castellano owns the Majestic. Eddie is his partner, and they plan to renovate and reopen it. Frankie took everyone except Eddie and me to his resort in the Gulf of Mexico. Frankie's grandson Jojo bonded with Venus, and I let him take her to the resort with him." J.P. said.

"So you lied to me," Susie said.

"No way!" J.P. said. "I explained to Frankie about Venus."

"Are you talking about Frankie Castellano, the Don of the Bayou?"

"That's him," J.P. said.

"You plan to sell Venus to a mob boss?" Susie asked.

"If he comes up with fifty-grand. Why not?" J.P. said.

"Because that wasn't part of our agreement when you took Venus," Susie said.

"I don't see your point," J.P. said.

"My point is you promised me you would train Venus to be a service dog," Susie said.

"Was that a verbal commitment, or do you have a contract?" Eddie said.

"Of course, I have a contract," Susie said. "J.P. signed one with the Chalmette Animal Shelter."

"You have a copy of that contract with you?" Eddie asked.

"No," Susie said.

"Does it specifically say J.P.'s training facility can only sell Venus to someone you first approve of?"

"Of course it doesn't," Susie said.

"Have you ever been sued, Ms. Larsen?" Eddie asked.

"Why would anyone want to sue me?" Susie said.

"Fraud," Eddie said. "Sounds like I could rake you over the coals in a court of law. Are you prepared to be sued for everything you're worth?"

"Are you J.P.'s lawyer now?"

"More than simply J.P.'s lawyer, I'm counsel for Oyster Island Canine Training, Inc."

"Is that true, J.P.?" Susie asked.

J.P. nodded when Eddie glanced at him.

"Every successful business needs a lawyer. Eddie is ours now."

"When did you incorporate it?" Susie asked.

"I just arrived on the island. The paperwork will have to wait until I get settled into my new abode," Eddie said. "Now, if you're through posturing, I could get back to ogling your gorgeous bod."

Susie's smile returned. "Let's drink some more beer and worry about Venus later."

"Sounds like a plan to me," Eddie said.

"Give us a ride up the hill to the little house beside the lighthouse," J.P. said. "I'm thirsty for more than beer, and the owner, Jack, left several bottles of rum."

"My Firebird only has room for two. Eddie can ride with me. You'll have to walk," Susie said.

Susie and Eddie were sitting at Jack's plank table drinking rum and chasing it with Lone Star Beer when J.P. walked in the door.

"What took you so long?" Susie said.

J.P. pulled up a chair across the table from

them and poured himself a mug of rum.

"I don't know Meika's number. I'm pretty sure someone on the force could find it for me," he said.

"Call her," Susie said. "I'm not doing anything wrong?"

J.P. grabbed his cell phone. "Let's just see about that."

Susie got out of her seat, sat on J.P.'s lap, and kissed him on the neck.

"Truce?" she said.

Chapter 21

Susie was sitting in J.P.'s lap when someone pushed open the door to Jack's house and entered without knocking. It was Heather Boudreaux, the waitress from Claws and Craws.

She smiled when J.P. asked, "Heather, what are you doing here?"

Heather's laughter filled the room. Eddie was ogling her tanned legs on full display in her cutoff jeans and cowboy boots. Her white tee shirt said Chalmette Fighting Owls.

"Don't you two ever get enough?" she said.

"It's not what you think," J.P. said.

"Heather," Susie said. "Give me a hug."

When Heather broke away from Susie's embrace, she saw Eddie. Walking around the table, she extended her hand.

"Guess no one is going to introduce us. I'm Heather." Eddie kissed it.

"Eddie Toledo," he said. "At your service, pretty lady."

"How do you know these two?" Heather asked.

"J.P. and I have known each other for years. Pretty Miss Susie and I just met," he said.

Susie poured Heather a mug of rum and patted her ass when she handed it to her.

"Love those long legs of yours. What are you doing on Oyster Island?" she asked.

"There's a problem. My boyfriend Basil is on his way here to kick J.P.'s ass. I came to warn him."

"He doesn't have a gun, does he?" J.P. asked.

"Basil doesn't need a gun," Heather said. "He's the star quarterback at L.S.U. and the best athlete in Louisiana."

J.P. grinned when he said. "I'm impressed."

"You'd better be scared," Heather said. "I came to give you a chance to get the hell out of here. Basil's six-three and weighs two-forty-five."

"This is my home now," J.P. said. "I'm not going anywhere."

"You aren't afraid?" Heather asked.

"I was a police officer for years. This isn't my first rodeo."

"You're not going to shoot him, are you?" Heather asked.

"Only if he's packing," J.P. said.

"You aren't worried?" Heather asked.

"Basil is an amateur. I'm a pro," J.P. said. "When's he going to get here?"

"Don't know," Heather said.

"Then relax and enjoy your rum," J.P. said. "When Basil arrives, I'll explain to him he has nothing to worry about where I'm concerned. How does he even know I spent the night at your apartment? I didn't tell him."

Heather lowered her head and said, "I did."

"Why in the hell did you do that?" J.P. asked.

"I knew he'd find out somehow if I didn't tell him," Heather said.

"We didn't do anything. I slept on your couch."

"No one's going to believe that," Heather said.

"Then why didn't you take me to a motel?" J.P. said. "Wait a minute. I think I get it. You used me, didn't you?"

Heather began to cry. "Basil's the campus stud. He's a shoo-in to enter the pros as a first-round pick. His family is already rich, and he will make millions on top of it."

"More power to him," J.P. said.

"I'm just a country girl with a high school education who waits tables for a living," Heather said. "Why would he want me?"

"You're the prettiest girl in the parish. If Basil can't see what he's got, then the asshole doesn't deserve you," J.P. said.

"That's not the way it is," Heather said. "He thinks he loves me but has every pretty girl on campus to choose from."

Susie put her arm around Heather's slender waist. "J.P.'s right, girl. If your boyfriend can't see all the special qualities you have to offer, he doesn't deserve you."

Susie held the mug of rum to Heather's mouth until she began to drink. When the alcohol started working on her, she turned her attention to Eddie.

"What do you think, Mr. Toledo?"

"I think I'm going to help J.P. kick your asshole boyfriend's ass when he gets here. He doesn't deserve a prize like you. And please, my name is Eddie."

Heather sat in Eddie's lap and laid her head on his shoulder.

"Thanks, Eddie," she said.

Susie caught J.P.'s eye and motioned him to follow her outside.

The sun was low on the horizon, the tide subsiding. Susie made sure they were away from the open door before speaking.

"I think she set you up," she said.

"You think?" J.P. said.

"Why are you grinning?" Susie asked.

"Because she snatched a page straight out of your playbook," J.P. said.

Susie's arms crossed tightly across her chest. "I can't believe you think I set you up the other night."

"Seems to me like you did," J.P. said. "Heather saw what happened, and I guess she thinks so too."

"Heather looks comfortable in Eddie's lap. She's still so young. She probably hasn't decided if Basil is the person she wants to spend the rest of her life with."

"Me and Eddie have the same problem," J.P. said. "I'll handle Basil when he gets here. You still haven't explained what you're doing here without Meika."

"She's working, and it's my day off."

"Having second thoughts on your committal?" J.P. asked.

"Maybe," Susie said. "I got to thinking about your fine ass."

"You are so full of bullshit," J.P. said. "It's obvious you want something. Cease the drama and tell me."

"I'm having a perception problem at the animal shelter. I think I need to change my image."

"You need a friendly journalist, or P.R. firm, and not a former cop," J.P. said. "I can't help you."

"Yes, you can," Susie said.

"How?"

"An interview with the local newspaper," Susie said. "You could explain the broad changes I've implemented, resulting in positive change for the community. Will you help me?"

"I'm here for you," J.P. said. "Do you have a reporter in mind?"

"A woman named Caila Clarkson," Susie said.

"I'm hip," J.P. said.

"Then I'll have Caila contact you," Susie said.

J.P. held Susie at arm's length. "Let me guess. You and Caila are soul mates. She doesn't know about Meika, and Meika doesn't know about her."

Susie stood on her tiptoes and kissed J.P. "You are very perceptive."

When J.P. broke away, he said, "Then why is it I feel as if I'm getting a dildo rammed up my ass?"

"Do you want to make love right here and now?" Susie asked.

"Sounds good to me, though I think you're screwing with my mind," J.P. said.

"You don't believe I'm serious?" Susie said.

J.P. grinned. "The thought crossed my mind."

A hand on J.P.'s shoulder prevented him from replying, a fist slamming into his chin when the person who grabbed him wheeled him around.

Eddie and Heather came running out of Jack's house. Susie was screaming as J.P. crumbled to his knees. Heather's boyfriend, Basil Doles, was standing over J.P.

"Don't you dare hurt J.P., Basil Doles," Heather screamed.

"Hurt him? I'm going to kill him,"

Basil Doles was much taller than six-three and weighed more than two hundred forty-five pounds, mostly muscle. The victim of a sucker punch, J.P. was out cold. Susie tore into the attacker with her fists. Eddie ended the confrontation by nailing Basil with the baseball bat Jack kept behind the door.

Heather glanced at Basil lying unconscious on the ground and then at Eddie.

"You didn't have to kill him," Heather said.

"He's not dead, though he'll be hurting when he comes to," Eddie said.

"You nailed him with a baseball bat," Susie said.

"Good thing I didn't have a pistol," Eddie said. Kneeling, he patted J.P.'s cheeks. "You okay, buddy?"

J.P.'s eyes opened. "What in holy hell?" he said.

Heather cried as she knelt over Basil Doles. "Why did you hit him so hard?"

Eddie brandished the bat. "If his attitude doesn't change, I will hit him again."

"You wouldn't," Heather said.

"You can't attack people without consequences," Eddie said.

Susie rushed into Jack's house, returning with a damp washrag which she used to revive Basil. He rubbed the knot on his head once his eyes opened.

"Where am I?" he asked.

"About to get banged again," Eddie said, waving the baseball bat over his head.

"Don't you dare, Eddie Toledo," Heather said.

"Give me a good reason why I shouldn't," he said.

"He's helpless," Heather said. "Please help me get him into the house."

Susie, Heather, and Eddie dragged Basil and J.P. back into Jack's and sat them on the couch. Outside, thunder and lightning had begun disrupting the night's solitude.

"I'm a former D.A.," Eddie said. "Do you have a reasonable excuse why I shouldn't sue you on Mr. Saucier's behalf?"

Heather stared at the floor when Basil said, "Officer Saucier raped Heather. I can't allow that to stand."

J.P. gave Heather a dirty look. "Heather," he said. "I think you better explain to your boyfriend what happened."

"I won't let you intimidate her," Basil said. "She doesn't deserve to be your victim."

"I spent the night on Heather's couch. I woke up with a backache and Heather's cat on my chest."

Heather was crying when she joined Basil on the couch.

"J.P. never laid a hand on me. He's a perfect gentleman. I'm so sorry."

"But you said. . ."

"I lied to you," Heather said.

"Why would you do that?" Basil asked.

"Because I couldn't bear to lose you," she said.

"I've asked you to marry me," he said.

"But you're going pro. You'll be famous, and every woman in America will be after you."

"I tore the hell out of my knee and am never going pro," Basil said. "I want to practice law and help people."

"That's another thing," Heather said. "You're so smart. I barely graduated high school and was too stupid to go to college."

"You have more common sense than any person I known," Basil said. "Second of all, I love you."

J.P. was massaging his jaw as Basil and Heather kissed and made up. Susie was grinning as Eddie continued brandishing the baseball bat.

Basil broke away from Heather and said, "I'm sorry I attacked you. Please accept my apologies."

"If I had done what you thought I did, I'd have attacked me too," J.P. said. "Eddie, you can put the bat down."

"Sure about that?" Eddie said. "I'm not apologizing for hitting you."

"I don't expect you to," Basil said. "I apologize for putting you in the position to do it."

"If you ever plan on becoming a lawyer, you're going to have to learn to control your emotions," Eddie said. "With the bad judgment you displayed, you'll be disbarred before the ink dries on your law degree."

Basil rubbed his head. "I'm not perfect and said I was sorry."

Eddie grabbed the bottle of rum from the counter and poured a mug for Basil.

"You're not all bad. Why don't you just tell Heather how you feel about her? Maybe then she won't be so insecure," Eddie said.

"I've asked her to marry me more than once," Basil said. "She told me she's not ready for marriage."

Eddie, Susie, and J.P. turned their attention to Heather. "Is that true?" Eddie asked.

"Maybe," Heather said.

"That's it!" Eddie said. "I'm throwing this case out of court."

"You can't do that without making a ruling, Your Honor," Basil said.

"All right," Eddie said. "Basil, you're free to date other women. Heather, you're free to date other men. I declare your relationship officially over."

J.P. and Susie were grinning, enjoying the pained expressions on Heather's face. Susie touched Basil's cheek.

"I have a few tricks I could show you," she said. "Dinner tomorrow night?"

"Basil Doles, don't you dare," Heather said, pushing Susie's hand away.

Basil grabbed Heather's arm and pulled her into his lap. "Seems to me, girl, we have unfinished business."

Thunder shook the roof of Jack's house. For a moment, the lights went out. Basil and Heather were in a lip-locked embrace when they came back on.

J.P. built a fire in Jack's fireplace, the dogs asleep in front of it as the storm continued.

"Wish we had some tamales," Susie said.

"Does sound good," J.P. said. "Wonder what Jack has in his refrigerator?"

Heather got out of Basil's lap. "I can cook. I'll fix us something. How about bacon and eggs?"

They soon feasted on Heather's scrambled eggs, bacon, and homemade biscuits.

"Wonderful," J.P. said.

"Best biscuits I ever tasted," Eddie said.

"Love it," Susie said. "If Basil doesn't want to marry you, I will."

The storm had passed, and Basil and Heather left in Basil's car shortly after finishing breakfast.

"I'll pick up my car later," Heather said. "Basil's taking me home tonight."

"Lucky him," Eddie said.

"I better go," Susie said.

J.P. grabbed her hand. "Sure, you don't want to spend the night with me?"

"Right now, I'm not sure of anything, cowboy," she said. "Thanks for putting up with me tonight."

"Great story, except for the ending," J.P. said.

"Maybe there's an unwritten chapter," Susie said.

"Hope so," J.P. said. "I'm getting frustrated."

Susie stood on her tiptoes and kissed him. "Don't be that way."

The moon was poking through the clouds as Susie disappeared over the bridge to the mainland.

"Just you and me now, pal," J.P. said.

"Just you," Eddie said. "I'm leaving it to you and heading for the Majestic."

"If you get scared, there's always the second bedroom in my Airstream," J.P. said.

"I'll keep that in mind," Eddie said as he walked away down the hill to the old hotel.

The rain had stopped, the air still damp, a breeze blowing up from the Gulf chilling Eddie's neck as he followed the plank walkway to the large deck in front of the entrance to the Majestic. The warmth felt good as he climbed the regal stairway to the top floor.

Jack had seen that plenty of Eddie's favorite scotch stocked the suite's wet bar. After pouring a drink, he relaxed in a recliner draped with an orange Afghan. The tumbler was half full when he dozed off in the comfortable chair.

Only the dim light of a single lamp lighted the room when Eddie opened his eyes sometime later. He'd left the hallway door cracked and heard something moving outside of it. After blinking to clear the fog in his eyes, he saw an ethereal light accompanying the movement. Lowering the footrest on the recliner, he got up to investigate.

An unearthly green light coming from the end of the hallway washed over him when he stepped out of his room. A young woman dressed in a white lace wedding gown turned to face him.

The spirit looked as if she could still be in her teens. Though she didn't speak, she uttered a sound reminding Eddie of the call of a night bird. Because of the veil, he couldn't tell if she was laughing or crying.

"Who are you?" Eddie said.

The young woman didn't answer, disappearing instead into the wall.

Chapter 22

When Eddie awoke the following morning, he barely remembered his encounter with the young woman's ghost in the hallway. He found J.P. hammering a nail into a portion of a wall taking shape on the dog training facility.

"Can I help?" he said.

J.P. grinned and said, "There's a hammer in the tool chest. Can you drive a nail?"

"You kidding me? My dad was a carpenter and taught me everything he knew. I've waited my whole life to build something."

"Then you've come to the right place," J.P. said. "Between me, Jack, Chief, and Jimmie, there's not a carpenter among us."

"Well, you got one now. I have a few suggestions to make."

"Don't tell me we need to start over," J.P. said.

"Nothing that drastic. I'll teach you a few tricks, and the finished building will be beautiful," Eddie said. "I can't believe you're up so early."

"A product of waking up before dawn for more years than I can remember," J.P. said. "Now, it's a habit. How was your first night in the Majestic?"

"Not bad," Eddie said. "I did see a ghost."

"You kidding?" J.P. asked.

"Nope," Eddie said. "A girl in a bridal gown."

"A girl?"

"She couldn't have been any older than sixteen or seventeen," Eddie said. "Maybe even younger."

"And she was in a bridal gown?"

"A beautiful gown. It looked like someone had dropped some serious money on it."

"Did she say anything to you?"

"She made a bird-like sound and then disappeared into the wall," Eddie said.

"Sure you weren't still drunk?" J.P. asked.

"I was sober enough," Eddie said.

"What do you mean she made a bird-like sound?"

"Like a warble," Eddie said. "It felt as if she was trying to tell me something. When I didn't respond, she went away."

"Disappeared into the wall?" J.P. said. "She was trying to tell you that you're nutty as a fruitcake."

"I know better," Eddie said. "You were a homicide detective for twenty years. I can only imagine the crazy shit you've seen."

"That's a fact," J.P. said. "Jack, Chief, Odette, and Paula swear up and down there were ghosts in the lighthouse. I believe them, and I believe you. I wouldn't want to spend the night alone in the Majestic."

Eddie wasn't just boasting about his carpenter's abilities. By noon, they had another part of the dog training facility framed.

"This would all go a lot easier if we were working off a plan," Eddie said.

"What do you mean?" J.P. asked.

"You know, like a blueprint that has the entire structure mapped out."

"Where would you get something like that."

"My dad used to draw them by hand on the kitchen table. Before he ever started, he knew exactly how many feet of two-by-fours he needed, how many squares of shingles, and so forth. Makes a difference."

"I can't draw anything like that," J.P. said. "Where would we get a plan?"

"Hire a designer to make it for you or buy one pre-made off the Internet."

"Thanks," J.P. said. "I'll look into it."

"It'll keep you from constructing something useless or that you don't end up liking," Eddie said.

"How much does something like that cost?" J.P. asked.

"Hell!" Eddie said. "I have no clue. A grand or so is my guess. First, you need to look at lots of pictures and find something you like."

"What if we can't find anything?"

"That's why you need an architect," Eddie said. "If you find something close, you can modify the plan as you see fit."

J.P. was pouring cold water into a red plastic cup when an approaching helicopter's sound disturbed the island's serenity.

"Must be Frankie and the crew returning from his resort in the Gulf," J.P. said.

"They'll be surprised about how much we've gotten done."

J.P. said, "No one's more surprised than I am. We've accomplished more in the past few hours than the rest of us have in the last week. You need to screw off Frankie's project and help us finish ours."

"I'll probably have lots of free time. We'll work something out. You better run the ATV down to the chopper," Eddie said.

The ATV wasn't big enough to bring everyone to Jack's house. When J.P. pulled up to the front of the house, Frankie, Jojo, and Venus exited. Eddie was waiting at the door with a glass of scotch for Frankie, a grape soda for Jojo, and a doggie treat for Venus. J.P. returned to the helicopter to transport the rest of the party.

When everyone was in Jack's house, it became apparent from Frankie's expression that all wasn't copasetic. Jojo was looking forlorn as he hugged Venus's neck.

"Say goodbye to the dog, Jojo," Frankie said. "Venus is staying here on Oyster Island."

"Venus didn't bite anyone, did she?" J.P. asked.

"Venus would never hurt anyone," Jojo said.

"Then what's going on, Frankie?" J.P. said.

"I decided while I was away. I'm going to sell Oyster Island and the Majestic. I'm sorry, Eddie."

"To whom are you selling the island?" Eddie asked.

"A group out of New Jersey," Frankie said.

"What group?" Eddie said.

"Trenton Dock Workers International."

"You kidding me?" Eddie said. "Everyone in law enforcement knows TDWI is an arm of the New Jersey mob. What are you up to?"

"They have the money and are ready to make the deal," Frankie said.

"Where does this leave me?" Eddie asked.

"I'm so sorry, Eddie," Frankie said. "Our deal didn't work out."

"You never gave it a chance," Eddie said.

"I didn't know what kind of money TDWI was willing to pay."

"At least our dog facility is off the table," J.P. said.

"Afraid not," Eddie said. "The lighthouse is part of the island and not owned by the State of

Louisiana. You'll see what I mean when you read the document."

"You're saying we're going to lose the island?" Chief said.

"Nothing I can do about it," Frankie said. "TDWI wants all or nothing. Come on, Jojo. Let's walk back to the helicopter."

Venus tried to follow Jojo out the door, and he had to hide his tears.

"Now wait just a minute," J.P. said. "What happened with Jojo and Venus? It's pretty damn obvious to me they are attached. It's one damn thing screwing us, but your grandson too?"

Frankie didn't look at J.P. or respond to his question. Instead, he said, "I'm so sorry, Jojo. I'm cutting all my ties with the island, including Venus."

"You don't have to walk," J.P. said. "I'll drive you to the helicopter."

Jojo's head was drooping when J.P. dropped them at the chopper. When J.P. returned to Jack's, he was visibly sad.

"We're screwed," he said. "What happened out there in the Gulf?"

Jimmie glared at Paula and Odette. "Maybe you better ask Paula," he said.

"Paula, you have something you want to share with us?"

"It wasn't our fault, Odette said.

"Shut up, sister," Paula said. "I got us into this mess. I'll explain what happened."

"Do we need more rum before you start your story?" Jack asked.

"Please," Paula said.

Light rain had begun falling as Venus stood at the door, waiting for Jojo's return. Odette put her arms around the dog's neck and coaxed her over to the fireplace with the other dogs. Everyone settled in, waiting for Paula's story as Jack served up multiple mugs of rum.

"The boys were gambling, so Odette and I found a quiet bar. Everyone there was smoking hashish from hookahs. Odette and I were already about half drunk, so we joined them. A few hours later, we somehow wound up in our suite and decided to explore the recreation deck we could see from the suite's window."

When Paula paused to drink some rum, J.P. said, "Go on."

"The deck had a beautiful infinity pool stretching out over the Gulf. There was no one out there except us. We decided to go skinny-dipping. Turns out, Frankie was sitting in an elevated spa and was watching us. He finally spoke up so we wouldn't think he was a voyeur."

"Paula and I joined him," Odette said.

"That doesn't sound like much of a reason for Frankie deciding to sell the island," J.P. said.

"Oh, the story gets better," Jimmie said.

Everyone's attention again focused on Paula. "Odette decided Frankie didn't need his bathing suit, so we pulled it off him. Odette tossed it over the ledge."

"You didn't," J.P. said.

"As I said, Odette and I were pretty-well lit. She decided to give Frankie a lap dance, and I helped her. Halfway through the dance, a woman showed up on the deck. It was Frankie's wife."

"Good God Almighty!" J.P. said. "You two are lucky Frankie didn't feed you to the sharks."

"Would have done him no good because his wife had already seen enough to incriminate all of us," Paula said.

"Is that it?" J.P. asked.

"We didn't have sex with him if that's what you're implying," Odette said. "I used to give table dances for a living when I worked at the strip club. Trust me when I tell you there was nothing sexually involved."

"Frankie's wife thinks there was," J.P. said.

"And now we're going to lose everything we've worked for," Jimmie said.

"Jack's losing his job, and I'm losing my tribal home forever," Chief said.

"Paula and I are so sorry," Odette said.

The rain had intensified, thunder shaking the house's roof and drumming the windows.

"Chief, why do you think you own Oyster Island?" Eddie asked.

"It's what my grandpa told me. He called this island tribal land and said our ownership was recorded. Problem is, I haven't been able to prove his assertion."

"I'll drive to the Parish courthouse tomorrow," Eddie said. "If there's a recorded deed, I'll find it."

"You think there's a chance we might keep the island?" Chief asked.

"White men had a way of screwing Indians out of things they promised in treaties. This may be the situation," Eddie said. "Whatever I find, it may take a Federal lawsuit to settle our point officially."

"That could take years?" J.P. said.

"Maybe if we prevent Frankie from making a quick sale of the island, he'll change his mind and offer us a settlement. At that point, it's all in the negotiating, and no one's better at that than me."

"So there is a chance, even half-a-chance, you could find something to prove Chief's ownership?" Jack said.

"More than a chance. "There is no doubt this involves Federal law," Eddie said. "No one on this planet knows Federal law better than I do."

"We'll find the money to pay you," Jimmie said.

"You'll pay me nothing. Frankie promised me the moon, and I'm as pissed as you are that he's trying to renege on that promise. I won't let the situation stand if I can do something about it."

"Frankie Castellano is the Don of the Bayou. Even if you are successful, he'll probably have us killed," Jimmy said.

"No. he won't," Eddie said. "I was fired from my job as Assistant Federal Prosecutor, but I still have many friends in high places. Frankie would be a fool to try something. I promise you, Frankie's no fool."

Jimmie was seated on the couch, and Paula took his hand.

"Baby, I'm so sorry for bringing all this trouble on us. Will you ever forgive me?"

Jimmie began to grin. "You know, I've never got a good look at your body all the years we've been married."

"And?" Paula said.

"I'll forgive you, though I'm going to need something in return," he said.

"Such as?"

"A naked lap dance with all the lights on before we go to bed tonight."

Chapter 23

When Odette and Asger returned to Noni's wagon, they found Noni, Alice, Bobbis, and Trysta sitting outside by the fire. Tis and Blossom were playing ball and jacks, Exo wrestling with Greatfall.

Greatfall was many times larger than Exo. It didn't matter because the giant dog wouldn't have intentionally harmed a hair on the little boy's nearly bald head. When Exo saw Asger and Odette, he stopped playing and greeted them at the fire. He didn't seem to notice the trickle of blood on his forearm.

Odette lifted him into her arms and said, "How did you get that scratch?"

"I didn't notice," he said.

"We need to put something on it," Odette said.

"It's okay," Exo said. "Alice will fix it."

"Bring the little brat to me," Alice said.

Odette waited for Alice to clean the wound and then apply topical antiseptic. Instead, she touched the wound with her index finger. As she moved her finger, the length of the scratch, the blood disappeared.

Exo smiled when Alice said, "All good."

"What did you just do?" Odette said.

"Healed Exo's scratch," Alice said.

"I saw what you did. How did you do it?" Odette asked.

"Alice has the touch," Trysta said.

Odette glanced at Trysta, then took hold of Exo's arm and said, "Let me see."

The scratch hadn't just stopped bleeding. It was healed, no sign of an injury having ever occurred.

"Alice is a touch healer," Trysta said.

Asger and Odette joined them by the fire. "That's wild. I've never seen anything like it. Who taught you how to do it?"

"I was born knowing how," Alice said. "Energy flows through my fingers. It's a gift."

"That isn't all Alice can do," Bobbis said. "She can converse with the dead,"

Odette asked, "Are you a witch?"

"Not a witch. A healer."

"And you can summon the spirits of the dead?" Odette asked.

Alice nodded. "I have the power."

"Can you contact any dead person?" Odette asked.

Alice said, "Only if I have some personal connection."

"What if that isn't possible?" Odette said.

Alice could only shake her head. "There are billions of spirits in the void. Contact with the dead requires some personal connection."

"Have you eaten?" Noni said.

"No," Asger said. "And I'm starved."

"Have you ever tried Vienna sausage?

"Is it good?" Asger asked.

Noni speared a Vienna sausage from a small can with a plastic fork and handed it to Asger.

"Try it and see for yourself."

Asger popped it into his mouth. "Tasty."

Odette turned up her nose when Noni handed her the can.

"I've never eaten one of these things in my life," she said.

"Why not?" Asger said. "They are wonderful."

Spearing one with his fork, he put it into Odette's mouth.

"Tastes better than I thought it would," she said. "Too bad you don't have any mustard."

"I have jars and jars of mustard," Noni said. "I didn't know what it was for." Noni went into his wagon, returning with a jar of German mustard. "How do you eat it?"

"Dip you Vienna sausage into it," Odette said.

Noni's smile told everyone he liked the combination of Vienna sausage and German mustard. He had a dozen or so cans of Vienna sausage. The little group, including the kids, licked their lips as they finished all of them.

As the lights had begun dimming over the Biowomb, Noni, Trysta, Bobbis, and the kids disappeared into Noni's wagon.

Alice grinned when Odette said, "You're not sleeping with Noni?"

"We aren't married," Alice said.

"Do you plan to marry him?" Odette said.

"He hasn't asked me," Alice said.

"Men can be dumb sometimes. Maybe you should ask him."

"I could never do that," Alice said.

"Then I'll do it for you."

"Don't you dare," Alice said.

"You two were meant for one another," Odette said. "What's your problem?"

"I don't want to push him into something he's not ready for," Alice said. "Are you and Asger married?"

"We've only known each other for a couple of days," Odette said.

"It seems as though you've known each other for years," Alice said.

Odette nodded. "I've never been as close to a man as I am with him."

Asger wasn't listening to their conversation and had already fallen asleep. With darkness came the peaceful symphony of crickets and tree frogs. The gentle night sounds put Odette to sleep. Sometime later, when she blinked open her sleep-crusted eyes, she found Alice was holding her hand.

"You cried out," Alice said. "Did something frighten you?"

"I reached for Asger, and he wasn't there," Odette said.

"He's asleep between the two dogs," Alice said. "I don't think we should wake them."

"Aren't you sleepy?" Odette asked.

"I sense you need my help, and I couldn't sleep thinking about it."

"Extra sensory perception must be another one of your gifts. Are you up for a little bit of adventure?" Odette asked.

"What kind of adventure?" Alice said.

"A midnight visit to Dead City?"

Alice smiled and said, "To hunt for ghosts?"

"A particular ghost," Odette said.

"I can't walk very fast," Alice said. "Lead the way, and I'll try to keep up with you."

"I won't leave you."

Asger was sound asleep between Duchess and Greatfall and never awoke as Alice and Odette left the warmth of Noni's fire. Darkness in Dead City wasn't something they had anticipated. The dim streetlamps cast moving shadows on the cobblestone streets. All was silence except for the sound of escaping air, like from a balloon. Odette tried not to imagine what it meant. Alice was out of breath when they reached the building encompassing Einstein's hologram.

"You okay?" Odette asked.

Alice smiled. "I'm not built for moving very far."

"We're here," Odette said. "You did fine."

The hum of escaping air ceased when the steel door shut behind them. Odette could see from the light that Einstein's hologram was active.

"Professor Einstein," she said. "I brought someone with me."

"Someone other than the young Viking you were with earlier?" Einstein said.

"This is Alice," she said. "She has special powers."

"Such as?" Einstein said.

"She can converse with the dead," Odette said.

Einstein nodded. "Glad to meet you, Alice. You're from the Nether World. What do you think of the Biowomb?"

"There is life here, though it seems all the plants and creatures here are. . ."

"Trapped in a fishbowl?" Einstein said, finishing Alice's sentence.

"Trapped is the correct word," Alice said. "Though I have no idea what a fishbowl is."

"Do you know who I am?" Einstein asked.

Alice shook her head. "No," she said.

"Good," Einstein said. "Why are you here, Alice?"

"I don't know," she said. "Odette said I might be able to help her."

Einstein glanced at Odette. "Maybe you should explain," he said.

"I know you and Tesla didn't like each other. I want to channel his spirit. Perhaps the two of you can figure out how to save the world."

"What makes you think it needs saving?"

"There are no birds or trees, and you can't see the moon, stars, or sun."

"Two men can't restore what it took millions of men to destroy," Einstein said.

"The earth will restore itself," Odette said. "You said as much yourself. I just need you to speed up the process a bit."

"I have ideas, though no way to implement them," Einstein said. "My strong point is theory. When it comes to practice, I had trouble changing a light bulb."

"That's where Tesla comes in," Odette said. "He devised hundreds of inventions that brought theories to life."

"Tesla detested me," Einstein said.

"We need your help to conjure his spirit," Odette said.

"Even if we successfully channel Tesla's ghost, there's no guarantee we could devise a way to reverse earth's damage."

"I can think of a way," Odette said. "Break the Biowomb. Set the creatures and plants inside of it free to propagate the earth."

"What makes you think they would survive?

"The people populating Dead City and the Biowomb migrated to the Nether World," Odette said.

"And didn't survive," Einstein said.

"Yes, they did. They suffered, evolved, and prevailed. Alice is a survivor and an heir to the earth."

"I'm not convinced," Einstein said. "The Nether World is fraught with indescribable dangers, and plants can't live without light. The atmosphere is thin, the ozone layer all but destroyed."

"Man damaged the ozone layer. Can't they also repair it?" Odette asked.

"Theoretically," Einstein said.

"That's where Tesla enters the picture."

"Tesla's long dead," Einstein said.

"With your help, Alice can summon his ghost," Odette said.

"If I assist you, will you terminate my brain?"

"I can't " Odette said.

"Not good enough," Einstein said.

"Then do it yourself. Fracture the Biowomb and Dead City will disappear, this building and your brain along with it."

"Maybe," Einstein said. "How do you propose we channel Tesla's ghost?"

Alice took a step closer to the hologram. "I'm a mystic, touch healer, and medium. Give me something to work with, and I will summon him."

"Like what?" Einstein asked.

"A personal possession of the person I'm channeling," Alice said.

Light from Einstein's hologram briefly intensified. "I have nothing like that."

"Then perhaps you have a memory you can share with us," Alice said.

Odette's smile had disappeared. "Isn't there another way to channel Tesla's spirit? Professor Einstein and Tesla weren't friends. It seems impossible he has a personal memory to share."

Alice glanced at the hologram. "You do, don't you?"

Einstein bowed his head. "A memory I had all but forgotten."

Alice was smiling when Odette looked at her. "Seems my partner knows more than I do. Will you share the memory with us?"

Einstein began speaking in a monotone voice as he recalled an almost forgotten moment in time.

"I had a tobacco addiction that plagued my health and lasted my entire life. I acquiesced when my doctors and family pleaded with me to quit smoking. Though I tried to keep it hidden, I never really quit. I bummed cigarettes whenever I could and took to picking up butts on the streets, smoking the tobacco in a pipe.

"It was in the forties, before the war in Europe. I was in New York City on business and walked through the park looking for tobacco. I sat on a park bench, extracting tobacco from the butts I'd found on the ground. I was surprised when the old man beside me spoke. It was someone who knew who I was because he used a nickname I hadn't heard since I was a young man in Germany."

"'You're as addicted as people say, Dopey,'" the man said.

"Tesla was older than me. He'd aged since the last time I'd seen him, his hair gray, his body thin and his voice reedy. Our paths had crossed more than once, and it was common knowledge he didn't like me.

"He smiled when I said, 'What are you doing here, Niko?'

'Conversing with the pigeons,' Tesla said.

"Many people unfamiliar with Tesla called him an eccentric genius. He also had a mental illness." Einstein chuckled. "Toward the end, he was nutty as a fruitcake.

"Want me to walk you home, Niko?"

"Why not," he said. "I have a bottle of Schnapps at my apartment. Let's have a drink."

"Sounds good to me," I said.

"Tesla lived on the third floor of an old high-rise building. We were both out of breath when we reached the door. His apartment was stark with almost no furniture. An old dog didn't bother greeting us when we entered.

"Piles of dog shit were all over the floor, and the poor beast hadn't left the apartment in ages.

205

Tesla grabbed the Schnapps from a cabinet without commenting on the dog. He retrieved two dirty glasses from his kitchen sink and poured me a drink.

"I'm dying," he said. "Are we all destined to end like this?"

"I have no answer for you, Niko," I said. "Questions of my own haunt me.

Tesla drained his Schnapps and poured himself another.

"In the end," he said. "What does it all mean?"

"Tesla chuckled when I gave him my answer.

"Pour me some more Schnapps, and I'll try to develop a theory."

Odette glanced around when it was apparent someone, or something, had joined them in the dimly-lit room. It was a thin young man with dark wavy hair and a bushy mustache.

"Who summoned me?" he said.

Chapter 24

A lice didn't speak to Odette on the way back to Noni's wagon. Odette noticed.

"What's the matter? Why aren't you talking to me," she said.

"Just when I thought things were changing for the better, I realize they are about to take a turn for the worse."

"How can you say that?" Odette said. "Don't you want to see the earth renewed to its former glory?"

"I don't know," Alice said. "The concept is foreign to me."

"It will be better. Much better, I promise you," Odette said.

"Are you a hundred percent sure of that?"

"I'm not sure of anything," Odette said. "I know we're going to repopulate the earth with its creatures and vegetation."

"By destroying the Biowomb?" Alice asked.

"It seems the only way."

"What if the Biowomb with all its beauty and lushness is all you succeed in destroying?"

When Odette said, "That's not going to happen," Alice didn't respond."

The light had returned to the Biowomb, and

they found the group sitting in a circle around the fire. Noni got to his feet to greet them, Alice's despondent look causing him to grasp her hand.

"Is something wrong?" he said.

"The Biowomb is going to be destroyed," Alice said.

"That can't be," Noni said. "By whom?"

"Two men from the past," Alice said.

"For what reason?" he asked.

Noni frowned when Alice said, "To restore the earth."

When Alice didn't return his frown, Noni turned to Odette for an explanation.

"Is it true?" he asked.

"Please don't look at me like that," she said. "It's for an excellent reason."

"What reason?" Noni demanded.

"There are few creatures and no plants in the Nether World. We need to fracture the Biowomb to restore the earth to the way it was," Odette said.

"The way it was?" Noni said. "A cesspool?"

"To its pristine state before it became a cesspool," Odette said.

"And the Biowomb must be destroyed to accomplish this rejuvenation?" Noni said.

"Asger, can you help me with this?" Odette said.

"Noni is right. Why would you destroy something alive and beautiful for the chance of creating something better?"

Odette turned her gaze to Bobbis and Trysta. "Trysta?" she said.

Trysta stood. "I'll tell the kids they'll never have ice cream again."

"Holy fuck!" Odette said. "What have I done?"

She turned away from the fire and ran toward Dead City. Asger followed, grabbing her arm when he caught up to her.

"Where are you going?" he asked.

"To stop Einstein and Tesla," Odette said.

"Then let's hurry," Asger said.

Along the way, Asger ripped a long piece of rebar from a half-finished building.

"What do you intend to do with that?" Odette asked.

"Resort to violence, if need be," Asger said.

"You can't kill a spirit that's already dead," Odette said.

"Watch me," Asger said.

Asger swung the metal length like a baseball bat as they entered the dimly-lit building. They found Einstein's hologram and the ghost of Tesla laughing as they sat on the floor.

"I'm sorry I brought the two of you together. I can't let you destroy this world in an attempt to create another," Odette said.

"Very profound, young lady," Einstein said.

"Please don't terminate the Biowomb," Odette said. "I can't live with myself if that happens."

Tesla said, "Dopey and I aren't your puppets. This world is as it is and not meant for mortal man to destroy."

Tesla laughed when Odette said, "Then it's beyond your capabilities?"

"If that's what you want to think," he said. "I never knew what real power was until I spoke with Herr Einstein. He opened my eyes to questions I never dreamed would be answered."

"Nonsense," Einstein said. "Niko has the greatest mind of any human ever born. I had no idea someone could put my theorems into practice."

"Together, we could have ruled the world," Tesla said.

"Then you aren't going to fracture the

Biowomb?" Odette asked.

"That was your idea, young lady, and not mine or Niko's," Einstein said.

He and Tesla laughed when she said, "My name is Odette. Stop calling me young lady."

"I meant no disrespect," Einstein said.

"If you don't fracture the Biowomb, how will you restore plant growth to the world?"

"The nuclear war didn't destroy all the seeds scattered over the earth," Einstein said. "A little light and rain and vegetation will begin growing before you know it," Einstein said.

"There is no light or rain in the Nether World," Odette said.

Einstein put his hand up to silence her. "Come sit with us, and we'll explain."

Asger was still wielding the length of rebar. Odette took it from him and gave it a toss. It skidded across the concrete floor, banging to a stop when it hit the wall.

"We don't need it," she said.

"Are we missing something?" Tesla asked. "The Viking boy looks ready to fight."

"A misunderstanding," Odette said. "Please tell us your plan."

"Explain it to them, Niko," Einstein said.

"The Nether World is the result of numerous nuclear detonations. World War III destroyed everything, the earth's atmosphere a casualty. The earth isn't doomed and is healing itself, though it's possible to speed the process along."

"That's encouraging to hear," Odette said. "How do you intend to accomplish it?"

"Lightning," Tesla said. "A lightning storm creates oxidants that react with pollution and methane, causing them to drop out of the atmosphere, dissolve in water, or stick to the earth."

"Lightning creates nitrogen oxides that increase ozone levels," Einstein said.

"The ozone layer protects the earth from harmful radiation and ultraviolet light," Tesla said. "It made the earth habitable for humans, plants, and other animals."

"There is lightning in the Nether World," Odette said. "Asger and I have seen it."

"But insufficient to restore the earth's protective layer," Einstein said.

"To accomplish our goal, we must generate a worldwide lightning storm that lasts for a significant period."

"Is such an event possible?" Odette asked.

"Niko?" Einstein said.

"There were no supercomputers or the Internet when I was alive. They weren't yet in their infancy when Dopey died," Tesla said with a smile. "If either of us had wielded the power such devices provide, there's no telling what we might have accomplished."

"Niko and I have spent the past few days studying the immense database available on the supercomputer that controls me."

"Consuming information with a passion is a better description," Tesla said. "We have a plan to cleanse the earth."

"If it isn't too complex for us to understand, please tell us," Odette said.

"Scientists have known for decades about the phenomenon known as volcanic lightning," Tesla said.

"Volcanic eruptions produce fantastic light shows," Einstein said. "What we need is something to create worldwide volcanism. Niko has a way to do it."

"We're listening," Odette said.

"It starts with the 'Ring of Fire,' a zone of

211

faulting, earthquakes, and volcanoes encircling all the continents," Einstein said.

"We're going to trigger a massive earthquake which will, in turn, generate volcanic activity."

"How and where?" Odette asked.

"California," Tesla said. "The Big One."

"There's a beach on the Pacific Coast between Los Angeles and San Diego," Einstein said. "At San Onofre State Park, owners of a depleted nuclear power plant buried 3.6 million pounds of nuclear waste about 100 feet from the shoreline. Erosion has exposed the site, which overlies a fault zone that is part of the 'Ring of Fire' and near the San Andreas Fault."

"Scientists learned decades ago they could induce earthquakes by injecting nuclear waste into fault-fractured boreholes," Tesla said.

"Surely there's no way California would have allowed such a condition to occur," Odette said.

"But they did," Tesla said. "All we need to do is direct the nuclear waste into the fault system. Massive earthquakes along the 'Ring of Fire' will trigger a worldwide volcanic event."

"The resultant lightning storms will cleanse the atmosphere," Einstein said. "When the storms subside, renewal and restoration will begin in earnest."

"How will you trigger the earthquake?" Odette asked.

"Nuclear explosion," Einstein said. "Through Dead City's supercomputer, we have access to every unfired nuclear missile in the United States. We intend to detonate one over the nuclear waste."

"The poison that polluted the earth will begin the process to cleanse it," Tesla said.

"The San Andreas and other surface faults will serve as our open conduits to the earth's bowels," Einstein said.

"Volcanic activity along the 'Ring of Fire' will create a chain reaction. The resultant volcanic lightning will result in the biggest cataclysmic event in earth's history," Einstein said.

"The lightning will restore the ozone layer," Tesla said. "Light will return, the ensuing rain nourishing the seeds scattered across the earth. Rebirth will begin."

"When do you intend to start?" Odette asked.

"We are ready now," Tesla said.

"When the storms begin, you and the Viking must leave the Biowomb," Einstein said. "The resultant energy we create will open a portal to your world. It won't stay open long."

"What about the creatures living in the Nether World?" Odette asked.

"They will take shelter," Einstein said. "Most will survive."

"At first, the rain will be acidic," Tesla said. "That will change."

"What about the radiation?" Odette asked.

"The radiation has already dissipated," Tesla said. "It will continue to do so until it is harmless."

"What about you two?" Odette asked.

"For now, I'm happy to assist," Tesla said. "When the world no longer needs me, Alice will help me cross over."

"I'm excited about my contribution," Einstein said. "When I'm no longer needed, I'll have someone sever the wires and tubes feeding my brain. Like Niko, Alice can help me cross. Go now. You have lots of life to live."

"Thank you," Odette said.

Odette and Asger didn't bother shutting the door to the research lab as they exited the building.

"What now?" Odette asked.

"Leave the Biowomb forever and find our way to Vinland," Asger said.

"Or my world," Odette said.

"We'll never find either one in Dead City," Asger said. "We need to leave."

"I'm scared shitless," she said.

"We have to tell everyone," Asger said as they made their way back to Noni's wagon

Noni and Alice were holding hands as they sat by the fire. Neither of them would make eye contact with Odette.

"The Biowomb is safe," Odette said. "Tesla and Einstein refused to destroy it."

"Wonderful news," Noni said.

"They have an alternate plan to restore the Nether World. It involves generating a great storm. It would help if you remained in the Biowomb until the storm subsides," Odette said.

"A storm?" Noni said.

"This isn't our world, and Asger and I are leaving," Odette said.

"When do you plan to go?" Alice asked.

"When the storm begins," Asger said.

"Can you wait a while?" Noni said. "Another day or so?"

"For what reason?" Odette said.

"Alice and I wouldn't have met except for you," Noni said.

"And?"

"We're getting married and want you to stand for us."

"When is the wedding?" Odette asked.

"Today," Alice said. "The children are gathering flowers, Noni and Trysta planning a feast after the ceremony."

"Wonderful," Odette said. "We wouldn't miss it for the world and are honored you want us to celebrate with you. Who is going to perform the ceremony?"

"Bobbis," Noni said.

Alice spent the time before the wedding between Asger and Odette, the three holding hands. Soon, the ceremony began, Alice wearing a swath of lace as she and Noni stood in front of Bobbis.

"Grasp hands," Bobbis said. "This ceremony is for life. Hold on to each other, or let go now. There's no in-between."

Neither Noni nor Alice relinquished their grip. "I'm so happy for you," Odette said.

"I can perform the ceremony for you and Asger," Bobbis said.

"We are from different worlds," Odette said. "There are many things we need to resolve first."

Noni was all smiles as he opened a canned ham served with fresh fruit the children had gathered in a nearby grove. When they finished eating, Alice and Noni begged them to stay for one more day.

"The storm is already rocking the Biowomb," Asger said. "We must leave now."

"Will you ever return?" Alice asked.

"Maybe someday," Odette said.

"We can't let you go out into the dangerous storm," Noni said. "I will take you in Mona."

"I'm going with you," Alice said.

Asger glanced at Odette and said, "Now or never."

Chapter 25

Robert's Body Shop called Eddie at seven the following day. Still, in bed, he fumbled for his cell phone, knocking over the half-full glass of water he'd poured for himself before going to sleep.

"So much for trying to rehydrate before bedtime," he said.

"What did you say?" the person on the other line said.

"Just mumbling to myself," Eddie said. "Who is this?"

"Robert from Robert's Body Shop in Chalmette. We got your car fixed."

"Wonderful," Eddie said. "I'll have to catch a ride into town to pick it up," he said.

"I'll send my son Barrett to get you. You still on the island."

"Yes," Eddie said. "When can I expect him?"

"Give him an hour or so. He's a good boy though kind of slow," Robert said.

"Thanks, Robert," Eddie said. "I'll be waiting."

Eddie pulled on a pair of dress pants, a white shirt, and wingtips and started up the hill to Jack's. The aroma of bacon and eggs elevated his appetite when he walked through the door.

"What the hell!" Jack said. "Are you on your way to a funeral?"

"What?" Eddie said.

"You're at a resort island on the Gulf of Mexico," J.P. said . "Where are your shorts and teeshirt?"

"I've never been on vacation," Eddie said.

"You kidding me?" J.P. said. "How old are you?"

"Old enough," Eddie said.

"Jack has a closet full of beach clothes," Chief said.

Jack came out of his bedroom with a handful of Hawaiian-style shirts."

"You're on the island now. Put on one of these."

"I'm good," Eddie said.

Odette began unbuttoning his shirt and then pulled it off of him.

"No, you aren't," she said. "Only old men wear white teeshirts. You need to throw it away and never wear it again."

Pulling the white teeshirt over his head, she tossed it into the corner.

"Which one do you like, Eddie.?" Jack asked

"The red and white one with the yellow hibiscus."

"Good choice," Jack said, helping Eddie put his arms through the colorful shirt. "Now, the pants."

Jack returned with another handful of clothes, this time shorts.

"Sit down and let me get those brogans off your feet," Odette said.

"They're my favorite shoes," Eddie said.

"Trash," Odette said, tossing them into Jack's waste basket.

"Those shoes cost a hundred bucks," Eddie said.

"You're living on an island resort. You don't need black wingtips," Odette said, unbuckling Eddie's belt.

She'd pulled Eddie's pants off and tossed them into the trash. He sat on the ottoman, looking embarrassed in his white boxer shorts.

"Now, wait just a minute," he said when Odette grabbed the shorts. "I'm not a shrinking violet, but I don't usually strip my clothes off in a room full of people. Especially before eight in the morning."

"You can't wear old man's underwear," Odette said. "I'll get you something sexy next time I'm in Chalmette."

"These will do until then," Eddie said.

Choosing a pair of khaki shorts, he pulled them on. Jack handed him a pair of sandals.

"These should fit you," he said.

"Odette took my socks," Eddie said.

"You aren't in a courtroom. You don't need socks when you're wearing sandals," Odette said.

Eddie smiled when he stood and pirouetted for everyone to see his new duds.

"Now, you look like an islander," Chief said. "Where were you going?"

"I had an accident on my way to the island," he said. "The body shop in Chalmette has repaired my car. Someone's on their way to pick me up."

"Are you going to the courthouse after you get your car?" Chief asked.

"I'm planning on it," Eddie said.

"Can I go with you?" Chief asked. "Maybe I can help."

"Why not," Eddie said. "Has everyone here had breakfast except me?"

"Grab a chair at the plank table," Jack said. "I'll fix you a plate."

Eddie was sopping up the last of his sausage

gravy with one of Jack's 'from scratch' biscuits. A bottle of Dominican rum was on the table, and he poured some into his black coffee.

"Where's Jimmie and Paula," he asked.

There was almost a grin on Chief's face. "They either killed each other or celebrated with another lapdance," he said.

Paula and Jimmie entered the front door with ear-to-ear grins. "Were you talking about us?" Jimmie said.

"How did you guess?" J.P. said.

"I thought so," Jimmie said. "My ears have been burning all morning."

"You hungry?" Jack asked.

Jimmie was still grinning. "You kidding me? I need some protein."

Paula was also smiling and gave Odette a wink. "I feel you're not the only one in need of protein," she said.

Someone was honking outside the door. "I think our ride is here," Eddie said. "You ready, Chief?"

"Soon as I fill my flask," he said.

Everyone was laughing when Eddie and Chief went outside and found the little truck with the Robert's Body Shop sign on the door.

Eddie greeted the smiling young man with dark hair and black hornrims in the truck's driver's seat.

"I'm Eddie, and this is Chief," Eddie said. "You must be Barrett."

"That's me," he said. "You ready?"

"Absolutely," Eddie said.

They joined Barrett in the cab of the little truck. They were soon across the bridge and on their way to Chalmette. The land beside the blacktop road was marshy, a snowy egret lifting out of the shallow water.

"My dad is interested in buying your car,"

Barrett said.

"What makes him think I want to sell it?" Eddie asked.

"He calls it an old lady's car," Barrett said.

"Then why does he want to buy it?"

"For my mom," Barrett said. "She loves it."

Eddie's car was a black Lincoln Continental sedan, a luxury car with all the extra bells and whistles he'd bought from a friend in the department who was retiring and moving to Peru.

"Why doesn't your mom just buy one from the Lincoln dealership?" Eddie asked.

"Lincoln quit making sedans in 2020. The model you have is as scarce as hens' teeth. Would you consider selling it?"

"Not really," Eddie said. "I got a hell of a deal on that car."

"What about trading it?" Barrett said.

"The Continental drives like a dream and has every luxury addition Lincoln offered that year," Eddie said.

"Yeah, but you're not an old lady."

"What's that supposed to mean?"

"I don't see a wedding ring on your finger. Why do you need a four-door sedan?"

"Believe it or not, it's the first car I've ever owned," Eddie said. "I always had a company car to drive when I worked for the Feds."

"Let me guess," Chief said. "They were all black four-door sedans."

"What should I be driving?" Eddie asked.

Barrett was quick to reply. "My dad's 1992 Porsche 911. Mom hates it. If she put the pressure on him, I think he'd make you an even trade for the Continental.

"My Continental is a 2020 model. It's 28 years younger than your dad's car."

"The 911 has less than 40,000 miles on it, and it has been taken good care of," Barrett said.

"I don't know," Eddie said.

"Your Continental's worth around $80,000. Dad's 911 would go for around $140,000."

"Then why in the world would he trade me?" Eddie asked.

"Because your Continental is rarer than his 911. Mom wants it, and he can't talk her out of it. She hates the 911 because she suspects dad is driving it to attract younger women."

"As I said, I'm not a car person. What's so special about this 911?"

"You kidding me?" Barrett said. "It's every man's wet dream; candy apple red with beige leather seats and so much power under the hood it'll give you an orgasm just revving the engine. And did I mention there's not a woman in the world who can resist a man driving a 911?

"You'd make a hell of a salesman," Eddie said. "If the Porsche 911 is half the car you say it is, your dad's never going to part with it."

"Yes, he will," Barrett said. "Mom is at the body shop. If you tell Dad you'll trade him even for the 911, he won't be able to say no."

When Barrett got out of the vehicle and started to walk away, Eddie said, "Did your mom tell you to set this up."

Barrett didn't answer but smiled as he disappeared into the back of the body shop.

"You gonna do it?" Chief said.

"Why hell no. No one in their right mind would trade an almost new car for one going on thirty? years old."

"There's the Porsche," Chief said. "Let's take a closer look." Chief circled the two-seater sports car. "Like Barrett said. You can almost have an orgasm just looking at this thing."

"What are you trying to tell me?" Eddie said.

"Your Continental is nice, but the Porsche is the ultimate middle-aged-crazy car. You're never going to get another chance like this. Remember what Yogi Berra said."

"What?" Eddie asked.

"When you reach a fork in the road, take it."

"That makes absolutely no sense," Eddie said. "I'll see what Robert says. He probably wants the Porsche himself."

"Because you can't look at the 911 without thinking pure sex," Chief said.

"Then maybe you should buy it," Eddie said.

"Would if I could," Chief said. "If you trade for it, maybe you'll let me borrow it to take my granddaughter's for a spin."

Eddie looked at the Porsche and stroked its sleek surface with his finger.

"You think I need a Porsche?" he said.

"No one needs a Porsche," Chief said. "It's more visceral than that. Don't you feel it?"

As he moved away from the car, he took another look. He could feel it. Robert and his wife were waiting for Eddie in the office.

"The car Is beautiful," Eddie said. "You can't even tell another car bumped it."

Robert was short, had a full set of bushy black hair, and was likely in his mid-fifties. His wife was an inch or so taller than him, her permed hair dyed blond.

"I'm a hammer and dolly man," Robert said. "No filler in this body shop. This is my wife, Imojean."

"Nice to meet you, Imojean," Eddie said.

"Want to sell that Lincoln of yours?" Robert said.

"You kidding me?" Eddie said. "It's a classic. Lincoln doesn't make sedans anymore. It's irreplaceable."

"What do you want for it?" Robert asked. "I'm prepared to pay top dollar."

"I don't want to sell it," Eddie said.

"I have a lot across the street. Go over and browse around. I'm sure they have a car that will make you happy."

"I like the 911 at your front door," Eddie said.

"That one's not for sale or trade," Robert said.

"Oh? Your son Barrett seemed to think differently. He informed me how rare the Continental is. It's in perfect shape and top of the line. Imojean could take all her friends to luncheons at the country club. I can't imagine anyone you know having a more beautiful car."

Robert was frowning, and neither Eddie nor Chief missed the dirty look Imojean gave him.

"The 911 is worth more than your Continental."

Imojean frowned again when Eddie said, "Then let me pay my tab, and I'll get out of your hair."

"I'll give you eighty thousand dollars for your Lincoln," Robert said. "My final offer."

Eddie grinned. "As I said, give me the bill. I'll pay it, and we can all go about our business."

"I'm offering you more than the Lincoln is worth," Robert said.

"And I'm turning you down. I'll take the 911, you pay for the body repair, and you give me ten thousand dollars to boot. You're trying to short me on a classic Continental. You've heard my final offer." Eddie glanced at Imojean and said, "Ma'am, you'd look stunning in my Lincoln."

"Five thousand, the repair work, and the Porsche," Robert said.

Eddie extended his hand and smiled. "Deal," he said. "Let's exchange titles and keys. Chief and I have other business and must be on our way."

Chapter 26

Eddie revved the engine in the shiny Porsche a bit too much, almost losing control when he pulled out into traffic.

"Want me to drive?" Chief asked.

Eddie's grin was ear-to-ear. "I love it," he said. "I may never get out of this damn thing. Which way is the courthouse?"

"We're on St. Bernard Highway," Chief said. "The courthouse is just up the road. What did you pay for the Lincoln?"

"Thirty grand, cash," Eddie said.

"You bought a car worth seventy-thousand dollars for thirty grand?" Chief asked.

"I had no idea how much it was worth," Eddie said. "I'd just been let go from my job and had a pocket load of severance pay. My buddy Dan was retiring and moving to Peru. He had a car and needed cash. I had cash and needed a car, so we made a good deal for both of us."

"Hell, remind me never to horse trade with you," Chief said.

"What?"

"You got your bodywork for free, a car worth almost twice as much as the one you had, and five grand to boot. Dayum!" Chief said, exaggerating the word.

"I'm a lawyer. I negotiate for a living," Eddie said. "It's what I do."

"I'm not complaining," Chief said. "I'm in awe. Next time I need someone to clinch a deal for me or need a high-powered attorney, you're the one I'm going to call."

"You already did," Eddie said. "We may not win the fight for the island, but I'm not letting it go until I taste blood."

"You sound pretty damn confident," Chief said.

"If I can't find a hidden clause, something else to thwart Frankie Castellano, I'm going to damn well make something up. He's not coming out of this deal unscathed. I'll promise you that."

They found the courthouse open and doing lots of business despite the early hour. Eddie asked a clerk where to find the deeds. The young woman pointed down the hall.

"You know what you're doing?" Chief asked.

"The rules in every state except Louisiana are based on British common law. Louisiana law employs French civil code," Eddie said.

"Is that good or bad?" Chief asked.

"Depends on who you ask. It makes it tough for out-of-state lawyers to represent a Louisiana client."

"You aren't from Louisiana," Chief said. "How long did it take you to adjust to our system?"

"I never adjusted because I practiced in the Federal Court system."

Eddie laughed when Chief said, "Then you're flying by the seat of your pants?"

"I'm savvy enough to know where to start. Every county, or parish, courthouse records changes of ownership. Index books begin with first ownership. They tell you what book to pull to check specific documents detailing ownership, mortgages, etc."

"So, what are we looking for?" Chief asked.

"Title to Oyster Island," Eddie said. "I'll run the chain of title and then have you pull the books so I can view copies of the original documents. When done, we'll have an idea of who owns Oyster Island. Hopefully, it'll be you."

"If I had clear title to the property, there'd be no problem," Chief said. "You must be looking for something more specific."

"An unexplained gap in the title," Eddie said. Title is like a resume. You have to explain why you went three years between jobs. There has to be a logical sequence of events."

"Is something like that easy to spot?"

"Unless we're dealing with a pro who knew how to cover up discretions in the records," Eddie said.

"And if we are dealing with a pro?"

"It's like the perfect murder. There's no such thing. It's not good enough to tie up one or two loose ends. You have to tie them all up or have your lie exposed," Eddie said.

Eight or nine people occupied booths and tables and were checking records. Chief and Eddie staked out a couple of chairs at an unoccupied table.

"What now?" Chief asked.

"We check the wall map to locate the Oyster Island index book."

Eddie studied the map and then pulled the correct index book, opening it to the page where title began on Oyster Island."

"How do you know where to start?" Chief said.

"In Louisiana, it's not easy. The ownership tracts are all strangely shaped because the French tried to give everyone access to water. A novice land person might contemplate suicide when they first start indexing Louisiana property."

"Have you ever done it?" Chief asked.

"I'm getting ready to," Eddie said with a grin.

It was half-past noon before Eddie finished indexing the title to Oyster Island and joined Chief at the table. Chief had never seen anyone run title though he could tell Eddie was fast and efficient. Soon tiring of watching Eddie add information to the yellow pad, he returned to the table and scanned the internet on his cell phone.

"You done?" Chief said.

"Just getting started. Hungry?"

"I'm always hungry."

"Know where we can get a good lunch and an adult beverage?"

"J.P. and Susie took us to Chico's when we first met her. Great gumbo."

"What's not to love?" Eddie said.

As they were leaving the records room, Eddie saw someone he recognized. It was Basil Doles, and Eddie tapped his shoulder.

"Mr. Toledo," Basil said. "What are you doing here?"

"Just Eddie and I could ask you the same thing."

"I'm finishing my Masters in Energy Management at L.S.U. When I'm not in class or rough-necking offshore, I work at a local brokerage house one of my professors owns. I'm checking a tract for him. You?"

"Running ownership for Oyster Island," Eddie said.

"Everyone knows Frankie Castellano, the Don of the Bayou, owns the island," Basil said.

"I'm trying to prove he doesn't," Eddie said. "Chief and I are on our way to Chico's for lunch. Care to join us? I'm buying."

"Love the place. Every landman in St. Bernard

Parish congregates there after the courthouse closes."

"Good drinks?" Eddie said.

"The best," Basil said. "Maybe while we're eating, you can explain why you want to prove Frankie Castellano doesn't own Oyster Island."

Eddie said when they were in the parking lot, "We'll have to take your car or follow you. My Porsche only holds two, and Chief is so big he counts for more than two."

"Beautiful car," Basil said. "I didn't picture you as a sports car guy."

"How did you picture me?" Eddie asked.

"When I realized who you are and the power you possessed in New Orleans, I pictured you driving a Mercedes or Bimmer."

Chief almost grinned when Eddie said, "I'm more of a sandals, Hawaiian shirt, and Bermuda shorts kind of guy."

"I'm glad," Basil said. "Most people with your kind of power are usually starched-shirt country club snobs."

"My kind of power has flown the way of the goonie bird," Eddie said, grinning. "But thanks for giving my ego a lift."

Basil followed Eddie and Chief to Chico's in a black, late-model Range Rover.

"He's one to talk about expensive cars," Chief said.

"Good-looking vehicle," Eddie said, glancing at it in the rearview mirror. "Expensive?"

"You don't get around much, do you?" Chief said.

"Never had time to do anything except work all day, drink most of the night, and repeat the next morning," Eddie said.

"Basil's daddy is the richest and most influential person in St. Bernard Parish," Chief said.

"That's what I heard," Eddie said.

"Basil was the president of the Chalmette senior class, the homecoming king, the most popular person in his graduating class, and valedictorian."

"Now I understand why Heather is so insecure," Eddie said.

"Around here," Chief said, "he could have any woman he wants."

"If he's rich, why is he bothering to work?" Eddie said.

"Hell, he wants to be president of the United States and has a plan to get there."

"More power to him," Eddie said as he pulled into Chico's broken shell parking lot.

Basil was smiling when he exited his sleek S.U.V. "I love this place," he said. "I'll have to leave before five or catch hell from my cohorts."

"You don't want everyone to think you're the hardest worker, do you?" Eddie asked.

"Don't get the wrong idea about me," Basil said. "I can party with the best of them."

"But. . . ?"

"I don't like setting bad examples," Basil said.

"I get it," Eddie said. "You want to be a politician and don't want your reputation soiled."

"There's some truth to what you say. I don't deny it."

Lunch hour had come and gone, the little café, except for the bartender and the people bussing the tables, all but empty. Meika exited the kitchen, smiling when she saw she had customers.

"How you doing, Basil?" she said. "Late lunch?"

"You bet," Basil said. "Got any gumbo left after your lunch crowd?"

"We always have extra for you, baby," she said. "I remember Chief, here. Who's the owner of

229

that gorgeous car?"

Eddie grinned and said, "Eddie Toledo. I'll give you a ride anytime you like."

"Don't want a ride. I want to drive it," Meika said.

"Eddie tossed her the keys and said, "Knock yourself out."

"You kidding me?" Meika said.

"Try not to get a ticket," Eddie said.

Meika's short skirt highlighted her tan legs. She flipped it up as she strutted out the front door, giving them a glimpse of her red thong bikini underwear.

"Damn!" Eddie said. "That's one hot mama."

"She's taken," Chief and Basil said in unison.

"I've never let a little thing like that stop me," Eddie said.

"Hope she doesn't wreck your new ride," Chief said.

The bartender was frowning when he arrived at the table to get their drink orders.

"Can't find good help these days," he said. "What are you drinking, Basil?"

"Ice tea, Isaac," he said. "I'm still on the clock."

Isaac's mustache wiggled when he shook his head.

Chief said, "Abita Amber."

"You got Monkey Shoulder?" Eddie asked.

Isaac smirked and shook his head. "You're mistaking this place for Antoine's. I got scotch, though."

"Then bring me a double, neat," Eddie said.

Before their drinks arrived, Meika returned, a grin on her pretty face. She flipped Eddie the keys.

"You're my new favorite man. What are you having for lunch?"

"Gumbo and half an oyster po'boy," Basil

said.

"Make that two," Chief said.

"Why not?" Eddie said. "Same here."

Meika returned with their drinks and two dozen raw oysters.

"Oysters are on me," she said. "Thanks for the ride."

"Anytime," Eddie said.

"If Frankie Castellano doesn't own Oyster Island, who does?" Basil asked.

"Chief says his grandfather told him he did. Chief is the last of the Atakapa Indians and his grandfather's sole heir," Eddie said.

"You were running title in the courthouse," Basil said. "What did you find?"

Eddie gave Chief a nervous glance before he answered Basil's question.

"Oyster Island was unassigned property owned by the Americans after the Louisiana Purchase in 1803. Recorded title began in 1919 when the Chief of the Atakapas sold the island to a syndicate from Chicago. Part of the agreement was that they were allowed to occupy the island until the death of the last Atakapa," Eddie said.

"My grandfather was the chief of the Atakapas in 1919," Chief said. "He would never have sold the island."

"Unfortunately," Eddie said. "The records say he did."

"Grandpa couldn't even write," Chief said.

"He affixed his mark: the letter x."

"Anybody can make an x," Chief said. "How does anyone know it's Grandpa's x?"

"There were two witnesses and their signatures were notarized," Eddie said. "Frankie bought the land from the syndicate about ten years ago."

Eddie and Chief looked at Basil when he said, "Was Oyster Island considered tribal land?"

"Since the beginning of time," Chief said.

"I just took a course in American Indian law," Basil said. "The Atakapas would have held Aboriginal Title, also known as original Indian Title, or Indian Right of Occupancy, to the island."

"But Grandpa sold it," Chief said.

"You can't sell something you have no title to," Basil said. "In this case, Oyster Island would be held in Federal Trust because Louisiana never extinguished Aboriginal Title."

"So they were overlooked in the Indian Removal Act of 1830?" Eddie said.

"Exactly," Basil said.

"What the hell does all that mean?" Chief asked.

"Sounds to me like Oyster Island is tribal land that your grandfather had no authority to sell," Eddie said.

Basil and Eddie smiled when Chief said, "Am I going to have to give the money back?"

"You can sue anybody for almost anything," Eddie said. "If they had done their due diligence, they would have realized your grandfather had no legal authority to sell the island. They induced him to sign a fraudulent deed that no court in Louisiana or the rest of the country would find valid."

"What about Frankie?" Chief asked.

"If all this is true, he got scammed, though he should have known better if his attorneys had done their due diligence."

Chapter 27

The conversation concerning Oyster Island ownership ceased when Meika brought them fresh drinks and lunch.

"I love your Porsche," she said.

"How was your drive?"

"Fantastic," Meika said. "I've never driven a car with that much power."

"Me either," Eddie said.

"I get off work in thirty minutes," Meika said. "Let's go somewhere in it."

"Chief's my passenger, and the car isn't big enough for three people," Eddie said.

"Where are you headed?"

"We live on Oyster Island," Eddie said.

Meika was smiling. "Give me your credit card. Before leaving, I'll tab out your table and join you for a few drinks. Isaac will serve us until Kathy comes on."

"I need to get back to the courthouse," Basil said. "One of my professors at L.S.U. is an expert in American Indian Law. I'll ask him about your case."

"I have a question before you go," Chief said. "Where did the lighthouse come from? If the state has no authority over Oyster Island, who gave them the right to put a state-owned facility there?"

"Good question," Basil said. "I'll look into it when I return to Baton Rouge. My guess is someone on the faculty has the answer."

"Great, Basil. You've been a tremendous help," Eddie said. "I'd forgotten almost everything I know about American Indian law."

Chief and Eddie were alone at the table as they watched Basil walk out the door of the little café. Chief downed his Abita and motioned Meika to bring him a glass of rum.

"Don't guess you know it, but Meika and Susie are a number. If you have romantic plans, you'd better forget them. Meika doesn't even like men."

"She likes my car," Eddie said. "Maybe I can parlay it into a change of heart on her part."

Chief shook his head. "Acorns don't fall from pecan trees," he said. "You're going to screw our dog adoption deal with Susie."

"If we don't find a way to change Frankie's mind about selling Oyster Island, there won't be a dog training facility."

"Wish you hadn't brought that up," Chief said. "I don't want to live anywhere other than Oyster Island."

"I have no place to go either," Eddie said. "I'd planned to make a home on the island and turn the old casino into a destination."

"Hope you succeed," Chief said. "What's our odds of beating Frankie in the courts?"

"Where the law is concerned, there's no right or wrong. It's all about case law and precedents. We'll make this work or bog Frankie in the court system until he has it coming out his ears," Eddie said.

"What about our ears?" Chief asked.

Eddie smiled. "In the end, it'll probably be up

to a jury to decide. Unless."

"Unless what?" Chief said.

"Unless Frankie blinks before we do."

"Is that likely to happen?"

"We may have to play some dirty pool. You okay with that?"

"I don't know what you're talking about, but I'm all in with whatever it takes to keep the island," Chief said.

Meika joined them with a big smile and a lime mojito in her hand.

"You boys look so intense. Lighten up, or you'll spoil the party."

"What party?" Eddie said.

"After work, every landman in the parish comes in for drinks. I can't begin to tell you how much I make in tips."

"Because they all think they're going to get into your red thong panties?"

Meika grinned. "You've been looking," she said.

"I confess," Eddie said. "You're tabbed out. How will you earn those big tips if you aren't working?"

"Because I'm only going to stay long enough to make them all jealous and then leave with you and Chief. Tomorrow, my tips will double."

"My car only has two seats," Eddie said.

"Let Chief drive. I'll sit in your lap," Meika said. "It'll make these boys jealous."

"Then what?" Eddie asked. "Are you coming to the island with us?"

"You drop me at my house. This is just a game."

"A game?"

Meika kissed him. "You don't play games?"

"Not really," he said.

"How old are you?"

"Old enough," Eddie said.

"I don't see a ring on your finger. Looks to me as if you've played games all your life."

Eddie opened his mouth to reply but thought better of it. The old clock on the wall said a quarter past five as several young men entered the door.

"Three dirty martinis, Meika," one of the men said.

"Kathy will wait on you tonight," she said. "I have places to go."

The young man's smile disappeared, his black mustache looking out of place with his tinted mullet.

"Where?"

"A party," Meika said.

"You can't desert us," he said.

"I'll be here tomorrow. Kathy will take care of you tonight."

Kathy rushed out of the kitchen to take the orders of the new arrivals. Her long blond hair draped to the shoulders of her white satin blouse and highlighted her green eyes. Though an attractive woman, she was probably ten years older than the young men she was waiting on. Realizing as much, she cast Eddie a sad smile when she brought them fresh drinks.

"Doing okay?" she asked.

"Can't complain," Eddie said. "How about you?"

"I was as young as Meika once," she said.

"Wine gets better with a little aging," Eddie said.

Kathy smiled and said, "Thanks, sweet talker. I needed that."

Meika was busy chatting with the young men filling the little café and bar. Chief leaned over to say something only Eddie could hear.

"Long as you can pay for all the drinks and drive a candy-apple red Porsche 911, you have something better than sex appeal."

"Like what?" Eddie asked.

"Checks appeal," Chief said.

Meika was half-sauced and smiling as she traded innuendos with her admirers.

"You okay?" Chief said.

"You're making me feel old," Eddie said.

"You can't be much older than forty," Chief said. "Way younger than me."

"Ever been married?" Eddie asked.

"Once," Chief said. "I have a daughter and three granddaughters."

"Are they pretty?"

"Beautiful," Chief said.

"Where do they live?"

"New Orleans. I haven't seen them in years."

"Why not?" Eddie said.

"My ex never forgave me for walking out on her. She poisoned my relationship with my daughter."

Eddie grinned as he slugged his scotch. "Then I guess we're both losers."

"Hell!" Chief said. "There are fifteen or so young men in here right now that would give anything to trade places with us."

"That's the difference between perception and reality," Eddie said.

"Quit bitching," Chief said. "Maybe Meika will let you cop a feel on the way to her house."

"You think?" Eddie said.

"Hell no!" Chief said. "Doesn't hurt to dream, though."

Kathy finally tabbed out Eddie, and he and Meika headed to his 911 to the protests of all the young men in the bar. Chief was almost too big to drive the Porsche as Eddie climbed into the passenger seat, and Meika crawled into his lap.

Chief grinned when Meika looked at Eddie and said, "I may be sitting in your lap but keep your hands to yourself."

"Yes, ma'am," he said.

Chief and Eddie were both grinning after dropping Meika off. Eddie drove as they followed the rural road back to Oyster Island. When they crossed the bridge to the island, they realized there were visitors.

A black Navigator sat in front of Jack's house. From the look of things, the occupants of the big Lincoln had just arrived. When Eddie saw who it was, he almost choked.

Jimmie, Jack, Paula, and Odette were all standing outside the house talking with the occupants of the Navigator, three people Eddie knew well. It was his ex-fiancée Josie, her son Jojo, and Adele, Frankie Castellano's wife. Eddie pulled the Porsche beside the Navigator and got out of the car.

"What's going on?" he asked.

Jojo smiled and ran to Eddie, hugging him. The hug brought frowns to Adele and Josie.

"Is this your car?" Jojo asked.

"Yes, it is. Like it?"

"Love it," Jojo said. "I want one."

"How are you?" Eddie asked. "Looking for Venus?"

Jojo nodded. "Is she here?"

Eddie opened the front door to Jack's house and whistled. A half-dozen dogs responded. When Venus saw Jojo, she approached the boy, her long tail wagging a mile a minute. Jojo knelt and put his arms around her neck. Josie and Adele continued glaring at him.

Despite the warm day, Adele and Josie wore matching black dresses reaching their knees. Both had gorgeous dark eyes. Adele was probably twenty years older than Josie. Like her step-daughter, Adele's hair was dark, though probably with the help of a dye job at the local beauty shop.

Eddie had met Adele when she was the owner, along with her father Pancho, of an Italian restaurant in Metairie. Adele had smitten Frankie Castellano with her pretty face, curvy body, and talent as one of the best Italian cooks in Louisiana. She still spoke with a Metairie-flavored accent.

Josie was the mother of Jojo, and Frankie Castellano's only child. She was brilliant as well as attractive. Eddie thought he loved her until it was time to tie the knot. She never forgave him for jilting her at the altar of the biggest wedding held in St. Tammany Parish.

Hoping the marriage would somehow still work out, Frankie had offered Eddie a potentially lucrative partnership in the Majestic Hotel and Casino on Oyster Island. Odette and Paula's moment of indiscretion at Frankie's resort in the Gulf of Mexico had changed all that.

When Eddie took a step toward Josie and Adele to hug them, they both stepped away.

"No hug for an old friend?" Eddie said. "Something wrong?"

"You know damn well there's something wrong," Josie said. "It wasn't enough to break my and Jojo's heart. You had to sway my dad so he could ruin the relationship with the woman who loves him."

"So now all this is my fault?" Eddie said. "I was here on the island. I'm not even sure what happened."

"Yes, you do," Josie said. "I'm so glad I didn't marry you. You're a sorry excuse for a human being."

Eddie turned to the others standing transfixed at the conversation.

"Isn't anyone going to help me out here?" he said.

Odette stepped forward. "Frankie Castellano is a good man. He never laid a hand on either Paula or me. It was partly his fault, though."

Adele uncrossed her arms as she glared at Odette.

"Tell us what he did," she said.

"Paula and I smoked some hashish in a bar at the resort. To say we were screwed up is an understatement," Odette said. "We stripped our clothes off and went swimming in that glorious pool on the upper deck where our rooms were. Frankie was alone in the hot tub and told us he was there. Paula and I thought the whole thing was hilarious in our whacked-out state. We pulled off Frankie's swimming trunks, and I gave him a lap dance."

"He could have gotten out of the water and left," Adele said.

"Your husband is a normal male," Odette said. "Jimmie, Paula's husband, is as straight as an arrow, but if you and Josie stripped off your clothes and put your arms around him, he would have been putty in your hands. That's the way men are."

"I've never been so humiliated in my life," Adele said.

Adele didn't move away when Odette and Paula put their arms around her.

"We're so sorry," Paula said. "Frankie is a wonderful man, and as Odette said, he never touched us. Jimmie has forgiven me. Frankie did absolutely nothing out of line. Can't you forgive your husband?"

Josie tried to separate them. Eddie took Josie's hand and pulled her away from the three women.

"Except for my mom, you're the only woman I ever loved," Eddie said. "When it came time to marry you, my problem with commitment raised its ugly head. I don't know if you and I have a future together. I want to give it a try."

Jack stepped forward. "Another storm's kicking up in the Gulf, and I'd love to learn how to make spaghetti carbonara from the best Italian cook in Louisiana."

Lightning flashed over the beach's breaking waves as everyone piled into the house. Eddie grabbed Jack's arm.

"I owe you one," he said.

"Don't know where you got that pussy wagon of yours. You better raise the top and pull it beneath our new overhang before the storm gets here and ruins your interior," Jack said.

241

Chapter 28

Thunder wasn't the only thing Noni, Alice, Asger, and Odette noticed when they motored out of the Biowomb in the big electric vehicle. Flashes of lightning dancing across the sky revealed the utter starkness of the Nether World.

"Where are we going?" Noni asked.

"To Bobbis's tent," Asger said. "It will provide shelter."

The thundering light show had become even more spectacular, the swirling wind pulling dirt from the ground high into the air and rocking the vehicle.

"It's too dangerous to leave you there," Alice said. "Return with us to the Biowomb."

"The storm will provide a path to our world," Odette said.

"If you must leave," Alice said. "We have something to give you to remember us by."

Reaching under the front seat, Alice retrieved one of Princess's puppies and handed it to Odette.

"Ohh!" Odette said. "We can't take one of your wonderful puppies."

"He's weaned and ready to leave his mother,"

Alice said. "His name is Bruiser."

"He's adorable," Odette said.

As Odette and Asger exited the vehicle, the wind continued whipping dirt off the ground. After last hugs, they said their goodbyes and hurried into the shelter provided by the wall of rock. Sitting on Bobbis's fur, Odette cuddled Bruiser as wind whipped the flaps of the teepee.

"What now?" she said.

Asger touched Odette's cheek and stared into her eyes.

"We may face an ordeal leaving the Nether World," he said.

"I'm not afraid," Odette said.

"I am, and your bravery humbles me," he said.

Asger smiled when she said, "I'm shaking like a leaf. Where are you going?"

"Outside, to watch the sky," he said.

"It's too dangerous."

"Doesn't matter. Our eternity depends on it," he said.

Asger wasn't gone long when it started to rain. As he stared upward, the clouds began to part.

"Odette, bring Bruiser and hurry," he said.

Shielding her face from the downpour, she said, "It's raining. Tesla's plan is working."

Asger pointed toward the angry sky. "And Pegasus has come for us."

They watched the white unicorn glide to a halt in front of them. Asger hoisted himself onto his back, took Bruiser, and pulled Odette up.

Lightning flashed as the white steed ascended into the sky. Odette remembered flying in a small plane during a storm. The craft had moved like a rollercoaster as it went in and out of the clouds. It suddenly did when Odette began thinking the ride couldn't get any bumpier.

A circular break appeared in the clouds ahead of them, Pegasus's strong wings pumping as he flew toward it. An ear-busting noise like a roaring freight train encompassed them, and Pegasus began to wobble and then to roll over, Odette pressed against his neck, barely hanging on, Bruiser beneath her, and Asger crushed against her back. The rolling ended with a thunderous explosion. Closing her eyes, she readied for death.

When the loud noise abated, and Pegasus righted himself, Odette opened her eyes. The thunder and lightning were gone, the sky bright. They were high in the air amid blue sky and above the beautiful greenery of another world.

"Vinland," Asger said. "Pegasus has brought us home."

The earth was alive with color, and majestic mountains marked the horizon. Far below, a large river with a lone man in a canoe flowed. Odette patted Pegasus's big neck.

"It's gorgeous," she said.

"This is my home," he said.

She kissed him when Pegasus landed on a bed of thick pine straw.

"I'll never know how you got us through that terrible storm. Thank you, magnificent beast."

As if acknowledging Odette's words, Pegasus knelt on his two front legs and bowed his head before lifting into the air. Neither Odette nor Asger spoke until the unicorn disappeared into the puffy clouds.

"Guess we're walking from here," he said.

"I already see why you love this place," Odette said.

"Compared to the Nether World, it's paradise."

"Paradise when compared to any place on earth," she said.

The river they had flown over stretched before them, and the man in the canoe was paddling toward them. From the smile on his face, it seemed likely he knew Asger. An old man wearing feathers and buckskins climbed out of the canoe. Above them, green-headed ducks circled to land.

The dark-eyed man with gray hair clasped Asger's shoulders and said, "Where you been?"

"A journey to a place far away," Asger said. "Atepa, this is Odette. Why aren't you at the celebration?"

"We are from different tribes. Your ways aren't those of mine," Atepa said.

"Nonsense," Asger said. "There are members of every tribe. Join Odette and me at the celebration."

"You can borrow my canoe. I'm staying here."

"Where are you camped?" Asger said.

"Downriver," Atepa said.

The old man smiled when Asger asked. "Have anything to eat?"

"The bounty along the river is good," the old man said. "Are you hungry?"

"It has been a while since we've eaten," Asger said.

"Climb in. It's late, and I was about to return to camp. You can spend the night with me and make your way to the celebration tomorrow."

Odette found the canoe trip to Atepa's camp magical, fish breaking the river's clear surface, a herd of whitetail deer grazing on its banks. A large meander in the river formed an oxbow lake. Beside it was Atepa's camp.

Atepa's teepee reminded Odette of Chief's domicile on the ridge above Oyster Island. Much like Chief, Atepa had chickens and a dog. Atepa's dog looked like a husky though nothing like any breed Odette had seen. The dog wagged her tail when she sniffed Bruiser. Odette put the big puppy on the ground, and the two dogs touched each other's noses.

"You like trout?" Atepa asked.

"I'm so hungry I could eat the backend of a donkey," she said.

She smiled when he said, "I think my trout will taste better."

Atepa had trout slow-roasting over a low fire. The three soon feasted on roasted fish, vegetables, and spring water.

"Wonderful," Odette said. "What's your dog's name?"

"Storm," Atepa said. "She is good company. I have never seen a dog like yours."

"He's unusual," she said. "His parents were huge."

"As will he be," Atepa said.

It was barely dark when Asger stood from the fire.

"I'm going to check on the canoe," he said. "Atepa will keep you company while I am gone."

When Asger disappeared into the darkness, Odette said. "Sure you won't change your mind about coming with us?"

"Asger's tribe has strange rituals with which I do not agree," he said.

"Like what?"

"Though your hair is the same color as his, your eyes are dark like mine," Atepa said. "You come from different places."

"Much different," Odette said.

"Maybe you should return to that place."

"I'm in love with Asger," Odette said.

"Love is an emotion. Reality is truth," Atepa said.

"What do you mean?" Odette said.

"Asger's people practice unthinkable rituals," Atepa said.

"Like what?"

"Asger is returning, and I am going to bed. If you're still interested, ask me tomorrow."

Atepa retired to his teepee. Odette and Asger stripped off their clothes and went swimming in the warm water of the oxbow lake. Sated by food and exercise, they fell asleep in each other's arms and didn't awaken until the morning sun grew bright.

After breaking their morning fast with Atepa, the old man said, "Return the canoe when you can."

"Come with us," Asger said.

"I'm at peace with the Great Spirit," Atepa said. "Go. I'll be fine."

Odette broke away from Asger when he began pushing the canoe into the lake.

"I have a question I must ask Atepa before we go," she said.

"I'll come with you," Asger said.

"It's private. Please wait for me."

Atepa was waiting when Odette approached. "I'm unsure if I should share what I know," he said.

"Please," she said.

Odette's hand went to her mouth when the old man said, "Asger's people practice human sacrifice and ritual cannibalism."

"You're lying," she said.

"I wish I were," he said.

"What should I do?" she asked.

"Go with Asger. There are answers for the questions you seek, though perhaps not the ones you hope to hear."

Asger and Odette headed downriver in Atepa's canoe. The farther they went, the more people they began to see.

"What's this celebration we're on our way to attend?" Odette asked.

"The Summer Solstice Ceremony," he said.

"Every year, old enemies unite and congregate to trade goods, play games, drink, feast, and pray to our gods. You will see many people, and they'll all be wearing smiles."

"Asger, there is something I must tell you," Odette said. "I'm frightened."

"Don't be afraid. You'll love my people, and they will love you."

Odette said, "Then I can't wait."

"What were you and Atepa talking about?"

"Nothing much," she said.

"You looked intense. Do you have something to tell me?" Asger said.

"I want to meet your family," Odette said. "I've never loved another man as I love you."

"But you have questions."

"Most Native Americans have dark hair and eyes. Your skin and hair are fair, your eyes the color of the sky."

"My grandfather came from a world far away from here. The tribe integrated him."

"A Viking?"

"I don't know, though I've heard that word," Asger said. "Father raised a Cahokia, and that's what I am. Is there something wrong with that?"

Odette clasped Asger's hand. "I hope not," she said.

The place where Asger lived was more than a village, a city stretching for a half-mile in all directions. A timbered palisade surrounded the city, a moat circling the tall fence.

Hundreds of teepees surrounded the fortified city, and Native Americans from many tribes danced, celebrating and trading goods. Sensing Bruiser cradled in Odette's arms, a friendly dog wagged its tail as it sniffed her bare legs.

"Bruiser is heavy," Asger said. "Let me carry him for a while."

Asger took the big pup as they crossed the

bridge over the moat. The guards at the entrance to the city recognized Asger as he and Odette followed the circular corridor to the city. What Odette saw when she entered the walled city was hundreds of wooden houses atop earthen pyramids.

"This is my city," Asger said.

"It's huge," Odette said. "I would never have imagined."

Like the outside of the wooden fortress, hundreds, maybe thousands of people lined the trail, selling and trading turquoise, jade, spear tips, arrow points, and assorted jewelry. Food vendors sold tortillas filled with fish and venison.

"The city is huge," Odette said.

Asger smiled and said, "Try not to tire before we reach our destination."

Colorful wooden houses sitting atop earthen pyramids occupied much of the space inside the enclosure, some larger and more ornate than others.

"Do families live in those houses?" Odette asked.

"The Chief of our tribe and his family live in the largest pyramid. You'll see it."

When they walked past an extensive excavation, Odette noticed the ornate altar.

"What is this?" she asked.

"The Plain of Death," he said.

"Why does it have such a name?" Odette asked.

"Maidens brought here give their lives to the gods, so the rest of the tribe remains safe and prosperous," Asger said.

"Human sacrifice?" Odette said.

"Gifts to appease the gods," Asger said.

"Are you kidding me? How are they killed?" Odette asked.

"Priests rip their hearts from their bodies,"

Asger said.

"How barbaric! You don't condone such a practice, do you?"

"The girls have no fear or anxiety after drinking tea from the dark cup," Asger said.

"They are drugged?" Odette asked.

"Tea from the Dark Cup eases any fear they may have had," Asger said. "They suffer no pain and pass directly into Paradise. It is a great honor to die for your people and make your families proud."

Foot traffic along the path Asger and Odette followed was light, most of the people gravitating toward the festivities near the entrance to the city. The crowd roar had diminished, and Odette jumped when she heard something sounding like a banshee scream. Asger was still carrying Bruiser, and a stray dog they passed sniffed Asger's leg.

"What's that horrible sound?" she asked.

"The shriek of a Death Whistle."

"Death Whistle?" Odette asked.

"A musical instrument shaped like a skull blown to signal the death of someone important."

Upon entering the Plain of Pyramids, Odette was impressed by the size of the structures. The farther they went, the bigger and more ornate they became. They soon reached the largest of the pyramids.

"This is my father's home, the Chief of the Cahokias," Asger said.

"You're father is the Chief?" Odette asked.

Asger nodded. "I will become Chief when he dies."

"Are you frightened?"

"He is still very young, and his death a long way away."

Asger grew visibly disturbed when a man standing on the ledge outside his house began blowing a Death Whistle. Odette squeezed his hand.

Though Asger's family was happy to see him, it was apparent their hearts were heavy. They entered the pyramid and proceeded up a winding stairway to the large wooden house on top of a deck encircling the house. Asger's siblings took them to a room fit for a king, complete with colorful rugs and tapestries where a regal woman sat on a throne-like chair. When she rose to greet him, she burst into tears.

"Your father contracted a fever and has died."

She led them down a hall to a small room where a body draped in a golden cloak lay prone on a table. Dozens of chanting mourners made way for them to approach the body. A mask of Jade covered the man's face. After showing Asger the body, the woman reacted to Odette for the first time.

"Mother, this is Odette," Asger said.

Odette didn't know whether to bow or shake the woman's hand. Instead, she hugged her. When they broke the embrace, Odette saw the tears in the dark eyes of Asger's mother.

"I'm Colel," she said. "My husband Kukulcan died suddenly. Our family is still in shock."

Unlike her son, Colel bore the physical characteristics of a Native American, her nose arched, her hair and eyes dark.

"I'm so sorry," Odette said.

Asger removed his father's death mask to reveal his blond hair and Nordic features. Stretching himself across the corpse, he lay there until Colel tapped his shoulder.

"You must prepare for the ceremony," she said.

Taking Odette's hand, Asger led her through the crowd of mourners. One of the mourners, particularly a beautiful young woman with Native

American features, turned away when she made eye contact with Odette. Before leaving the room, Odette felt their frowning stares.

Asger took Odette and Bruiser to a large room with a window overlooking the plain below. Like the other rooms they'd passed through, this one featured a polished wooden floor covered with woven rugs and colorful tapestries on the walls

"This is my room," he said. "I must prepare for the ceremony beginning at dawn. I am the eldest son and must take my father's place."

"One of the young women in the room with your father was staring at me," Odette said.

"Itotia," Asger said. "She and I were betrothed."

"Did something happen between the two of you?"

Asger shook his head. "I will tell her and the others about you tomorrow. I intend to marry you and make you queen."

"What about Itotia?"

"She'll understand."

"What if she doesn't?"

Asger smiled and said, "Then I'll marry her as well. A great Chief needs many wives."

Odette took Asger's comment as a joke. "What does the Death Ceremony involve?"

"Death drums and death whistles begin. The Summer Solstice celebration will temporarily end while everyone prays for my father's spirit as it ascends to Paradise. Priests will remove Father's heart and brain, which I will consume to share his wisdom and intelligence. Now, I must begin the cleansing ritual.

"What about Bruiser and me?" Odette asked.

"I will check on you before the ceremony begins."

Odette reclined on Asger's sleeping pallet, falling in and out of sleep. It was dark when someone with a candle entered the room. It was Itotia.

"Who are you, and where did you meet Asger?"

"I come from a different world," Odette said. "Asger and I met by accident."

"You know I am his betrothed," Itotia said.

"I'm so sorry," Odette said.

"I don't think you understand. Lineage is essential to the Cahokia. We preserve it at all costs. Since Asger has no sister, he must marry his first cousin, and they must bear children. I am Asger's first cousin."

"It's not my choice to be here," Odette said. "If I could leave this place, I would."

"Do you mean that?" Itotia said.

"Yes."

"I must help with the ceremony. I will return before dawn with someone who will escort you out of the city and take you wherever you want."

Itotia slipped away but left the candle. Odette's eyes were red when Asger returned shortly after midnight.

"Why are you crying?"

"I'm sorry," she said. "Our love isn't meant to be. I'm leaving you."

"No," he said.

"Your people have customs I don't understand. There are too many issues for us ever to be happy together."

"We can work out our differences," he said.

A creature appeared through the darkness before Odette could reply. It was Buttercup, Chief's time-walking cat."

"It's Buttercup," Odette said. "She's come for me."

"Buttercup?"

Odette jumped off the pallet after Buttercup rubbed her leg and started across the floor.

"Chief's cat is here to lead me back to my world. It's my only chance, and I'm taking it. Though we'll never see each other again, I'll always love you."

Asger scooped up Noni's big puppy and said, "Wait. Take Bruiser. Whenever you hold him close, think of me."

Odette smiled and gave him a quick kiss before she and Bruiser followed Buttercup through a time portal in the wall.

Chapter 29

Eddie managed to raise the top of his Porsche before it began to rain. During an exploration of the Majestic, he'd discovered an extensive wine larder, most of the bottles old and rare. Anticipating his first good Italian meal in many months, he returned to the old hotel for a few bottles to contribute to the festivities. He found the Majestic dark and spooky.

The storm already rocking the old wooden structure hadn't affected the building's power, the hall lights working when he flipped the switch. The rumble of thunder and the silence of the Majestic were eerie as he made his way to the wine larder behind the regal bar on the first floor.

A wave of cold air swept over him when he opened the door to the wine room. The shiver it sent up his spine caused him to wonder what else he would find there. He quickly discovered the answer to his question.

Despite the fact he was confronting a ghost, Eddie was mystified and not frightened. The spirit of the young woman in the lace wedding gown he'd seen the previous night had joined him. Gone was the veil that had covered her head, its

255

absence revealing her red hair and lustrous blue eyes.

"I'm Eddie. Who are you?" he asked.

The young woman smiled. Instead of answering, she chirped like a bird. Eddie thought she was playing tricks on him until she peeped again.

"I don't understand what you said, but you are beautiful. Do you live here?"

The red-haired young woman continued smiling, her image flickering as she floated across the chilly room. Eddie took a bottle from one of the rows of wine bottles and read its label.

"This room is a treasure trove," he said. "I don't need anything this exclusive."

The ghost warbled again and floated to a corner of the wine locker where wooden crates sat in stacks. Eddie found a hammer and opened one of the crates, filling it with bottles of Chianti vintage 1929.

The spirit smiled again when Eddie said, "Just what I need. Thank you, pretty lady."

Finding a dolly, he loaded two crates of the Chianti and wheeled them out to his car. The trunk of the Porsche was more extensive than he'd thought. The two crates fit, but barely. The rain had intensified when he pulled the Porsche beneath the covered parking. Chief helped him take the crates inside. The aroma of frying bacon melding with the electric smell of crackling ozone flooded his senses when he entered the house.

"What you got?" Chief asked.

"Two crates of Chianti, vintage 1929."

"Oh my God!" Adele said when Eddie handed her a bottle. "Where in the world did you find this?"

"There's more where this came from," Eddie said. Odette and Paula exchanged glances when he added, "The spirit of a red-haired young woman helped me find it."

"Was her name Laurel?" Paula asked.

"She didn't speak," Eddie said. "She made noises like a bird."

"Eddie, you're so full of shit!" Jimmie said.

"Adele's teaching me how to cook spaghetti carbonara," Jack said.

"Only five ingredients," Adele said. "Pasta, bacon, eggs, garlic, and black pepper."

Adele was drinking a mug of Jack's rum, her smile telling Eddie her mood had lightened since arriving on the island. The wind outside Jack's little house had strengthened, and rain peppered the roof.

Eddie forgot about the wonderful aroma emanating from Jack's galley as he glanced around the room, looking for Josie. Like Adele, she smiled as she sat by the fireplace with Jojo, Venus, and J.P.

"Old friends already?" Eddie said.

Not answering his question, Josie asked, "Where did you go?"

"The Majestic has a world-class wine collection. How about a glass of Chianti?"

"Jack's rum is divine," Josie said. "I've never tasted anything quite like it. I'll switch to Chianti when the carbonara is ready."

"You dog," J.P. said. "You never told me how gorgeous Josie is."

Not liking J.P.'s tone, Eddie said, "She's taken."

"By who?" J.P. said.

"Me," Eddie said.

"You're fantasizing," Josie said. "I saw your red Porsche. I know what it means."

"What?" Eddie asked.

"I think it's called the Peter Pan Syndrome," Josie said. "The inability to ever grow up."

J.P. was grinning and glanced in the opposite direction when Eddie tried to make eye contact with him. Jojo hugged Venus's neck, hiding his face to keep Eddie from seeing his smile.

"How you doing, Jojo?" Eddie asked.

"Good," the boy said.

Josie, J.P., and Jojo all shook their heads when Eddie said, "I'm going for a mug of rum. Does anybody need anything?"

Paula grabbed Eddie's arm when he backed into her and Odette.

"Tell us more about the ghost you saw," she said.

"As I said, flame-red hair, blue eyes, and wearing what looked like a wedding gown," Eddie said.

"How old was she?" Odette asked.

"Hard to say," Eddie said. "Twenty-one or two, though she could just as easily been younger. Why?"

Eddie shook his head when Paula asked, "Did she have wings?"

"No wings," he said.

"That explains why Christopher was alone," Odette said.

"What in Holy Hell are you two blabbering about?" Eddie asked. "And who is Christopher?"

"Laurel is the name of the ghost you saw. She has returned to the Majestic."

"The daughter of the lighthouse keepers back in the thirties," Paula said. "Gangsters from the Majestic killed her parents and forced her into prostitution. She became a vampire by contacting one of the men who paid for her services."

"You're kidding me," Eddie said.

"Before you arrived on the island, all sorts of ghouls and spooky spirits occupied the Majestic. Paula and I performed a cleansing ceremony and ridded the old building of all the spirits."

258

"All except one," Eddie said.

"Christopher and Laurel crossed over," Odette said.

"Who the hell is Christopher?" Eddie asked.

"Someone who worked for the mob here on the island during the Depression. He took care of Laurel and was also a vampire. He's now an angel."

"Because of the trauma she endured, Laurel is non-verbal and only communicates in chirps and trills," Odette said.

"Did Laurel frighten you?" Paula asked.

"Hard for me to fear a beautiful young woman who never stops smiling," Eddie said.

"We'll have to visit the Majestic," Paula said. "Maybe we can find out what happened between her and Christopher and why she returned."

"Tell me again who Christopher is," Eddie said.

"A gorgeous man covered with tattoos. When the ghouls in the Majestic attacked us, he came to our rescue," Odette said. He was originally a New Orleans lawyer sentenced to Angola prison because of trumped-up charges. He escaped and hid out on Oyster Island.

"When Odette and I smoked hash at Frankie's resort and were attacked by people in the bar who morphed into wolves, Christopher saved us again and flew us to safety."

"It was just before we gave Frankie the lap dance and got caught by Adele," Odette said.

"Uh-huh!" Eddie said.

"You don't believe us?" Paula said.

"Sounds as if you're both still smoking hash," he said.

Thunder shook the little house, followed by an immediate flash of lightning through the windows.

"Damn!" Paula said. "That was close. You and Mudbug must stay the night in the camper with me and Jimmie."

"I'll be lucky to get Mudbug to leave the comfort of Jack's fireplace," Odette said.

Paula and Odette grinned when Eddie said, "Pardon me. I need a mug of Jack's rum if I'm going to catch up."

After pouring a mug, Eddie joined Chief sitting at Jack's plank table.

"Mind if I join you?"

"Why not?" Chief said. "I'm starving, and it'll help take my mind off Jack and Adele's cooking."

"Does smell good," Eddie said. "It's been a while since I've had a home-cooked Italian meal."

Everyone stopped what they were doing when the blare of a horn outside the door sounded over the thunder. Chief, Eddie, and everyone else went to the front door when Eddie opened it to see Meika and Susie hastily exiting Susie's baby-blue Firebird.

"Hurry before you both drown," Eddie said.

Meika's miniskirt, the same one she wore at Chico's, was wet when she burst through the door. Susie's well-worn jeans, western shirt, cowboy boots, and Stetson were also wet. Both were laughing uncontrollably and drunk, the open whiskey bottle in Susie's hand their first clue.

"What the hell!" Eddie said. "Couldn't you have picked a better night to go for a drive in the country?"

"That's a fact," Meika said. "The roads are slicker than owl shit. If Susie weren't such a good driver, we'd have been in the ditch a half-dozen times."

"Meika says you have a new car," Susie said.

"I'll give you a ride next time the sun comes out," Eddie said.

"Something smells wonderful," Meika said, gravitating to the stove to join Jack and Adele. "I'm Meika," she said. "The little café I work at in Chalmette never smelled so good."

Adele hugged her. "What are you two girls doing on a night like this?"

"Susie and I were drinking when I told her about Eddie's car. She got a wild hair, and here we are."

Adele just shook her head. "I was a waitress for twenty years, baby. I learned to cook along the way."

"I'm trying to learn," Meika said. "I'd love to be a chef someday."

"You'll get there, baby. I'm Adele, and this is Jack. You remind me of my daughter, Toni."

"Can I help?" Meika said.

Adele squeezed Meika's hand. "You bet you can."

"Whatever you're cooking smells wonderful," Meika said.

"Spaghetti carbonara," Adele said. "Jack and I are frying the bacon. We'd love for you to help."

Susie spotted J.P. sitting by the fire with Josie and joined them, sprawling in J.P's lap.

"Aren't you going to introduce us?" she said.

"Susie, this is Josie," J.P. said.

Susie slurred when she said, "You didn't tell me you have a new girlfriend."

"I didn't know you cared," J.P. said.

Ignoring J.P.'s levity, Susie said, "J.P.'s my dance partner. We won the dance contest at Claws and Craws."

"I think Adele and I need to leave," Josie said. "It's past Jojo's bedtime."

"I doubt Adele's going anyplace until she finishes cooking and everyone eats," J.P. said.

Jojo had his arms around Venus when Susie turned her attention to him.

"I'm Susie," she said. "What's your name?"

"Jojo," he said. "This is Venus."

"I know Venus very well," Susie said. "She came from my dog shelter in Chalmette. She's the smartest dog in St. Bernard Parish."

"I love her," Jojo said. "Grandpa won't let me have her."

"Shame on him," Susie said. "I have many wonderful dogs at the shelter that would love to go home with you."

"I don't want another dog," Jojo said. "Venus loves me, and I love her."

"All my fault," J.P. said. "I told Jojo's grandpa we'd sell her for thirty-thousand dollars. Guess he thought we were trying to rip him off."

"Were you?" Josie asked.

Susie didn't let J.P. answer. "J.P.'s establishing a service dog training facility on Oyster Island. Service dogs are priceless to the people for whom they provide care. A good service dog sells for thirty-thousand dollars. As I said, Venus is the smartest dog in St. Bernard Parish. She's easily worth fifty-thousand dollars."

"Is that true, J.P.?" Josie asked.

"Susie may be a little tipsy, but she's smart, savvy, a great business person, and the most knowledgeable dog expert I've ever met," J.P. said. "She's the person I go to when I need advice on business and dogs."

"I'm impressed," Josie said. "Adele, Jojo, and I will wait until we eat, and then we have to leave."

"The roads are slick and starting to wash out," Susie said. "Meika and I barely made it. With all this rain, it'll be even worse."

"You can spend the night in my Airstream," J.P. said. Jojo beamed when J.P. added, "Venus can go along and protect you from the storm."

"I don't know. I'm already uncomfortable being on the island with Eddie," Josie said.

As if suddenly realizing who Josie was, Susie said, "You aren't the one he left standing at the altar, are you?"

Chapter 30

S usie regretted her remark when Josie's eyes began to tear.

"Sorry," she said. "I had a relationship with an asshole like that once. We were engaged."

"What happened?" Josie asked.

"I like men. Don't get me wrong, but women make far the best partners," Susie said. Sensing J.P.'s grin, she said, "What are you smirking at?"

"Nothing," J.P. said.

Their conversation ended when Jack banged on a pot with a spoon and said, "Chow's up. Let's eat."

Chief was the first in line, and Jack gave him a double portion. Hungry diners soon filled the couch and plank table. Outside, the storm continued to rage.

"Adele, this is wonderful," Jack said. "I've never tasted better spaghetti carbonara."

"You did all the work," Adele said.

"I take good directions," he said. "I couldn't have cooked it without you."

"You need to start another restaurant," Chief said. "Jack and I would be your best customers."

"My dad Pancho has a little pizza joint in Covington. He taught me everything I know about cooking. My daughter Toni and I join him weekly and cook Italian specials."

"Then let us know the next time you'll be there," Chief said. "Jack and I will make the trip across Lake Pontchartrain and join you."

"You flatter me," Adele said. "If you're serious, come next Wednesday. Toni and I will be there."

When they'd finished eating, Josie said, "I need to put Jojo to bed."

"After he's asleep, come back and join us," J.P. said. "Venus will keep Jojo company and protect him from the storm."

"We'll see," Josie said.

J.P. had installed a covered walkway to his Airstream. After dinner, Josie, Adele, Jojo, and Venus retired to the luxury trailer for the night.

"The wine went good with the spaghetti," Chief said. "Now, It's time for more of the world's finest rum."

"I'm all for that," Jack said as he began breaking out mugs.

"Not us," Paula said. "Jimmie and I are returning to Chalmette tomorrow and plan to get an early start. Odette and Mudbug are staying with us."

"Dibs on the couch," Chief said.

"Meika and I will sleep in my car," Susie said.

"Sounds better than Jack's wooden floor," J.P. said.

"There are plenty of rooms for all of us at the Majestic," Eddie said.

"We'd drown before we got there," Susie said.

"Not if Jack lends us the ATV," Eddie said.

Jack tossed him the keys. "Knock yourself out," he said. "It's early, and Adele made tiramisu we forgot to eat. Stick around for a while."

Heavy rain continued drumming the roof as they sat around Jack's plank table, drinking rum and eating Adele's tiramisu.

"What happened in Chalmette?" Jack asked.

"Yeah," Susie said. "Meika told me you were at Chico's after spending the day at the Parish courthouse. What's going on?"

"Do we need to start packing our bags?" J.P. asked.

Susie gave J.P. a troubled glance. "Are you somehow in danger of losing the island?"

"Chief's ancestors, the Atakapas owned Aboriginal Title to Oyster Island," Eddie said. "From there, it gets complicated."

"How so?" Jack asked.

"Chief's granddad sold the island to the group that subsequently turned it to Frankie. The transaction is covered by what is now considered American Indian Law. Chief probably owns the island. It will need litigating."

"That could take years," Susie said.

"Unless we settle," Eddie said. "Frankie's not going to want to drag this out in court. To Frankie, public exposure is like daylight to a vampire."

"So, what's your prognosis?" Susie asked.

"Kick ass and take names," Eddie said. "Make Frankie's life miserable until he starts seeing things our way."

"Then it doesn't sound good for a reconciliation with Josie," Susie said.

Eddie was smiling as thunder rattled the shingles on the roof. "Guess I'll have to live with it," he said.

"Josie's a beautiful woman," Meika said. "Sure about that?"

"There are many beautiful women in the world," Eddie said. "J.P. and I are doing our best to go through all of them before we die."

Seeing the frowns around the table, J.P. said, "Eddie's only joking."

"We aren't laughing," Meika said.

"Chief said young Doles had doubts about the ownership of the lighthouse," Jack said.

"It's an unanswered question," Eddie said. "How did Louisiana get control of the land under the lighthouse and Jack's house?"

"What's the answer?" Jack asked.

"No idea," Eddie said. "All I know is Frankie will sink us if he can, though public opinion is on our side. No matter who prevails, it could take years."

"Maybe there's another way," Susie said.

"Like what?" Eddie said.

"Blackmail," Susie said. "He couldn't resist Paula and Odette. I doubt he can resist Meika and me."

"How do you intend to trap him?" J.P. asked.

Susie smiled and said, "Men's dicks always seem to get in the way of their good sense. Shouldn't be hard to come up with a plan."

Talk of losing the island to Frankie Castellano diminished as the group became more raucous and inebriated. Chief soon snored on the couch, Jack having abandoned the festivities and adjourned to his bedroom.

"Maybe we should head to the Majestic," Eddie said. "We don't want to keep everyone awake all night."

"Little worry of that," J.P. said. "Adele's spaghetti wiped out Chief and Jack, and the dogs don't care how long we party."

"I'll get everyone a room at the Majestic, and then we can continue this party. Frankie's an asshole, but he has me fully stocked with every alcoholic beverage a person could ever need."

"Then let's do it," Meika said. "Can we take a go cup?"

"Why not?" Eddie said.

Thunder boomed as someone entered the front door of Jack's house. It was Josie.

"No one's going anywhere without me," she said.

Josie had taken a bottle of Chianti to J.P.'s trailer. Her drunken smile indicated she'd drank the entire bottle and was ready to consume even more.

Meika frowned when Susie said, "Hey, girl. Where you been?"

"I'm here now," Josie said. "I can't remember the last time I was a bad girl. I'm testing the boundaries."

"Good for you," Susie said.

Jack's little ATV seated four comfortably. Eddie pulled away from the protective overhang, he and J.P in the front seat, Meika, Susie, and Josie in the rear. Josie was sitting in Susie's lap, Meika none too happy about it. Eddie pulled to a stop when they reached the front of the Majestic.

"We'll have to run from here," he said. "There's no cover over the walkway to the front door."

The wooden walkway to the entrance was long and slick, and everyone was soaked when they reached it.

"Damn!" Eddie said. "I'm drenched."

"You aren't alone," Meika said.

"There are a dozen rooms on my floor," Eddie said. "Enough for all of us."

"Susie and I only need one," Meika said.

Eddie fumbled with a set of keys. The room gasped warm air when he opened the door.

"It's lovely," Susie said. "Just what we need."

"This place is too creepy to sleep alone. Can I stay with you?" Josie asked.

"You bet you can, baby," Susie said.

"There's plenty of booze in my room," Eddie said.

J.P. and Eddie weren't even out the door before Susie, Meika, and Josie began shedding their wet clothes.

"Maybe we ought to hang around," J.P. said.

"You're fantasizing," Eddie said. "Let me get you a room, and then you can join me for some more drinks."

"You have all the booze," J.P. said. "I'll sleep on a chair or couch in your room."

Eddie's room was stuffy, and he flipped on the air conditioning. He and J.P. stripped off their wet clothes.

When Eddie saw J.P.'s red briefs, he said, "You look like you're auditioning for a job as a male stripper."

"Never know when you're going to get lucky," J.P. said. "What have you got to drink in this place?"

"None of Jack and Chief's rum. I have scotch, including my favorite Monkey Shoulder."

"Never tasted it," J.P. said.

"Then you're in for a pleasant surprise," Eddie said.

Except for the lightning through the open window, only the weak beam of a nightlight illuminated the room. They listened to the sound of the storm as they drank scotch. Both men sat bolt upright when they heard a scream.

J.P.'s police training kicked in, and he was the first to the door, Eddie following. Someone screamed again, the sound coming from the room where they'd left Susie, Meika, and Josie. Eddie and J.P. burst through the door without knocking.

The room had gone dim, the overheads not working. A flickering lime-green light barely illuminated the room. Meika and Josie had towels wrapped around their bodies and damp hair. Susie was naked by the bathroom door. By now, she, Meika, and Josie were all screaming. J.P. and Eddie immediately saw the cause of their horror.

"Help us," Meika said. "It's a ghost, and she's

a vampire, fangs and all."

Eddie stepped between the ghost and the women.

"It's okay," he said. "It's Laurel. She won't hurt you."

When Eddie tried his hand at making a bird call, Laurel smiled and began chirping. He extended his hand, an electric pop occurring when their fingers touched. In barely a moment, the lime-green glow disappeared, and the overheads came back on.

"Relax," Eddie said. "Laurel is the only ghost in the Majestic. She won't hurt you."

Suddenly realizing J.P. was staring at her, Susie reentered the bathroom, slamming the door behind her. She returned, her hair and body wrapped in towels like Meika and Josie. She glanced at J.P.'s red bikini briefs.

"Here to give us a table dance?"

Susie grinned when he said, "I'm game if you have some dollar bills."

"You still wearing those boxer shorts?" she said to Eddie.

"Good thing for you. I had something on and didn't embarrass myself after seeing your naked tush."

Susie smiled when she said, "You loved every minute of it, you pervert."

Eddie didn't miss a beat. "I guess that so did you."

"Guilty as charged," Susie said. "I'm in dire need of something alcoholic."

"Then get dressed and join J.P. and me in my room."

"We're all friends here and know how the cow eats the cabbage," Susie said. "Lead the way. I'm not staying in this room tonight."

When they reached Eddie's, he and J.P. began pulling on their damp pants.

"Stop," Susie said. "You're fine the way you are."

They were all soon lying on Eddie's large bed and drinking alcohol from his extensive supply.

"How did you know the ghost?" Meika asked.

"I met her the first night I spent here," Eddie said.

"She looks so young," Josie said.

"Sixteen," Eddie said. "Gangsters murdered her parents, the lighthouse keepers, and then forced her into prostitution. I apologize for putting you in her room. She never got far from that bed her whole life."

"That poor girl," Meika said. "How did she become a vampire?"

"One of her clients infected her," Eddie said. "Odette and Paula released her soul. For some reason, she's returned."

"What reason?" Susie said.

"Don't know," he said.

The group crowded the bed. When Eddie bumped into Josie and touched her, she didn't move away.

"Keep your hands off of her," Susie said.

"I barely touched her," Eddie said

"Don't," Susie said. "Josie needs space. Give it to her."

Chapter 31

Josie's towel had come loose sometime during the night, Eddie's hand cupping her right breast when she awoke. He didn't awaken when she pulled away from his grasp.

Susie and Meika were scrambling eggs at the stove, their breast exposed and towels wrapped only around their waists. They didn't seem to care. Still dressed in only his red bikini briefs, J.P. was assisting them.

"Naked eggs and bacon," Susie said.

"Love it," J.P. said with a smile.

"Hell yes, you do," Susie said. "Good food and half-naked women. What more could you ask for?"

"I can think of something," J.P. said.

"You have all you're going to get," Susie said. "Ogling my titties will get you nowhere."

"Doesn't stop me from ogling," J.P. said.

The aroma of bacon and eggs soon awakened Eddie. He joined the others at his tiny kitchen table.

"Damn!" he said. "Now I'm regretting having slept late."

"That's the only thing you regret?" Meika asked.

"Did I do anything I should be ashamed of last night?" he asked.

"No, and neither did J.P. We waited to see his dance act. He never performed," Susie said.

"Are you making me dance for my breakfast?" J.P. asked.

"Don't chance it," Susie said.

"Next time I get a dog from you at the shelter, you'll know what I'm smiling about," J.P. said.

Susie grinned when she said, "I may have to slap you right now."

Josie's eyes grew large when she exited the bathroom.

"Didn't mean to shock you," Susie said.

"Don't change a thing," Josie said. "If my head weren't splitting because of a massive hangover, I'd say this is the most fun I've had in years."

Eddie sat on a leather loveseat in the corner of his apartment. Josie joined him and offered him a bite of her buttered biscuit.

"Does this mean I still have a chance?" Eddie said.

"You helped me realize something for which I'm grateful," she said.

"Like what?"

"I've dealt with tons of guilt since my ex left me for another woman," Josie said. "I put myself under so much pressure worrying about Jojo that I forgot to worry about my mental health."

"You're the strongest person I know," Eddie said. "I've never seen you at a loss."

"I thought I loved you. I was looking for a lifevest."

"Josie, I'm sorry," Eddie said.

"It's okay. Last night forced me to realize I have lots of life to live and that Jojo is making it just fine, even without a father." Josie stopped Eddie before he could speak. "Our marriage would have ended much as my first one did. Now, instead of an ex-husband, I have a lifelong friend. Are you all right with that?"

"I wanted to be the person you trusted to care for you and Jojo. I'm not that man. I'm sorry."

Josie grinned. "Does this mean we can have sex from time to time with no commitment?"

"When do we start?" he said.

Josie didn't answer, asking another question instead. "And you won't get jealous if I have sex with J.P.?"

Eddie wasn't smiling when he said, "I'll have to think about it."

After breakfast, Josie, Susie, and Meika returned to their room to get dressed. J.P. and Eddie's clothes were dry, and they were doing the same when they heard Frankie's helicopter landing in the flat area outside the old hotel.

"Wish you had your three-piece lawyering suit on," J.P. said. "I have a feeling Frankie's here to evict us."

"Flip flops or wingtips," Eddie said. "We're going noplace. At least not today."

Susie said when they were all in the ATV, "I have an appointment at the shelter, and Meika is late for work. Good luck with the island."

Eddie drove them to their car, and then he, J.P., and Josie returned to the helicopter to pick up Frankie. Unlike Eddie, Frankie wore a suit and looked ready to meet a judge in the courthouse. He never smiled when he kissed Josie.

"I have something to tell you, Papa," she said.

"That you and Eddie are getting back together?" he said.

"Anything but," Josie said. "I've been so worried about Jojo, I've forgotten I'm a single woman with needs of my own. From this day on, I will allow myself to go out and get shit-faced drunk if I want to. You and Adele can watch Jojo when I do."

She grinned when Frankie said, "Remember one thing, little girl. I can still paddle your ass if I have to."

Josie kissed him. "You never paddled my ass."

"Maybe I should have," he said.

Frankie stayed in the ATV after Josie exited. "This makes things easy for me," he said. "I'm selling the island next week. The new owners want you to vacate it immediately."

"You can't sell something you don't own," Eddie said.

"What kind of fast one are you trying to pull?" Frankie said.

"Chief owns the island by the right of Aboriginal Title," Eddie said. "His grandfather had no authority to sell it to anybody."

"That's bullshit, and you know it," Frankie said. "How does Louisiana have a lighthouse here if that's the case?"

Before Eddie could answer Frankie's question, a black Land Rover crossed the bridge to Oyster Island, Basil Doles, Jr., and Heather emerged after parking beside the ATV.

"Maybe Basil ought to answer your question," Eddie said.

"Who the hell is Basil?" Frankie said.

"Basil Doles, Jr., the son of the richest man in Louisiana, not to mention the most powerful senator in this state."

Heather went inside the house. Basil climbed into the back of the ATV when Eddie opened the plastic flap and yelled at him.

"Basil, this is Frankie Castellano."

Basil pumped Frankie's hand. "Pleased to meet you, sir," he said.

Basil surprised Eddie when Frankie said,

"The counselor here says you know something about the lighthouse."

"Yes, sir, I do," Basil said. "The State holds the land in trust for the Atakapas because they never overturned Aboriginal Title like Mississippi and other states did. They rent the lighthouse from Mr. la Tortue."

"I don't agree with you," Frankie said.

"Doesn't matter what you believe," Eddie said. "Chief owns the island. Not you. If you try to sell something that isn't yours, I'll sue you for everything you own."

"You underestimate me. If Louisiana controls the island, as you say, you're in deep shit. I own the legislature from the governor on down."

"Now, wait just a minute," Basil said. "My dad is a state senator, and no one owns him."

"We'll see about that," Eddie said.

Adele and Jojo were waiting outside the ATV. Frankie glared at Eddie, Basil, and J.P. before getting out of the little vehicle.

"This isn't over," he said.

"I didn't expect it to be," Eddie said.

Adele and Jojo hugged Frankie.

"I heard you were here to check on me," Frankie said.

"I've been so upset since I saw you in the hot tub with those naked women. I thought our marriage was over."

"Adele. . ."

"Let me finish," she said. "Paula and Odette convinced me you weren't at fault. I'm so sorry I accused you of infidelity."

Remembering Paula's advice, Frankie said, "I'm not a perfect person. When I was in the hot tub, I had carnal thoughts, and those two young women were rubbing against me."

"Frankie. . ."

"Let me finish. You are the best woman I've ever known, and I've never considered having sex with anyone other than you. Will you please forgive me?"

When Frankie and Adele grabbed each other, Jojo made a face. Eddie gave him a wink.

"Let's give your grandparents some space," he said.

When he approached, Josie was at Jack's front door, handing something to J.P.

"What is it?" J.P. asked.

"A check for fifty-thousand dollars," she said.

"For what?"

"The smartest dog in St. Bernard Parish, and maybe the entire State of Louisiana," she said. "Nothing but the best for my son, Jojo."

"We were only asking thirty-thousand dollars," J.P. said.

"She's worth fifty thousand dollars, and you know it. I don't need charity."

"You mean it?" Jojo said.

"If I have anything to say about it," Josie said. "Venus is never going to leave your side."

"Josie, Jojo, Adele, and I are leaving in the helicopter," Frankie said. "I'll have someone pick up the Navigator."

Eddie drove them back to the helicopter in the ATV, Venus's tail wagging as Jojo refused to stop hugging her. Frankie waited until everyone was in the chopper before speaking.

"You're going to get your ass kicked on this one, counselor, and I'm going to enjoy every minute of it."

"Get it on, big boy," Eddie said. "We'll see who comes out on top."

Eddie watched the helicopter disappear into the clouds above Oyster Island before returning to Jack's. Jimmie waited outside his truck as Paula greeted them.

277

"Where's Odette?" she asked. "She and Mudbug stayed the night in our camper. They were gone when we awoke."

"Maybe she returned to her tent on the beach," J.P. said.

"I'd better check," Paula said.

The storm had passed over the island, the sun warming Paula's bare shoulders as she walked across the sand toward Odette's little pop tent. She found the door flap zipped, Odette and Mudbug asleep. Odette opened her eyes when Paula shook her.

"Jimmie and I didn't hear you leave."

"You planned to go early. The storm let up, so I decided to come here and sleep in," Odette said.

"You had me worried," Paula said. "What's that beside you?"

"You mean Mudbug?"

"The puppy. He's going to be a monster when he's full grown."

A colossal puppy was wagging its tail and licking Odette's ear.

"This is Bruiser," she said.

"Where did he come from?" Heather asked.

"Someplace long ago and far away," Odette said.

"He's adorable," Paula said. "Though I have no idea what you're talking about, I can tell from his size he's going to cost you a fortune to feed."

Odette hugged the squirming puppy to her heart.

"And I'm going to love every minute of it."

End

Book Notes

I hope you liked *Oyster Bay Tango* as much as I enjoyed writing it and that you liked all the eccentric characters. Though fictional, many of its historical details are factual.

The pathologist performing Albert Einstein's autopsy stole his brains and eyes. The body parts were supposedly found years later in the safe of the pathologist, though it isn't clear if this is true.

Einstein was younger than Tesla though they lived simultaneously for parts of their lives. Tesla supposedly railed against Einstein because he was a theoretical scientist rather than a hands-on inventor such as he. Tesla believed the earth itself could produce inexhaustible supplies of energy not associated with burning fossil fuels.

The disposal of nuclear waste in boreholes indeed causes earthquakes. The United States Geological Survey discovered as much when disposing of nuclear waste deep in the earth.

3.6 million pounds of nuclear waste lies buried in a shallow pit beside the Pacific Ocean at San Onofre Beach in California. The beach, a part of a California State Park, overlies an extensive fault system and is close to the massive San Andreas Fault. Could seepage of nuclear waste into the fault system generate enough energy to result in a volcano? I'd love to pose that question to Nikola Tesla and Albert Einstein.

There is evidence in Oklahoma at Runestone State Park that Vikings visited the United States long before the Spanish did. Oklahoma and western Arkansas have significant Native American populations; many have blond hair and blue eyes.

A large settlement of Mississippian Indians existed near what is now Spiro, Oklahoma. There are mounds preserved there, such as I described in *Oyster Bay Tango*. Pottery and arrow tips produced by the Mississippians are found as far away as California and South America.

In southern Illinois, the remains of a large city exist with mound-like pyramids such as described in *Oyster Bay Tango*. Mass graves there bear the remains of sacrificial victims. The Death Whistle exists and sounds much like the shriek of a banshee.

If you loved *Oyster Bay Tango* and all of its perfectly imperfect characters, please consider leaving a review and reading the next book in the series. You may also like my French Quarter Mystery Series and Paranormal Cowboy Series.

Thanks for being a fan. My stories would be little more than morning fog wafting across a forgotten lawn without beautiful readers like you. Thank you.

About the Author

Born on a sleepy bayou, Louisiana Mystery Writer Eric Wilder grew up listening to tales of ghosts, magic, and voodoo. He's the author of three series, seventeen novels, four cookbooks, many short stories, and Murder Etouffee, a book that defies classification. His first two series feature P.I.s adept in the investigation of the paranormal. He lives in Oklahoma near historic Route 66 with his wife Marilyn, two beautiful dogs, and one remarkable cat.